3

Ashes to Ashes

Ashes to Ashes

MELISSA WALKER

KATHERINE TEGEN BOOKS
An Imprint of HarperCollins Publishers

Katherine Tegen Books is an imprint of HarperCollins Publishers.

Library of Congress Cataloging-in-Publication Data
Walker, Melissa (Melissa Carol), 1977–
    Ashes to ashes / Melissa Walker. — First edition.
        pages   cm
    Summary: Sixteen-year-old Callie McPhee, a ghost existing in the Prism between
Earth and the next dimension, is torn between Nick, the boyfriend she left behind when
she died, and Thatcher, the spirit who is teaching her how to haunt.
    ISBN 978-0-06-207734-9 (hardcover)
    [1. Ghosts—Fiction.   2. Love—Fiction.   3. Future life—Fiction.   4. Supernatural—
Fiction.   5. Charleston (S.C.)—Fiction.]   I. Title.
PZ7.W153625Ash   2014   2013005069
[Fic]—dc23   CIP
                                                                         AC

Typography by Ellice M. Lee
13 14 15 16 17   LP/RRDH   10 9 8 7 6 5 4 3 2 1
❖
First Edition

For Tommy Walker, my favorite nephew

One

I WAKE UP WITH A JERK, not certain what startled me. I was having a good dream, the kind you want to hang on to after you wake up, and I try to re-create everything that was happening. I think Mama was there, but I can't get the details clear in my head.

Wanting to recapture them, I snuggle down deeply into the warmth and comfort—

The alarm blares.

The warmth and comfort beside me bucks. "Geez, Callie! Why the alarm? It's summer."

Horrified, I quickly slam the Snooze button, then twist around and shake my boyfriend, who's already drifting off again. "Nick, you gotta go. Dad's up."

That jars him out of his drowsy haze. He bolts out of bed and starts searching frantically for his shoes. His brown hair sticks up in all directions and his eyes are sleepy. *Adorable.* I bring the covers up to my chin, trying to keep the warmth cocooned around me, to delay having to deal with the unnatural chill of the morning as long as possible.

Nick snatches up his sneakers and drops down onto the edge of my bed to put them on.

"So what did you want to talk to me about?" I ask. Late last night, he snuck in through my bedroom window like he has a hundred times before. We watch TV, talk, gorge on honey barbecue Fritos and mini peanut butter cups. We kiss, make out, but always, always stop short of going all the way, even though I'm more than ready.

Nick once told me, "If your dad catches me spending the night, he'll kill me. If he catches me and thinks we've done more than sleep, he'll kill me slowly."

He glances back over his shoulder, his brown eyes softening. "Later."

He said the same thing when he arrived a little after midnight and realized I was snuggled beneath the blankets, having my own private *Walking Dead* marathon. He crawled into bed with me and got caught up in the story. With his arms wrapped securely around me, I fell asleep first. At some point he must have turned off the television.

I hear Dad's heavy step across the kitchen tiles below, and I wait for the clink of his coffee cup in the sink. When it comes, I know it'll be exactly twenty-seven minutes before he leaves for work—that's how long it takes him to read the paper, which he does *after* coffee so that he can fully concentrate.

Clink.

"We still have a few minutes if you're going to sneak out before Dad leaves," I tell Nick. "Give me a hint."

"Not enough time for even that."

He leans over and gives me a quick kiss, but I put my hand on the back of his neck and pull him closer.

"I gotta go," he whispers. Reluctantly, I release him.

He bounds toward the window as I throw off the covers. A blast of coldness sends a chill through me.

Perched on the window seat, Nick raises the window. He clambers onto a sturdy branch of the oak tree.

I rest my folded arms on the windowsill. "I love you."

"Same here." Reaching out, he tucks my hair behind my ear. "Just remember that."

Something sad touches his eyes, and a sense of foreboding rushes through me. "Nick—"

"See you tonight."

Then he's gone. I watch him scramble down the tree, then dash across the front yard. I know he parked his car down the block, just to be sure that Dad doesn't discover he was here when he wasn't supposed to be.

I close the window and wrap my arms around myself, listening as my dad walks over to the hall closet and pulls out his shoes. He shined them last night, like he does every night, in front of some History Channel documentary about bombs. It's not like his shoes have to be perfect—he's a professor now, head of the physical science department at the Citadel, not a full-time military man anymore. But the spit shine—like his precisely timed morning and his insistence that my alarm go off at seven a.m. even when I'm on summer vacation—is something that has stuck with him from his days as a naval officer.

I wonder if any of Nick's warmth is still in my bed. I want to curl back up beneath the covers, but Dad has no tolerance for a daughter who doesn't get up and get going. I stomp into the hallway and check the AC. Dad has it set to sixty-two degrees. It's sweltering outside, as it always tends to in the Charleston summer, but do we have to keep the inside of our house set to morgue temperature? I turn it up to seventy and jump into the shower.

When I get downstairs, I catch Dad leaning against the counter and reading the Features section of the *Post and Courier*, which means he's almost ready to go. He always reads news, then sports, then business, then features.

This morning the paper was riveting enough to provide Nick with a chance to slip away undetected. As I pass by, I lift up on my toes and give Dad a quick kiss on the cheek. Usually he doesn't react, but today he homes his gaze in on me, like a sniper lining up his sights.

"What?" I ask, guilt gnawing at me because maybe he knows that Nick was here.

He nods toward a small, perfectly wrapped package next to the always empty ceramic cookie jar that's there just for show, to give the impression that we have someone here who might bake. The white marble countertop is gleaming. Our housekeeper, Carla, comes every other day to keep our lives spotless.

Last week I got a letter informing me of my acceptance into a visiting students summer program at the University of North Carolina, a few hours north of Charleston. Dad was flatlined, as usual—no high five, no down low, no fist bump—but I could tell he was really proud. They don't take many high school kids. I was a little unsure about whether or not I'd really go—the program starts in two weeks. I knew I should, for my transcript, for summer enrichment, blah, blah, blah, but I had a difficult time with the fact that I'd be away from Charleston—and Nick—all summer.

Dad talked me into it, though, with one very big promise.

"Oooh." I pick up the package, tug on the black bow, and open the lid of the cream-colored box.

Keys.

On a BMW key chain.

The note says, "For Callie May. From your loving father."

The formal tone is so Dad. Breaking into a smile, I throw my arms tightly around his neck and release an excited scream. "Is it outside?"

"Yes." Dad pushes back from the counter, away from me, and straightens his tie. I'm bursting with anticipation, but I know rules are definitely coming. "Callie, this is for you to drive up to Chapel Hill this summer. It is not for cruising around with your friends; it is *not* for joyriding." His voice is gruff.

I nod obediently. "Yes, sir."

"One other thing: no one drives it but you."

My father taught me to drive with military precision. I had to learn on a stick shift, and before I got my license, he required me to pass an exam of his own creation, which involved things like pulling my right front tire within one inch of a puddle ahead of me and parallel parking into a space that left me with less than half a foot around each bumper. It was way harder than the DMV's three-point turns and stop-on-red test.

I nod again, too excited to *sir* him right now. "Thank you, Daddy! Thank you, thank you, thank you!"

He gives me a quick pat on the shoulder before picking up his briefcase. "And don't let Carson talk you into burning any oregano or doing voodoo in the backseat—that new-car smell is half the joy of it."

I jiggle the keys in my hand. "Do you have time for a spin?" I ask, knowing that he doesn't. He's always at work at exactly "0800 hours."

But he surprises me this morning. "Just once around the block."

I grin and run upstairs to get my shoes—the sneakers my dad insists I wear when driving, for safety.

In thirty seconds, we're out the door, and I'm eyeing the sleek silver two-door 3 Series convertible and running my hand appreciatively along the driver's side door. "Thank you," I gush again. And I picture this scene in my head: a father and daughter, a new convertible just in time for her sixteenth summer. But there's a reason my father spoils me, and it's not because he's superwealthy or because I'm an entitled snob. It's because my mother's dead.

We cruise slowly around our sleepy neighborhood, and I revel in the fact that Dad is going to be late for work this morning—for me. We don't talk; we don't turn on the radio. Even though it's already nearly eighty degrees outside, I open my window to feel the air, and my father does the same. I watch his face relax as we listen to the bird tweets and hissing sprinklers and lawn mower engines over the BMW's soft purr. I've gotten good at seeing my father out of the corner of my eye, and I take advantage of any opportunity to do it, because when he thinks I'm not watching, he's more himself, more like the Dad I remember from before. It's like he believes that showing any emotion around me will make me sad. But I see him now, letting the warm air hit his face and ruffle through his military buzz cut, and I can sense a softening in him.

We pass Carson's bungalow-style house and her mother's prize roses, then the Sullivans' place with their carefully staked tomato plants. With my father in the car, I won't travel over twenty-five miles per hour. I watch the speedometer needle carefully, knowing that he's aware of it, too, and we're going so slowly that I have time to glance around for once. It's almost like we're walking.

Even though everyone has heard of Charleston, South Carolina, it still feels like a small town to me. I can't go anywhere without running into people who've known me since I was crawling, which means that a ten-minute errand can take up to an hour, depending on who I run into. Sometimes I resent the intrusions that delay my progress to the next adventure, but when I look around the neighborhood where I've lived my entire life, where Mama lived, I can't imagine leaving.

As we drive under the shadows of Spanish moss, along the slow bend of the Ashley River, I get used to the clutch. It's heavy, and it catches late, but after a couple of false starts I have the hang of it, and it's smooth as silk. Dad gives me a proud smile as I ease the car up the steepest hill in our neighborhood with a quick downshift—he loves that I drive stick—and I flash him a grin.

When we pull back into our driveway, I peer at the clock on the dash—8:17 a.m.

"What was it your mother used to say?" Dad asks me. And I'm surprised for a moment that he brought her up. He rarely does, even though I know we're both always thinking of her.

"You only live . . . once," he and I say together.

I shake my head as he gets out of the BMW. He's using Mom's motto to justify being half an hour late for work. That's not exactly the kind of "living" that thrills me.

My father gets into his car as I walk back toward the house, and when he pulls out of the driveway, I watch his Mercedes coupe turn around the bend before I race upstairs to change my shoes—it's way too hot for this closed-toe nonsense.

I just tooled around my neighborhood at twenty-five miles per hour, but my foot was itching the whole time. I climb back inside the BMW and smile at the speedometer, wondering how fast my new gift can go from zero to sixty.

The area where I live is a typical, well-kept development with cozy culs-de-sac and two-story houses built in the 1970s, but the heart of Charleston has a history that reaches back for hundreds of years. I pass the old mansions along South Battery and give a nod to the row of oak trees that makes people shiver even in this ninety-five-degree heat. Carson always holds her breath when she goes by the oaks—"So I don't breathe in their bad luck," she's told me—but I have no time for useless rituals. The story goes that back in 1718, twenty-nine pirates from Stede Bonnet's notorious crew were hanged from those giant oaks, and their eyes stared coldly as their bodies swung, rotting slowly in the hot Charleston wind. I know this tale by heart—everyone in town does. Hanging them right along the water was supposed to scare other pirates who thought about approaching our fair city, but I think it just worked to frighten the people in the mansions, which has always made me smile a little.

Superstitious types like Carson might be afraid to tempt fate in this spot where the horrific hanging happened—everyone says this part of town is haunted. But I don't believe in spooky stories. If there were such a thing as a spirit world, I think I'd be aware of it. The only ghosts I know are the ones that haunt the corners of my dad's mind. The ones that keep him quiet, unable to give me a real hug—instead of just a shoulder pat—on my birthday.

Not that I'm bitter. Dad has his own way of relating to things since Mama died.

I was six when it happened, and I remember little glimpses of her. The honeysuckle smell of her soft blond hair. A favorite blue cotton dress with tiny white flowers on it. Her fingernails—always cut short and painted a pearlescent pink.

I also remember glimpses of him. How he'd tuck me in at night—all the way up to my chin—to make me feel safe and warm. A laugh that rang out like a big brass bell. Arms that would scoop me up onto his shoulders to see what things look like "from the catbird seat."

"I want my little girl to live life at the top," he would say.

I guess this BMW is proof that he still wants that for me. But Dad hasn't tucked me in for years, his laugh—on the rare occasions when it rings out at all—is hollow, and he never swoops me into his arms anymore. He's still strong and larger than life; I've never seen him cry. In fact, I haven't seen much emotion at all since Mama got sick, except in moments when he thinks I'm not looking, like this morning when we rolled the windows down and he let the warm wind on his face soften his steely facade. I know he loves me, I know he's there for me, but I wish he'd show it more—it's like he's determined to convince me that he's a rock. Like he's forgotten how to feel anything.

I haven't. I know exactly how to get a rush.

The dock on the north side of Battery Park is long and narrow, but it widens at the far end as it juts out over the water. I start at the beginning of the pier, and though I'll want to steer around three storage structures built on the north side, I have at least three hundred feet to the other end, plenty of time to get up to sixty and then spin to a stop—I'm guessing I'll need about a hundred feet to brake. I half wish I'd called Carson and asked her to bring her camera for this one—she's always up for a thrill. But I want to break in the BMW on my own.

I glance in the rearview mirror as I remove the clip holding my waves back in a ponytail. A mess of dark blond hair falls over my forehead, frizzy from the humidity of Charleston in June. Stealing a glance in the rearview mirror, I see that my face is flushed with excitement, blue eyes shining with anticipation at what I'm about to do. "You only live once," I say to myself just before I rocket off the clutch and push the gas pedal to the floor with my bright yellow Havaianas. Dad hates it when I drive in flip-flops.

The car takes off with effortless determination, like it knows what I'm doing, like it's been waiting for me to let it run. I get closer and closer to the edge, and I see the point where I need to turn the wheel, ease off the gas, and start to brake so that I don't plunge into the Atlantic.

I let my foot linger for a split second longer than I should. As I release the accelerator, I jerk the wheel to the right, and the car responds immediately. I spin around the wide end of the dock, blue sky flashing abstractly in front of me. I wonder what it would feel like to hit the water in a violent splash.

And then, it stops. Everything is quiet for one perfect moment, and I let out a combined laugh-scream, a celebratory rebel yell at my latest stunt. This feeling—this nervous, excited, scared, happy, blissful, terrified feeling—is what I live for.

This and Nick.

Two

IT'S A LITTLE AFTER NOON when I pull up into Carson's driveway and honk twice. Dad said no cruising, but one little exception can't hurt. Besides, I'm on a mission of mercy.

She opens her front door, peers out, and shrieks excitedly. With her vintage straw bag flung over her shoulder, she rushes out and quickly paces around the car, studying it from every angle.

"You're so lucky!" she says as she finally opens the passenger door and slides in.

"I know," I say, patting the steering wheel.

"No, I mean to have me as a BFF." She reaches into her bag and pulls out what looks like a bouquet of withered leaves.

"Sage," she explains, responding to my questioning glance. "For cleansing."

I cock an eyebrow.

"Oh, Clueless Callie," she says breezily, running her fingers through the leaves. "You have to burn this in a new space to clear out any bad juju."

Juju, which I'm not even sure is a real word, is Carson's thing. She claims she can feel the vibes around her—good and bad.

"You're not thinking of doing that in my car," I say.

"Absolutely!"

"No way! Dad is too into the new-car smell—he'd die if we covered it up with burned herbs."

Carson pouts. "Is he still mad about last year when I burned those pine needles in his home office?"

I nod. "He said it smelled like a hippie had set up camp in there."

"Your dad just doesn't know the dangers of the dark side."

"He only believes in what he can see."

"That scares me," says Carson. "Because there's a lot we can't see." She frowns and throws the leaf bouquet back in her bag. I wonder what else is in there, besides the deck of tarot cards and the Magic 8 Ball key chain I know she always carries. She believes in being prepared for any unnatural emergency—not that we've ever encountered one, or ever will.

I back out of her driveway. "I dreamed about Mama last night." As soon as I say it, I wish I hadn't. Her face softens in sympathy.

After Mama died, for that first year or so, Carson used to insist that she felt Mama's presence. It was the start of her obsession with ghosts, the reason why every independent project she does at school is based on some haunting legend or ghoulish mystery—and Charleston is full of them. When you live in a hazy, hot place with hanging moss and sweet-smelling flowers and thick, humid air that almost feels like a living creature, it's easy to see ghosts everywhere you turn.

We were young, just in first grade, and the adults around us dismissed Carson's visions of Mama as wishful thinking. I did, too, because my dad told me Carson talked nonsense. *It is nonsense,* I think. But she knew how hard it was for me when Mama died —the way she died—and Carson helped me through my grief, she didn't let me wallow, and I know she is always just trying to make me feel better.

I consider lowering the top, letting the wind have its way with my hair, to distract me from Carson's sympathy, but I can tell she just straightened her glossy brown curls. "It's nice to dream about her," I say, making my voice upbeat. "Memories are good to have."

"So are guardian angels."

Although I'm wearing sunglasses, she still manages to catch my eye roll. She knows I don't really believe she ever felt my mom's ghost. She was just pretending.

"Who else are we picking up?" she asks.

"No one."

"Come on. You can't waste this sweet ride on just the two of us."

It's not that I'm not psyched about the car; it's just that I'm not the share-everything-with-everyone-I-know type. People at school think I'm antisocial, but Carson defends me, because that's not true. She's popular, she's friends with a gazillion people, she gets me invited to parties and keeps me in the loop. I appreciate all that, because it seems like what I'm supposed to be doing. You know, going to football games and dances and after-parties. I make appearances, I smile and nod at people, but they don't thrill me. I'm more into . . . experiences. Like climbing rocks at Kings Mountain State Park without ropes, or racing my car along the docks. High school just feels like a waiting room for something more real.

"It's not wasted. We're going to see Nick."

"Thought he was doing that Habitat for Humanity thing today."

"He is, but he has to eat." I point over my shoulder to the backseat.

Twisting around, she spies the two wicker baskets resting there. "Ah, the way to a guy's heart . . ."

I laugh. "I already own his heart, completely."

"Calpurnia McPhee," Carson says in a chiding voice.

"Carson Jenkins," I reply.

"You've got a secret." She reaches back—

"What*ever* are you talking about?" I ask. "You know I'm crazy about Nick. That's no secret."

She straightens. "I'm not talking about your amazing love life." Smiling, she holds up a hair clip before pinning back her own shiny brown blowout in a grand gesture. "You've already been for a joyride."

I groan. I tossed the clip back there after my pier adventure—to make a statement, to put an exclamation mark on the end of my stunt.

"Where'd you go?" she asks.

"To the harbor," I mumble. There's no use holding out on her now.

"You *didn't*. Please don't tell me you went out on the pier."

I give her a casual shrug that's in direct contrast to my victorious smile. I've talked about racing on the pier, but I never had the right set of wheels for it until now.

"Not without my camera!" she shouts, and rifles through her bag until she locates her phone and turns on the camera.

"Really?" I ask. "Now?"

"No better time," she says. "The open road is the perfect backdrop."

She films me while I tell her how I handled the car like a NASCAR driver, and how I'm pretty sure I got up to sixty miles per hour in under five seconds.

Hearing a click, I know that she hit the Stop button. Out of the corner of my eye, I can see her admiration. I bask in it. I do things she'd never dream of doing.

"You weren't afraid you'd get caught?" she asks.

"It was pretty early. It was just me and the spirits of the dreaded pirates."

"Don't say that!" She turns all serious on me.

"The historic district was a ghost town," I say, lowering my voice for effect. "Not a soul in sight. Not even Stede Bonnet."

I let out a ghoulish laugh and Carson swats my arm. "Stop it," she says in a hushed whisper. "Please tell me you held your breath when you went by the oaks."

A large gray cloud blocks the sun, and she peers through the windshield up at the sky. She's probably thinking that my joking about Charleston's storied ghost history has somehow caused this momentary shadow.

"Cars," I say. "It's a legend."

"Callie, it's *bad luck* not to."

I love my best friend, but this is a topic we don't see eye to eye on. I'm tired of the ghosts of the Old Slave Mart, the haunted house at 131 Church Street, the paranormal activity at the Battery Carriage House. It's all just old-people spook talk. Something to sell the tourists on the Lowcountry Ghost Walk.

Carson sighs. "You're so cynical."

"And you're gullible!" Carson imagines things. There is absolutely no such thing as ghosts. There can't be. I can't believe in them.

If I did, I wouldn't be able to explain why Carson somehow felt Mama's presence but I didn't. She told me that Mama sat with her, in her room, while she played with her dollhouse. Carson was compelled to tell me and my father that Mama was okay. But if ghosts were real, *I'd* have sensed her, haunting or hovering or giving me a sign that she's watching over me and Dad. I knew my mother for just six short years, but I know that she loved us. . . . I saw how much in her last breath. I know she'd visit us if she could—in whatever form.

Then, because I don't want this kind of awkwardness between us, I apologize. "Sorry I snapped."

"I know you didn't mean it."

Well, I did, but pointing that out will only put us into a dizzying circle. She always forgives me when I get moody. That's what you do for your best friend whose mother died.

Carson and I have been together our whole lives. When her parents moved to town, her mom was pregnant with her and Mama was pregnant with me. Carson's mom always tells the story of how they conspired to name their daughters after literary figures—Carson after novelist Carson McCullers, and me after the housekeeper in *To Kill a Mockingbird.* But if anyone besides Carson or Nick called me by my full name, I'd punch them. I'm more of a Callie than a Calpurnia. And to my dad, and to Mama once upon a time, I'm Callie May.

I turn in to a neighborhood that's seen better days. It's part of a renovation project, replacing crumbling structures with sturdier ones. I pull to a stop near a yard where the partial frame of a house has been erected. Several guys and a couple of girls are hard at work: hammering, sawing, clearing, carting. I'm always amazed by how organized they are and how quickly they can build a house. This is the third one that Nick has worked on.

"Thank goodness for the sweltering summer heat," Carson says. "It *is* our friend."

Laughing, I open the door and step out. I know she's appreciative of the scenery. Most of the guys have opted to go shirtless, and their bared torsos are glistening with sweat. One of them is Nick. I take a moment to appreciate the way his muscles bunch as he saws a plank resting between sawhorses. His concentration is intense.

A guy walks by, says something to Nick as he passes. Nick replies and the guy laughs.

Nick is always making people laugh. Even though he's working hard, he's relaxed here, obviously enjoying what he's doing. After the shorter end of the plank drops to the ground, he swipes the back of his hand across his brow as he straightens.

I know the exact moment when he spots me. He grins widely, sets aside the saw, and heads over. To my chagrin, he snatches a T-shirt that is one of several draped over a bush and works his way into it without breaking his stride.

"Hey, you!" he says, much more awake than he was the last time I saw him. His brown eyes sparkling with merriment, he jerks his head toward the car. "What's this?"

"Remember the deal I made with my dad?"

"You're kidding." His bristled jaw drops. "I figured he'd get you an old clunker that I'd have to spend way too much time repairing."

"Nope." I run my hand over the hood in a slow, sensual manner, the way I'd like to run my hand over his chest, shoulders, and back.

"Sweet. Hey, Carson," he says.

"About time. I was wondering if you were even going to notice me."

He gives her a wink and a grin. "A guy has to have priorities."

He turns his attention back to me, and it's like being hit with a spotlight. I love the way he gives me his entire focus. "What are you up to?"

"Other than showing off the Beemer"—I step up to him and trace my fingers over his biceps—"I could not possibly go the rest of the day without seeing you again. Tonight is too far away. I brought some lunch. Appetizer first."

I rise up on my toes and give him a big, energetic kiss. His hands come up to cup my face, his fingers threading through my hair.

Carson clears her throat. "Get a room, y'all," she says, and then she wanders over to say hi to some of the guys she knows. And no doubt burn her sage around the house so the area is cleansed for the family who'll be moving in once it's finished.

"Don't mind her," I whisper into his ear.

"Her and a couple of dozen guys."

I draw back to see Nick blushing. I can't help but wonder for the thousandth time how I ended up getting this lucky, with a boyfriend who's sweet enough to blush at me, even after a year.

"Come on, Fisher!" one of the guys calls out. "We have work to do."

"I've got food!" he yells back. Then he arches a brow. "You did bring enough for everyone, right?"

"Of course."

He pushes the front seat forward and grabs the baskets. I follow Nick to where he was working, and he sets the baskets on the plank of wood. The *thunk* serves as a dinner bell. Suddenly everyone is swarming over, grabbing pieces of chicken, and standing around eating. No plates, no napkins. I'm not sure four KFC buckets are going to be enough.

"Hey, Callie, you ever decide to dump this loser, give me a call," Michael Grayson jokes before biting into his already half-devoured drumstick.

"It'll never happen." I wrap my arm around Nick's and snuggle against his side. "I'm holding on to this guy like a drowning woman with a life preserver."

A strange expression flashes over Nick's face, like I've said something that upsets him. But it's gone so quickly that I can't be sure of what I saw.

"Callie!" Carson shrieks. "Don't invoke death in a conversation. It's bad luck."

I don't want to go back to the weirdness from the drive, so I capitulate. "Right, sorry."

I give Nick a secretive roll of my eyes. Grinning in understanding—he's not a big believer in Carson's theories either—he reaches out and tucks my hair behind my ear, his knuckles skimming along my cheek. We have plans for tonight, but that seems like an eternity away. I don't want to wait.

I lean toward him and say in a low voice, "Don't suppose you can head out early."

Regret softens his eyes as he shakes his head.

"But it's not like they're paying you or anything," I remind him.

"I made a commitment, Callie."

"Okay, yeah, I get that." His willingness to always help others is only one of the many things I like about him. I tried to assist with the first house but quickly discovered that my forte is bringing food, not hammering nails. Although I am pretty talented at hitting thumbnails.

When all the food is gone, everyone starts wandering back to work. Carson sweet-talks one of the guys into carrying the baskets back to the car. I know she's giving me some time alone with Nick— not that we can be truly alone here.

"I'm glad you came by," he said.

"Yeah, me, too. Do you have a marker?"

He pulls one from his jeans back pocket and hands it to me.

"Red. Perfect," I say. "Is this board going into the house?"

"Yep."

Right in the middle of it, with a flourish, I write, "Callie + Nick Forever" and the date. Then I draw a heart around it.

"You know that will get covered up with Sheetrock," he says.

"But we'll always know it's there. I like the idea of immortalizing us."

He puts his arm around my shoulders and leads me to the car. Once we get there, I move closer to him and run my hand down his strong back, resting it just under the bottom of his T-shirt. With my other hand, I trace his lower lip, a move he loves.

His eyes flicker with emotion, desire, I think. He wants this as much as I do. I take a deep breath. "So . . . I was thinking maybe tonight we could see how far the seats recline."

Nick gives a little laugh. "Let's stick to the original plan."

"You're making me dinner?"

He smiles, and it's like a heat lamp just hit my face. "Yeah," he says. "I need some time with you when no one else is around."

Oh, I need that, too.

"I cannot wait," I whisper, moving in again and letting my lips linger on his for one more moment before I reluctantly back away. "See you in a few hours."

"Okay." He gives my arm a squeeze before he opens the car door for me. I slide in behind the steering wheel.

"Bye, Carson," he says.

"Later, Nick." She wiggles her fingers.

I turn the ignition, rev the engine, and peel out.

"Speed limit!" Carson yells over the wind rushing by.

I slow down. It's one thing for me to chase after a rush, another when someone else is with me.

"He's cooking for you now?" Carson asks.

"It's nothing," I say casually. "He's making dinner."

"With his parents?"

"They're out of town." I can't stop myself from grinning so wide that my jaw aches.

"Shut *up*!" says Carson. "Are you sleeping over? Does your dad know? Do you have something special to wear? We need to stop and get you something sexy, something that will blow his mind. Victoria's Secret. Turn right at the next light."

I laugh at her rush of questions and commands. I knew she'd be excited, too. Nick and I have been dating for a little over a year, and last month I wanted to celebrate our anniversary by, um, taking the next step in our relationship. Nick, frustratingly, wanted to wait. Herein lies the problem with dating Southern gentlemen. They can be so . . . gentlemanly.

I take the right. "So you'll help me pick out something appropriate?" I'm suddenly just a little nervous. I want everything to be perfect.

"Absolutely. I'm thinking red."

"Nope. White. And lacy."

"So virginal," she says.

"Duh. You get to wear white honestly only once."

Carson giggles. "He *did* ask you to stay over, right?"

"Well, not technically."

"But he told you his parents would be gone, and he's making

you dinner, and anyone can plainly see that he *loooooves* you." She's being the best best friend ever. "Oh, Callie, tonight's the night!"

I'm glad the windows are up, because someone might call 911 if they heard the squeal she just released. Carson acts out what I feel inside. I never thought a guy would get to me, but Nick is definitely The One.

I've known him since kindergarten, but I didn't notice him until ninth grade—the year he got serious about soccer. Nick Fisher was always a skinny, goofy kid who made people laugh. But freshman year, he sat in front of me in earth science, and I suddenly noticed how broad his shoulders had gotten over the summer, how the back of his biceps curved into a delicious, muscular shape, how his soft brown eyes lit up when he turned around to pass back a worksheet or ask me for a pen.

The best part is that he's still that kid who makes people laugh. He's smart and he's kind and he has no idea how much every girl at our high school wants him. He just knows he wants me. At least, that's what I thought until he told me he wanted to wait to have sex.

A one-year anniversary in high school is pretty much like reaching the golden fifty in real-world relationships, so I was more than ready to kick things up a notch. I remember what I told him as I tried to pull him closer to me that night. "You only live once," I whispered.

But he didn't give in—he wanted to wait. I'm hoping that my leaving for the summer will make him more accepting of a going-away gift from me. Because tonight, I'm determined not to take no for an answer.

• • •

I slam the front door as I leave, overnight bag in hand. Carson went home an hour ago after helping me get ready for the night. I took another shower—complete with Carson's wild strawberry–scented body wash, which she swears is "like honey to a bear" with guys—so I'm extra clean and sweat-free. I feel a twinge of guilt knowing that my father would not approve of what I'm doing. I did tell him I was going over to Nick's, but I may have left out the part about Nick's parents being out of town. Still, there's no way I'd give up tonight's plan. Nick means everything to me.

When I get to Route 52, I put the BMW's top down. The shadows of the giant live oaks along the drive make the air feel slightly cooler, but it's the wind that really makes the heat bearable. I know my hair's blowing all over the place, but Nick likes it when I look a little wild. I'm wearing almost-too-short white shorts and a red-striped boatneck T-shirt. I press my white espadrille platform down on the clutch and shift into fifth gear, feeling a blast of air as I speed up to seventy. I wonder if being with Nick—really *being* with him—will curb my need for other types of adrenaline rushes.

My phone rings. I know I shouldn't pick it up while I'm driving, but I fish it out of my slouchy yellow Marc Jacobs bag anyway. I have to dig past a pack of gum, an extra hair band, and a sample of Chanel perfume that Carson made me take "for after."

"In case you get all sweaty and stinky," she said.

I find the phone and see his gorgeous face on the screen, all cheekbones and soulful brown eyes. "Nick."

I glance at the clock—7:26 pm. I'm late.

"Sorrysorrysorry," I say, putting my iPhone up to my ear.

"It's okay. I mean, if you can't make it, it's—"

"I'm on my way!" I interrupt. "I was making sure I packed exactly the right . . . outfit."

"Callie, you're so—" he starts. And he sounds serious and sexy, but I want to save that for when I'm with him in person.

"Hold that thought," I say, hoping he can hear the flirty smile in my voice. "I'll be right there."

I press down on the gas pedal, urging the speedometer up to ninety. There's no traffic on the road, and I want to get to Nick. *Now.*

"Guess how fast I'm going," I say, laughing.

"Callie, maybe you shouldn't . . ." His voice catches then, he pauses, and I wonder at the emotion I hear. It sounds . . . strained, like something is wrong. And it scares me.

"Nick? What is it?" I ask, and the smile is gone from my voice.

"Not on the phone. We'll talk when you get here."

"*Talking* is not on my agenda," I tease, trying to make this sense of foreboding go away.

"Callie—"

A truck suddenly looms out of nowhere, swerving in front of my car, and I slam on the brakes to avoid a collision. Every part of my body tenses and my senses heighten—I hear screeching tires, I smell a hint of magnolia over burning rubber, I see the flash of the truck's metal grille in the setting sun, and a shock of fear slices through me. My head crashes into the driver's side window and the windshield explodes, showering me with sharp glass. The whole world darkens; my body goes limp.

And then I'm gone.

Three

THE JOLT ISN'T PAINFUL; it isn't horrifying. It's a soft tug that becomes a strong pull, like when you slip your head beneath the water and the ocean current rushes by. But then a tidal wave grabs my ankles and drags me—fast, faster, beyond any speed I've ever known. A tunnel of white noise shifts and spins around me, like I'm in the middle of a cyclone, untouched by anything that might hurt me but at the very epicenter of an incredibly powerful force.

Then unexpected calm, as though everything is ripped away.

I land, untouched, onto soft ground, in the midst of a dark fog. It reminds me of early mornings in the Blue Ridge Mountains in North Carolina, where my parents used to have a cabin. We only went there a couple of times when I was little, but I remember that when I woke up each day, for a few minutes it felt like we were inside a cloud. It even smells like those mornings, I think, though I don't know how I can recall such a specific detail. It's colorless here, but not in the threatening gray of storm clouds—more a glistening silver, somewhere on the cusp between night and morning.

How did I get here?

Suddenly images rush at me—Dad shining his shoes, the keys to the BMW, speeding along the dock, Carson laughing in my car, my name and Nick's in a red heart, white lace, Nick's worried voice. *Huh?* I was on my way to Nick's. . . . He was . . . And then it hits me—a truck, shattering glass, the sickening way my body went limp when the impact came.

My skin prickles with goose bumps even though it's perfectly warm. *Am I . . . ?* I don't allow myself to finish the question, too scared to even voice it in my head. I sink to my knees on soft, spongy ground. A tear slips down my cheek, surprising me—I haven't really cried since I was twelve, and that was about Mama. I wipe at the wetness and fight back a wave of sadness that threatens to crash down over me. There has to be another explanation. I can't be . . .

I must be asleep. That's it. I'm still snuggled in my bed with Nick right now, safe and warm, just dreaming about this weird colorless place where I feel hopelessly alone. Sometimes in dreams you wonder if you're in a dream, you consider it, you ask yourself . . . It's possible . . . it's . . .

Just as I'm starting to believe that there's hope, that I'll wake up at any moment, I see a ripple of light out of the corner of my eye—a rainbow of colors, blurry, like it's underwater. A doorway appears in the distance.

Three figures emerge. The rainbow fades, and they stride

purposefully in my direction. I shove myself to my feet. I don't know who they are, but I have an immediate aversion to them. I glance around quickly, searching for some sort of escape. But there are no other doors. Nothing. No one else. Only us.

They're wearing light gray robes with a slight shimmer to them, like those rocks you can find that have a rainbow sheen—mica. One of the guys has a stocky frame with dark hair and deeply tanned skin, like maybe he's Native American. The girl, who bounded forward with the most energy, has a blunt brown pixie haircut and a constellation of freckles across her face.

The second guy is the most riveting. He exudes confidence, control. His blond hair whispers against his neck. His eyes are stormy blue, almost gray, like they've got a whole weather pattern of their own—swirling clouds, strong winds, and the glimmer of sun as dawn breaks over the horizon. I almost become lost in them before I shake off this intense pull and take in the sharp angle of his cheekbones and the soft arch of his full lips.

A soft buzz tingles through my body, like I'm holding the electric razor my dad uses to keep his buzz cut close to the scalp. I flash back to watching him in the bathroom as a little girl, sitting on the closed-lid toilet and helping him make sure to get the spots in the back.

"Calpurnia May McPhee," says the stormy-eyed guy, and his deep, rich voice breaks my reverie. It booms, like he's announcing something, but there is a familiar undertone that makes it seem like those three words—my name—mean something to him. I think that I must have met him before, somewhere, but I know that if I had, I never would have forgotten him.

Craning my neck back to meet his gaze—he's got to be over six feet tall—I wonder how he knows my name. His eyes draw me in, calming my erratically pounding heart.

"Welcome to the Prism," says the pixie-haired girl in a friendly tone. She smiles warmly, and so does the stocky guy. The taller one, though, keeps his lips in a firm, straight line. But his expression is softened by a tenderness—a knowing—that makes me instinctually lower my eyes. It's like he's trying to communicate without words, trying to force me to accept what I'm fighting not to acknowledge. I briefly wonder if I look crazy, like if there's dried blood all over me or glass stuck in my face or anything. I give my body a quick scan, and I realize that I'm cloaked in shimmering gray, too. But it's not a robe, it's just an illusion, like a metallic rainbow sheen that's covering my body—the clothes that I was wearing when I was on my way to Nick's are beneath it, and when I try to touch it, it's not really there.

"I'm Sarah," says the girl. "This is Ryan, and this is Thatcher."

A thousand questions spin through my mind. I can't seem to focus on just one.

"You're in the celestial plane between Earth and the next dimension," says Ryan, the stocky one. "You may feel a slight buzz of energy; that's the echo of your life force, the part that's still left in your body. Sarah, Thatcher, and I are Ghost Guides. Our job is to teach you how to use your new ethereal form and—"

"Wait." I hold up my hand so he'll stop, so I can take this in. *"Ghosts?* My *ethereal form?"*

"Calpurnia, we should start with—" says Sarah, and her voice is calm and soothing as she steps toward me.

"It's Callie," I interrupt. "And this is nuts. I'm in a totally whacked dream."

"No dream," Thatcher says. Regret is laced through his voice. More, I see it in his eyes.

"No. I just have to wake up. I just have to—" *Get out of this freaking dream!*

I start running, but nothing changes. It's just fog and mist and gray. It's like I'm on a treadmill or something, trapped, with no hope of escape. Thatcher is suddenly in front of me. An invisible wave slams into me. I bounce back and land in a sprawl. He didn't push me, he didn't touch me at all, but it was like my body was repelled by his, like a force field was surrounding him.

"What was that?" I ask, disoriented.

"Our form is protected by what you might consider an energy shield. It repels any ghost who gets too close."

"Cool trick, but look, I'm not a ghost. I'm alive. I'm gasping for breath from the running, my heart is pounding—"

"Those are just remembered reactions, phantom sensations, like an amputee who wants to scratch an itch on his toe even though his foot is no longer there. Your soul hasn't yet adjusted to the fact that you are no longer housed within a body."

No longer housed within a body? I shudder, and I don't care what he says about phantom sensations, my heartbeat kicks up a notch. I can hear blood rushing between my ears.

"Over time, the physical sensations will fade as you become accustomed to your new form," Sarah says kindly.

"No, no, you don't understand. I just need to wake up." I slap my face. It's there. I can feel it. And earlier, I was weeping. Tears. Real tears. Wet, warm. I pinch my arms, my legs. I experience the tiny pricks of pain, but they're surrounded by that weird buzzing sensation.

"It doesn't do any good," Thatcher says. "It won't change anything."

"What are you talking about?"

"Denying what's happened. Grieving your former life. It's better to move on quickly."

His voice doesn't waver, it doesn't catch, but I sense a sorrow underneath it, like he doesn't fully believe what he's saying.

"Wait. My *former* life? You're saying that I'm . . . I'm really *dead*?"

I whisper the word, not wanting to speak it aloud, not wanting it to be true, even though I'm beginning to realize that I'm not in a dream. I'm in a nightmare, but deep inside, I know it's not one I'm going to wake up from. I *feel* that I'm no longer living. You can't die in a dream, I've heard. If you do, you're really . . .

Thatcher opens his mouth, but I turn away before he can say another word, because I see the truth in his eyes. I'm dead. The painful knowledge nearly doubles me over. I wasn't ready to die. I wasn't supposed to die! Carson, she'll go off the deep end without me to ground her. Nick . . . we were on the verge of sharing something really special. And now I'll never see him again. My father has lost both his wife and his daughter. He gave me the BMW—he'll blame himself. I bow my head as the sorrow overwhelms me. *What will happen to my father? He's totally alone.*

A sob escapes my throat, because I know now for sure. I know what the truck did. I felt my body jolt. I felt my . . . my whatever, my soul . . . leave. I felt myself die. I hear a primal cry that sounds like it's coming from a wounded animal, someone whose anguish can't be contained with normal, human sniffles. And I realize it's coming from me.

The low electric buzz ramps up inside my body, and now it's less like I'm holding an electric razor and more like I grabbed onto a live wire, the energy twitching through me in shocks and starts. I don't feel pain but intense vibration.

The sensation frightens me so much that I stop screaming. I swallow the ache. I stay quiet, and the energy ebbs. Staring into the distance, I feel hollow and empty.

"What's wrong with her?" Ryan asks. "Why was she screaming?" He approaches me cautiously, bends down slightly, and studies me as though I'm some strange specimen that he's never before encountered. "Are you . . . angry?"

I glare at him, incredulous at his confusion. "I just found out that I'm *dead*. Of course I'm angry. Sad. Lost. Alone. How can you think for a single moment that I would be okay with any of this?"

He appears truly baffled. "But ghosts don't feel things the way the Living do."

Ghosts. The word sounds so unreal, so wrong. "I'm not a ghost."

"You're an echo of your former self," Thatcher says. "Once you're here, your emotions naturally dim."

"Excuse me?"

"This space anesthetizes you." He gestures at my surroundings, and I take in the foggy landscape, noticing that there are soft spots of light here and there that move across the bleakness, and it seems like they could cast a warmth over the gray background, if only they'd stay still.

"It's so . . . blank," I say.

"It's designed to help you detach from life." His words are practiced, flat, like he's said them a thousand times, and he's not meeting my eyes now. Was it easy for him?

"I don't want to detach from anything!" I shout, more tears coming now. I can't give up what I had without a fight.

"Anger isn't useful." Thatcher shakes his head like he's as confused as Ryan by my reaction—or maybe feeling threatened by it.

"Not *useful*?" I scoff.

"It won't help you haunt. It can hurt you."

"So can denial." My voice, cold and hard, echoes around us. The irony doesn't escape me: I'm doing exactly what I'm accusing him of—denying that this gray place is my reality.

Thatcher flinches slightly, almost imperceptibly. I don't know if he's reacting to my words or my tone. His face becomes an unreadable mask. "Do you remember your life?"

I focus on the bright spots that move across the surface of the mist. A flash of images races through my mind—Mama's pearl nails, Daddy's big brass laugh, my yellow tufted rug, Carson blowing bubbles in the yard, Nick in front of me in science . . .

"Of course I remember it," I whisper.

His forehead wrinkles with concern. "That's unusual but not impossible to deal with."

"Well, that's a relief. I wouldn't want to be *impossible* to deal with." If I weren't already dead, I'd die from the pain.

Sarah kneels in front of me but keeps her distance. "You're going to be okay. We know it's overwhelming at first. That's why you're given a Guide."

"But there's been a mistake, right?" I ask hopefully. "You're going to send me home."

"No mistake," she says gently, cautiously, as though she's afraid of setting off another emotional rampage.

I drop my head forward, confused, disbelieving, and the mist swirls around me quickly.

"So what do you think?" asks Ryan. He glances first at Sarah and then at Thatcher. "She seems extremely emotional. She shouldn't be so emotional."

Not be emotional? How can anyone not grieve when they've lost everything?

"I'll take her," says Sarah, her tone light and energetic. "It's my turn in the rotation, so . . ." She gestures for me to stand, but before I do, Thatcher says, "No."

He glances at Sarah hastily. "I mean, I'll take her."

"I don't mind," says Sarah. "You just finished with that boating accident guy and you probably need a break—"

"I said I'll take her," Thatcher repeats decisively.

Sarah shrugs and stands up, stepping back from me.

"Take me where?" I ask.

"Well, if you've got this, Thatcher . . . ," says Ryan, turning to go.

"Good luck!" says Sarah as she spins around to follow him. Then she glances back over her shoulder at me. "Don't worry, you'll do fine. Thatcher's a really skilled Guide—he's been here longer than any of us."

She smiles before disappearing into the mist with Ryan.

I give my attention to Thatcher, who's staring right at me. He's clenching his strong, defined jaw, his arms folded over his broad chest. If I concentrate, I can see beneath his shimmering robe to faded jeans and a tight black T-shirt that hugs his shoulders. He has a rangy, athletic build.

"How old are you?" he asks abruptly.

"Sixteen," I say. "You?"

"Eighteen forever."

His intense gaze slams into mine. A chill sweeps through me.

When he sees me shiver, he crouches near me, and I realize that warmth radiates, pulses, from his body. "You're warm. Or is that another phantom sensation?"

"It's real. The energy within souls generates heat. Sometimes it can provide comfort."

"I thought ghosts were supposed to be cold."

In one smooth motion, Thatcher unfolds his body and stands up. "You can't believe everything you hear on Earth."

I slowly push myself to my feet, my legs unsteady. "Earth," I say, and it sounds so weird. Am I not on *Earth*? "I want to go home. I have to see my dad, I have to—"

"It won't be the same. You must understand that. You can't interact with the Living."

"The Living? Oh, God, this is such a nightmare."

"It might prove helpful if we start your haunting," he says quietly.

"So what—now I'm supposed to rattle chains and scare people, try to be featured on *Ghost Hunters* or something?"

I can tell that he doesn't want to, but he can't help himself. He smiles. If he'd walked through the door with that grin on his face, I might not have taken an immediate dislike to him and this place. It's comforting, familiar. "That's not what haunting is."

"What is it then?"

"It's easier to understand if I show you. Please, come with me."

"Where are we going?"

His smile withers and along with it our momentary connection. I sense that he regrets both, that they were a mistake that won't happen again. "It'll make everything easier on both of us if you'll just trust me." He starts walking away from me.

Peering through the fog, I see nowhere, nothing. An endless sea of gray mist and emptiness. I follow him, moving one foot in front of the other in a hopeless march.

He leads me toward the doorway through which he came earlier, and I see the kaleidoscope of color rippling again.

"This is a *portal*—it's a gateway to another dimension," he explains. His gaze lands on me again, but I don't react. I have the sense that I'm trapped in a science fiction movie.

"We live in three dimensions on Earth, but the Prism isn't restricted that way," he continues, void of emotion, a teacher who has no passion for the lesson. So why did he volunteer to be the one to teach it?

I can't focus. I'm thinking about the last movie I saw—a 3D horror film with Nick. He tried to be the big strong boyfriend, but when the killer jumped out at a totally unexpected moment, he screamed and spilled our entire bag of popcorn. We both laughed in that silent-shake way that you do when you're trying to be quiet, and then he reached for my hand. "Never tell anyone about that sound I just made," he whispered. "I promise," I said, leaning in to kiss him. I was so happy, so content that day.

"Callie, are you listening?" Thatcher must have kept talking while I was lost in a memory.

I glare at him. "I don't want to be here."

"Then pay attention to what I'm telling you."

"So you're going to teach me how to escape this place?"

"Not *escape*, but move beyond it."

What does that mean?

He disappears through the portal, and I realize that if I don't go, I might be stuck in this misty no-man's-land. Alone. Who knows if it's safe? If it were, would I need someone to watch over me?

The portal looks like a gathering of all the sunspots I saw around us earlier—it twinkles and shifts, and I wonder if the Prism is called that because it's like one of those multifaceted crystals that you hang in the window to make rainbows. When I walk through, it feels like I'm traveling at the speed of light, like I just stepped onto a moving sidewalk that goes a thousand miles per hour. But I'm not jolted, not pulled, just *moved*. I don't see Thatcher—I don't see anything, really; I just sense pure motion.

And then I'm on the other side, and it's so familiar that I want to cry.

Home, I think.

Four

IT ISN'T MY HOME, but it's definitely Earth. The wind hits my face first, and I smell the familiar salty air as an involuntary smile crosses my lips.

The Charleston Harbor. It's midday, and the sun is high in the sky. I tilt my head back to see the sky and inhale deeply. "Love the way it smells—"

"You're not really smelling it. Scent is one of the strongest memory enhancers. Just like the smell of pecan pie can bring memories of Thanksgiving with family, so seeing something can cause you to remember a fragrance."

I glare at him, wanting to prove that I'm not like him, that I'm different, that I'm not really dead. "I *am* smelling it. I'm feeling the wind—"

I stop. Tall palmettos blow in the breeze, but my hair isn't whipping around my face. God, he's right. I'm only imagining these sensations, because past experience has taught me to expect them. "So you can't tell that I smell like wild strawberries?"

Before he blinks, I see longing reflected in his eyes. He slowly shakes his head.

"Don't you miss all the different aromas? Sunscreen, hot dogs, decaying fish?"

A corner of his mouth quirks up. "The rotting sea life, not so much. The other . . . I don't think about it. We're separate from Earth. Like being in a bubble. You have to realize that your outer shell is an illusion, a security blanket so everything isn't stripped away, so you have something familiar to anchor you. Don't focus on what's missing. Concentrate on what you can see, observe."

That's so hard. It's like all of a sudden, I can only think about the sensations that are absent: the grit of sand caught in a whirl-wind blowing across my calves, the tangy aroma of barbecue, the heat of the sun beating down. With a great deal of effort, I put it all aside and focus on what I can see.

Tourists pass by with ice cream cones, women wear big straw hats to protect their skin, and people hold hands, laughing. The scene before me is vivid and sharp—like we're watching a high-definition show from inside the TV.

I notice a little boy standing off to the side of a mother, father, and baby girl who sit together on a wooden bench with a lunch of pulled pork sandwiches and coleslaw. The boy attracts my gaze the most—he has a glow to him, almost like there's a subtle spotlight over his head.

Just down from the family, an older woman with tightly permed grandma hair sits next to an old man. She has the same glow as the little boy, and she stares at the man lovingly as he gazes over the water in front of them and into the distance. I drink in the scene, noting how she is so much more vibrant than he is, but he doesn't even seem to know that she's there.

I follow the old man's eyes out over the water, to a sailboat off the harbor with a family of four in the cockpit. As they take down the mainsail, I catch a glimpse of a girl my age—glowing—on the bow. "She's going to fall in," I say. "You can't stand out there when—"

I stop and catch my breath. Or I experience the sensation of catching my breath.

"Ella Hartley," I whisper.

"Yes," says Thatcher. "You remember her, too?"

"I need to sit down," I say to him as I start to realize what he's showing me and another wave of despair washes over me. *I am like Ella Hartley now.*

When Carson and I were little, Ella was in our ballet class—I remember she had the most incredible violet-colored eyes. She died last month when her body rejected the kidney she'd been given. It was huge news in town because everyone had been so hopeful when they finally found a donor. But it didn't take. Her friends decorated her locker with flowers and photos and poetry. Carson even added a sachet that included marjoram because she believes the herb brings serenity to the recently departed. I thought it was pointless to leave tributes for someone after they died—I thought the gestures were more for the Living than the dead.

Now I wonder if Carson will gather funeral herbs for me.

Thatcher and I sit on a bench near the very dock I sped down in my new BMW, and I watch Ella and her family motor in.

The Hartleys tie up their boat and step off, one by one, near where we're sitting. Ella trails after them with a soft smile on her face, lit up by that singular radiance. They walk right by us, unseeing, but when Ella passes, she gives me a slow nod, like we're in the hallway at school or something. I wave back, hoping my face isn't etched with the heartache that consumes me at the sight of her. Her eyes appear hollow, blank—their color muted. As she walks by, her long brown ponytail swings to the side and I see a small, green, half-moon-shaped tattoo on the side of her neck.

Immediately I shift my gaze back to the old woman on the bench. Her tight perm hovers over the same green moon symbol, but hers is a crescent. The little boy has an identical mark. My mind reels as a realization unfolds while I take in the full length of the dock and all the people on it.

In between the families strolling, the couples holding hands, the kids racing up the wooden planks, are some people who seem to be lit from within. They're in Technicolor—it's almost like I'm watching a movie where certain stars are in 3D while the others are flat. And the radiant ones . . . they share the moon mark. Their eyes reflect a mirror of placidity, an eerie calm.

"They're dead," I announce with certainty.

"Ghosts," says Thatcher, nodding.

"They seem so tranquil."

"They're echoes of their former energy."

"They glow," I say. "And they have a . . ." I move my eyes to his neck. He bends his head and turns slightly. His skin looks soft and radiates warmth as I lean in, wondering how this dead boy can seem so alive. And I see it. He has one, too—a nearly full moon mark. Was I so drawn to his face that I didn't notice it before?

He must decipher the question in my eyes, because he says, "You can't usually see it when we're in the Prism. Down here, though, the glow and the green moon are how we distinguish who's living and who's not."

"But we can see the Living, too, right?" I ask, grabbing onto the first glimmer of hope I've had since waking up in the gray mist. "The people I see without the . . . the moon and the glow . . . they're real?"

"They're *alive*," he says. "We're all real."

I don't find that as comforting as he seems to expect me to. "And I have the mark, too?"

Thatcher looks down at my neck, and I pull back my hair. I can feel his eyes on my skin and it makes me shiver.

"Yours hasn't shown up yet," he says, backing away. "It will. Sometimes it takes a little while."

"I always wanted a tattoo," I say lightly.

Thatcher studies me curiously.

"It's a joke." I can't believe I had to explain it to him. Nick would have gotten it immediately, but then he's not uptight. He's always finding the fun in any situation. Nick. I want to be with him. I want him comforting me. But then Thatcher gives me a small crooked smile, one side tipping up higher than the other, and locks of his blond hair fall over his forehead. I have a strange urge to reach up and comb them back. His face is like something out of an old painting—soft but serious, with strong angles and sharp lines. His eyes aren't like the others', though; they're not dulled at all—they're vibrant and . . . well, alive.

What must it be like to have to deal with the newly deceased all the time? In the beginning, does anyone truly accept this new reality?

A little white Westie comes bounding over, its purple leash trailing along behind it. It stops near our feet and starts sniffing around. Thatcher bends down and passes his fingers through its fur, over and over. But the fur doesn't move.

"Can it see us?" I ask.

"No, but she can sense us. Animals are much more attuned to the unconscious mind than humans are. We tend to drown out our instincts with too much thought."

I wonder about his instincts.

"Duchess, get over here!" A young woman rushes over and scoops the dog into her arms, continuing to scold her as she walks away.

Thatcher straightens, and for a just a moment he appears to be mourning.

"Could you feel her fur?"

He shakes his head. "Old habit." His hand is clenched on his thigh.

"How long have you been here?" How long have you been without sensations?

He narrows his eyes. "A while."

"Did you have a dog?"

He nods. "But he wasn't a sissy dog like that. Griz was a black Lab. Got him when he was a pup. I miss him sometimes, the softness of his fur, the stink of his breath, the roughness of his tongue." He releases a deep sigh, probably another habit, one of those muscle memories that you do without thinking and that I was told would fade in time. It's a little comforting to realize he hasn't totally let go.

He looks away, maybe embarrassed that he revealed all that. I can see him, roughhousing with a dog, tossing Frisbees for him to catch. I'm suddenly thinking of everything we can't experience. I need the familiar.

"Can you take me to my father?" I ask. "We live at Two thirty-six Blossom Drive on the Ashley River."

"We don't need an address," he says, relief reflected in his voice because I'm back on task. Maybe he needs the distraction from his momentary lapse, too. "The portals know where to go. They'll take us where we're needed—to the people who need you—and I'm sure your father will be on the list."

My chin starts to tremble as the sadness engulfs me again. Imagining my father alone is unbearable. Without me, without . . .

"Where is my mother?" I can't believe Mama wasn't my first thought once I realized where I was. Why didn't she greet me? If I can connect with her, maybe some of this awful emptiness consuming me will go away.

Thatcher clears his throat and narrows his eyes like he's

having a hard time reading the answer written on a blackboard somewhere.

"What's the matter? Wasn't this question covered in Ghost Guiding One-oh-one?" I ask.

He snaps his head around to glare at me. "You're not taking this seriously."

"I think you have serious pretty well covered for both of us."

"Callie—"

"Look, I just want to see my mom."

"She's not in the Prism anymore."

I don't know if I should be assured or worried.

"Where is she?" I ask. "Where did she go?"

"She moved on."

"To where?"

"Beyond the Prism is a realm that's something like what you probably imagine Heaven to be," he says.

"Heaven." I sigh. "So she's happy? She's okay."

"She's more than that," says Thatcher, and when I give him a doubtful glance he adds, "Yes, she's absolutely fine."

The conviction reflected in his eyes assures me that he believes his words, and his certainty is a relief. A weight lifts from my shoulders, one that I didn't even know was there. *Mama is okay.*

"But I can't see her?" I ask, just to be sure.

"No," he says. "I'm sorry."

"Hmm, you'd think one perk of dying would be reuniting with people you love, right? Isn't that what all the movies show?"

"It isn't like in the movies, Callie," says Thatcher, with the hint of a smile, a kindness in his face that eases some of the anxiety I'm feeling.

I study the slatted wood of the dock under my feet. The evening shadows are starting to fall now—the sky's golden glow is giving way to a blue twilight, and the Living are heading back to their cars. I see the ghosts shuffling among them, too, slowly, calmly. "Did you know her?" I ask.

"Your mother?"

I nod.

His mouth sets in a tight line, like he's trying to decide what to tell me. "She left just after I . . . arrived," he says.

"So you met her," I say.

"Briefly."

"And then she left because . . ."

"Ghosts move on when they've completed their haunting," he says.

"What do you mean?" I ask.

"Let me show you. Walk with me."

We head to the end of the pier, moving quietly side by side. I watch people pass us—mostly Living, but ghosts, too—sharing space and interacting with each other. A few of the glowing beings even nod at me and Thatcher, and I politely wave back. I'm confused, sad, maybe in shock. But I don't feel like my life is over. It can't be. And there was Ella with her family—sailing with them just as if she were alive.

"Everyone is so peaceful," I say, thinking back on each scene I just witnessed and the ghosts I see now. "It's not at all like the stories I've heard—the moaning and wailing and terrorizing that ghosts do."

"Ghosts are peaceful beings," says Thatcher. He furrows his brow like he's thinking about what he just said. Then he adds, "For the most part."

Five

THATCHER TRACES A PORTAL in front of us, using his hand to cut an opening through what was—only moments before—empty air. Hundreds of tiny points of light blaze into a glow like sunspots framing the portal. We walk through together. This time, I sense him with me in the space, traveling at a smooth speed almost like we're two bullets lined up inside the chamber of a gun. I wonder what this would feel like if I were still alive, if my body were really here and hurtling through dimensions like this. I bet it would be the ultimate rush, but as a ghost, the motion feels natural and almost calm. It's silent and effortless, and in some ways it seems instant, but I don't trust my notion of time.

When we get to the other side, I take in a sharp breath.

It's my bedroom, just as I left it. My middle dresser drawer is open, and a blue tank top hangs over its edge. Something inside me starts to crack. I'd considered bringing the tank top as part of my day-after-with-Nick outfit, but I went with a plain white T instead. Half a glass of lemonade rests on the nightstand—Carson's, left behind after she helped me get ready for my night with Nick—and my pajama shorts are balled up next to my pillow. The bed, as always, is unmade.

This is my room, these are my things, this is what's left from my life. But I'm absent. None of these objects means anything, really, but seeing them in this moment, they mean *everything*.

Thatcher is watching me carefully. He must read the heartbreak in my face, because he comes closer to me and says softly, "Tell me about them." He points to the photos over my bed. "This one looks like it has a story."

It's a shot of me and Carson on a ski trip in the mountains of North Carolina. My gaze skips over to a collage of moments spent with Nick. But I can't go there right now. I turn my attention back to Carson. Her left cheek is bright red because she's just face-planted on a black diamond—it was more like ice skating than skiing that winter because it wasn't cold enough for good snow.

"It was icy," I say. "She's actually a good skier."

Thatcher eyes me disbelievingly. "Like all girls from South Carolina," he says, and I laugh.

His face lights up at the sound, and I feel a flash of self-consciousness. But then he turns back to Carson's picture and smiles, and I appreciate his kindness. I think about my best friend and how she was right about this "other side" all along.

"Is the Prism like limbo?" I ask. "Is that why there are all these ghosts here?"

He looks at me again, the smile replaced by a serious expression.

"The Prism is a stage that souls pass through before traveling to the next dimension. Beyond the Prism is the big, thumping heart at the center of the universe. It's the place where we learn the true meaning of existence, once we merge with it. We call the heart of the universe Solus."

He spells it for me. *S-o-l-u-s*. But the way he says it, it sounds like he's saying *solace*. I was never really sure whether to believe in things like God or church or any of that. The way Thatcher's talking, though—even as he says these official phrases that he's obviously memorized and rehearsed—lets me know that he does believe. Like when you ask preachers about God and they give you a lot of information that sounds kind of made up, but they have so much faith in it that it all rings true, somehow.

"Giving the people we love a sense of peace around our deaths— that's our goal," he says. "Did you see how easily Ella walked alongside her family? That's because they're easing into acceptance of her passing."

I nod as Thatcher talks, not because I completely understand what he's telling me, but because I want him to keep talking. This room is filled with memories for me, pictures and objects and cor- ners I could get caught up in—memories that could devastate me if I let them. But there's something in the rumble of Thatcher's deep voice that's distracting and soothing, and after what I've been through—you know, dying—I could use some comfort.

As he explains more, my gaze lands on the framed photo of me and Mama that sits next to my bed. She's wearing a big sun hat and smiling right at Dad, who took the photo. Sitting in her lap, I'm staring straight up at her face with an expression of total love. If your mom dies when you're six, you never get to that time where you fight with her and go through all that hard stuff—you just get to the point of utter adoration. And that's when she was taken from me.

I wait for Thatcher to pause, to stop explaining things about Solus, which I know is this huge, answers-to-all-the-questions-in-the-universe thing. It's not that I don't care; it's just that I'm focused on something else. And when he finally does take a breath, I ask, "So you were going to tell me . . . why did my mother leave?"

"It was her time to merge with Solus," he says carefully. "She fulfilled her purpose for being in the Prism, which was haunting her loved ones—you, your father . . . she stayed with you to help you accept what happened to her and move on."

"So you mean my mother . . . she didn't leave until . . ."

"Until you let her go," says Thatcher, finishing my thought.

I sink down to sit on my bed.

Right after Mama died, Dad and I went to her tombstone in Magnolia Cemetery every day with fresh flowers. Dad stayed quiet, mostly, while I would tell Mama about what I'd done in school, because she used to always ask me about that when she was alive. After a while, though, we just went to her grave a few times a week, then only on Sundays after church. Eventually, we stopped with church altogether, and we stopped visiting the cemetery, too, except on her birthday.

But it wasn't like I never thought about her. It wasn't like that at all.

I whip my head around to glare at Thatcher. "I didn't let her go,"

I say, feeling defensive. "I wouldn't ever—"

"It doesn't mean that you forgot her," he interrupts. "It just means that you had healed enough and accepted her death so that she could move on. It's a good thing. It's what I'm going to help you do for the people you love."

Did I move on from Mama? I guess so. I found reasons to be happy again, moments of light. I even grew to love my life and all the potential that lay ahead. My mind flashes to Nick, my summer plans, maybe going away for college.

The knives of grief stab at me once more and slice into my heart, making me clutch at my chest as if I could protect it from their assault. The Future. The Possibilities. They're *gone.* Involuntarily I shake my head no—back and forth, faster and faster—and I don't know whether I'm trying to wake up from a nightmare or if I'm trying to clear away all the dreams I used to have. Everything I hoped for, all the experiences I never had, they're in the past tense now, or some tense where things don't even exist, they never did—they're just *what might have been.*

When I meet Thatcher's eyes, he turns away quickly like my sadness is an affront. He's uncomfortable dealing with my pain. His shoulders tense up as mine slump and I crumple to the floor. No support, no kindness, no outreach from him and I'm flailing. It dawns on me that he's trying to tell me that my purpose now—my *future* now—is to help everyone I love let me go. How can I possibly do that when *I* don't have the strength to let *them* go?

A rustling outside catches my attention. Nick is pushing open my window.

"Oh," says Thatcher quietly. "Is this your . . ."

"Nick." I say his name like it's the most important word that's ever crossed my lips and rush toward him.

"Callie." Thatcher protests, but I ignore him, getting to Nick just as he climbs inside and perches on the window seat. I reach out to hold him, but my arms pass right through his torso.

Nick hunches over, his body shaking. Is he . . . crying? It's so soft I can hardly hear it, but I think he is, and my heart takes another stab. He picks up the stuffed penguin he won for me at the state fair last year.

His dark brown hair is hanging down over his face, and I want to grab him, I want to say to him *I'm here*, I want to make him laugh by telling him that tears will just mess up that penguin's cheap fuzz-fur even more.

Thatcher moves closer to us. "You're not here to interact with him in a physical way," he says. "We're going to *haunt* him. That sounds like something out of an old ghost movie, I know, but what haunting really is—at least in its true form—is a practice that helps your loved ones grieve."

I drop to my knees next to Nick's feet, unable to listen to Thatcher, unable to focus on anything but this sensation of complete loss. It's like my throat is filled with glass as I fight against the tears that are piling up inside me. The grief is amplified by the fact that I'm feeling it alone, that I can't melt into Nick's hug, that there's no one to hold me. He has to be feeling the same. I'm not there for him any longer. I guess he came here to feel close to me.

I put my hand out to touch Nick again—I can't help myself—but my fingers just pass through his. Still, I feel a ripple of energy and I look up at him hopefully, but his face doesn't change.

"I don't understand," I say. "I'm sitting on my floor, right? I'm touching it. Why can't I touch him?"

"You're not touching the floor," says Thatcher, and when I look down I realize that I'm slightly above it, just a hair, hovering. "You're moving by memory, so it feels like you're on the floor, but you're not. You're in a remembered pose. Anything physical you experience is an illusion."

"I felt something, though. Just now. Our fingers tingled, not in a way I've experienced before."

"You still have an echo of your soul left in this dimension, and it brushed his soul, but the Living aren't usually conscious enough to notice that type of interaction."

I want to push my sadness down, and the best way I know to do that is through action. So far, everything I've tried has been pretty ineffectual.

"How does this haunting thing work?" I ask Thatcher. "Will it make him feel better?"

"When it's done right."

I look up at him, a definite challenge in the set of my mouth. "Then teach me how to do it right."

Thatcher kneels beside me. His warmth surrounds me almost as solidly as his arms might. "What your presence does is offer him a sense of peace. He may never realize that you're here, but your energy echoing in the space with his is enough."

I sigh, frustrated. "Isn't there a way to show him that I'm really here?"

Nick's phone rings, and we fall silent as he puts it up to his ear.

"Nothing," he says, plucking aimlessly at the penguin's fur with his free hand.

Sweeping his gaze slowly around the room, he quietly responds to the voice on the other end of the line: "Nowhere."

It's a while before he speaks again, and I try to decipher what the other person is saying, but I just hear muffled noise.

Then, suddenly, Nick's face crumples and he lets go of the penguin, covering his eyes as he doubles over on the window seat and chokes on his next words.

"It's my fault."

A new kind of pain hits me—it's guilt and sorrow and rage rolled into one storm of emotion at the unfairness of everything. *He thinks my death was his fault.*

"No!" I scream, but of course he doesn't hear me, doesn't even glance up. I search wildly around the room, wanting to throw an object to the floor, make my presence known. But when I swipe at the glass perfume bottle on my dresser, it's like I'm a hologram. It doesn't even rattle a little bit.

"Help me!" I shout at Thatcher in frustration. "Can't you see that I need to reach him?"

"Calm down." Thatcher's voice is maddeningly composed. "Your energy is intense, and your memories are strong, stronger than most. But if you're too worked up, we'll have to leave."

I stare at him hard. "You said you were here to help me make a connection. So do it already!"

"Callie, you—"

"Okay. I'll come." Nick's voice interrupts Thatcher.

With a tightening in my chest and an ache in my heart, I watch Nick pull himself together as he hangs up the phone. He's struggling to be brave, to be strong. I want to be there for him so badly. But I don't know how. He walks over to my desk and fingers a pendant he gave me—an amber heart on a silver chain.

When I was little, my mother gave me a heart-shaped jade charm, and I kept it on my desk. After she died, I lost it—but I never stopped hoping I'd find it, so I could hold on to that piece of her. When I told Nick that story, he bought me the amber heart, "not as a replacement," he said, "but as a reminder that other people love you, too."

He removes it from its chain and slips it into his pocket. Then he crawls back out the window onto the strong branch of the oak tree.

I try to rush after him, but Thatcher gets in front of me and I repel back, that strange sensation of undulating waves pushing at me.

"Get out of my way!"

"You can't reach him right now," he says sternly.

"I have to talk to him!" I'm pleading with Thatcher to understand, to help. "He didn't even realize I was here."

"You need to calm down. Relax."

"Don't tell me to relax." Nick's car rumbles in the driveway, and I scream at Thatcher. "He's leaving!"

"If you go after him now, you won't be able to do anything," he says, not getting out of my way, his stance one of a warrior protecting his turf. Even in death, he's stronger than I am. I know it; I can feel the power emanating from him. "Do you remember what I was telling you? To reach them, you have to be in a calm state, and it helps if they are, too. Then they're more open to sensing us."

The car's engine grows fainter. Thatcher steps aside, knowing he's won. I rush past him and lean out the window, trying to see where Nick is heading.

"Callie, listen!" This time Thatcher's voice isn't distant or calm—it's sharp and immediate.

I glare at him. "You're more of a bully than a Guide."

"And you're the most emotional ghost I've met in years."

"Are you telling me that other people just accept *dying*?"

"There's usually an obliviousness for new ghosts, an amnesia about life that makes it easier to haunt. The newly dead are calm by nature."

"Well *I'm* not," I say.

"Clearly."

"Are you saying I'm overly sensitive?"

"You're less . . ." He stops, and I can see him weighing his words, something real friends don't have to do. For some inconceivable reason, I wish we were real friends.

"Comatose?" I ask, thinking about Ella Hartley's dull eyes.

Thatcher scowls. "Something like that."

I drop my head back, sighing as I watch the shadows from the headlights of a passing car dance over the ceiling. Even shadows exist in this world with more solidity than I do. At least they're visible.

Thatcher sighs, too. "I'm on your side."

"Is that why you turned away from me earlier?"

His face falls, but just for a moment, and then he puts on his mask again. The one that hides his feelings. One of the things I love about Nick is his openness and honesty. He never hides anything from me. That's why he's hurting so badly now.

"Okay," I say. "If you're really on my side, then take me to my father."

"No."

"Why not?"

"There's an order to haunting," he says. "First you practice on people who aren't as close to you—the portals will lead you to them. And you work up to the ones who mean the most."

I consider this "order" for a moment. "But Nick is someone I love. He's as close to me as anyone in my life."

Thatcher doesn't respond; he just looks out the window.

"Did you hear me?" I say. "Nick is important!"

"I don't decide these things," says Thatcher. "The universe does."

"The universe does," I mock him. He sounds so crazy. This is all so freaking crazy. And terrifying. I don't want to be without the people I love, the ones who love me.

"Can't you just leave me here?" I ask. "I'll sign something saying that I take full responsibility for my actions. I'll figure it all out on my own."

"It's not that simple. I know it might not feel like it, but you did well. Your energy is extreme, but . . ." His voice trails off and then he meets my eyes. "Don't worry—you'll find ways to help everyone you love move forward."

His tone is gentle again. I soften, letting my frustration give way to sadness as I sink down onto my bed. Thatcher scans the room once, taking in each corner of my old life, and then he comes back to the bed and sits down with me. When I look up at him, I notice a tiny scar on the left side of his chin. I wonder how he got it.

"But how do I move forward?"

"I need you to be patient while you learn," he says. "You are not to haunt anyone unless I'm by your side. Do you understand?"

"Yes." I've always been independent, willing to explore new things, but it's not like I can research this realm on Google and figure out where I need to go or what I need to do. As much as I hate to admit it, I also seem to have no instincts when it comes to this haunting business. It felt horrible trying to make Nick see and hear me without any response from him. Thatcher is the only thing here that makes me believe that I still *exist*.

Then he stands up, and panic rises in my chest. I don't want to go anywhere, not now. "No, I'm not leaving my house. I need to stay here. I want to see my father—"

"Callie, I swear to you, you'll see your father," says Thatcher. "Right now let's just take a break."

I look down at my yellow area rug, all tufted and bright except for the worn-in spot where I step out of bed in the mornings. I want to lie down under my soft comforter and sleep forever, only waking up if I can start this day all over again.

"I don't want to go," I whisper.

"I know," he says, a tinge of regret in his voice, like he *does* know.

"Did you . . ." Within the depths of his gray-blue eyes is an openness, an honesty that draws me in. "Did you, you know, *haunt* your family?"

He turns away from me. "I tried."

The back of his neck stiffens.

"Do you still haunt them?" I ask.

"Not really," he says, turning to me again. "But sometimes I—"

His eyes meet and hold mine. I see him struggling to find the words. For the first time, he seems almost as vulnerable as I feel.

"Sometimes you . . . ," I prod gently.

Sadness flickers in his eyes, and he doesn't finish his sentence. Instead he says, "We'll come here again very soon."

I decide not to push him. "Promise?"

"I promise."

"It wasn't Nick's fault. My death, I mean."

"Of course not."

"You know how I died?" I ask.

"I know enough."

"I didn't mean to hurt anyone, to cause so much sorrow."

"We never do." Thatcher's voice holds an immense amount of understanding. I wonder who-all he hurt. Maybe I do need to trust him. It's clear that reaching out to Nick on my own won't work—I can't even connect with a perfume bottle, let alone a person.

"Will I ever be able to tell him that?" I ask. "That it wasn't his fault?"

"Yes," Thatcher says, creating a portal and motioning for me to stand up.

And I do, because I want to believe him.

Six

KALMIA, MAGNOLIAS, AND ROSES are growing in this perfectly kept garden. It's dark outside, but I'd know this spot even if I were blindfolded.

"Middleton Place," I whisper.

After speeding through the portal, I find the stillness of the historic plantation startling, almost like a quiet morning after a torrential rainstorm. We're on Ashley River Road, right along the water. There's a main house with wide-sweeping terraces that look out on acres of manicured grasses, gorgeous paths, and long, garden-lined vistas to the river and the marshland in the distance.

"I used to come here with Mama," I tell Thatcher, staring out at two swans swimming in the reflection pool in front of us. Lanterns along the dark shore cast a soft yellow glow. "We'd bring bread crumbs and sit by the water together."

I smile at the memory of my mother—it seems sharper in my mind now that I'm back here again. I spin around slowly, taking in the landscape and missing the light, powdery scent of the crepe myrtle all around us. Homesickness and a deep loneliness wash over me.

"Is there someone I'm supposed to haunt here?" I ask, wondering when I'll visit Carson. I want to see her, but I doubt she's out in the middle of the night.

"No," says Thatcher. "I just wanted to bring you, I mean . . . I wanted you to have . . ."

He fumbles over his words, like he's nervous.

"I wanted to give you a break," he finally says. "After seeing Nick. I know that was kind of . . ."

"Intense," I finish for him. I flash back to my bedroom, and I realize how suffocatingly sad it felt there, surrounded by all that I've lost. I'm grateful for the open night sky above me right now.

"Right. And this is the most serene spot I know of in Charleston, at least at night, so . . ."

He pauses again, and when I see his furrowed brow, I realize that he's waiting for my reaction. "Thank you," I say. "This place means a lot to me."

Thatcher gives me a quick smile and turns toward the path, away from the pond. "Shall we take a walk?" he asks, like he's an old-time gentleman come to call on the lady of the plantation.

He starts off on the path without waiting for an answer, and I watch him move gracefully, a few steps in front of me. I peer down at his feet, so close to the earth but not quite touching it, and I wonder if he always had this smooth rhythm to his walk or if it's a ghost thing. His motions are so controlled, so deliberate. It's like he's holding on to something—maybe his whole sense of the universe—very tightly.

I follow behind him, my eyes raking over the grounds. I've never been here at night, and as ironic as it sounds given my current ghost status, it's a little spooky without all the tourists milling around.

I rush to catch up to him, and for a second I almost take his arm, because it feels natural, but something holds me back. We walk together slowly and quietly. There's an ease to our silence that's almost more comforting than talking, and I'm suddenly glad that it isn't Sarah or Ryan who's with me in this strange new space.

"Why did you volunteer to be my Guide?" I ask.

He hesitates. Finally, he says, "Sarah and Ryan are new Guides. I could tell that Ryan was already nervous about your abundance of emotion, and Sarah is just so caring and sweet. She's not comfortable being firm when firmness is needed. She coddles. That's not what will help you. You have a strong aura. I knew you'd be a challenge."

"A strong aura? Is that a polite way of saying I'm a pain in the butt, so you decided I needed a hardass?"

Thatcher makes a sound like he's choking back a laugh. "You don't mince words, do you?"

I find myself wondering what his full-throated laughter sounds like. Why is he so closed up, so afraid to let loose his feelings?

"Your other . . . gosh, I don't even know what I am. Your student, I guess. Anyway, the others. Do you miss them?"

"No. We don't form attachments."

That might explain why he holds such a tight rein on his emotions. I can't imagine having people coming and going constantly through my life—or my death—and not feeling anything at all toward them. Or them not feeling anything toward me.

It seems like such a sterile existence.

About halfway to the main house, I hear a noise in the stable yards, where I *know* there aren't horses anymore.

"Ghost horses?" I ask.

And *that* makes Thatcher really laugh. The sound is deep and genuine, more full of life than anything else about him so far. But I guess it makes sense that he wouldn't be full of life.

Still, it echoes around us, seems to travel through my soul. I want to place my hand against his throat and feel the vibrations of joy that I thought he was incapable of making. He's so much more approachable in this moment, like someone I would know from school. It swallows up the distance between us.

"No," he says, still smiling. "Animals must go to another place."

"No pets in the Prism?"

"Afraid not."

So he'll never be reunited with Griz. That doesn't seem fair, and it makes me sadder than anything else has so far. I almost ask him about it, but there's no sense in bringing him down, too. "So what was that noise then?"

"It's just Miss Alice."

"Am I supposed to know who that is?" I ask.

"You've never heard of her?"

I think for a minute—Carson has definitely told me about supernatural activity at Middleton Place.

"She's the ghost who lives here?" I ask, unsure.

"Right," he says. "Let's test that exquisite memory of yours. Do you know her story?"

We step into the stable yards, and I try to recall the history of this place. "I think the Middleton family had, like, eight hundred slaves back in the seventeenth and eighteenth centuries. So I bet some of those ghosts are hanging around."

"Don't you think they'd rather pass through the Prism and leave this life behind?" asks Thatcher, eyeing the old farm tools on display in the stables. "There can't be that many happy memories for slaves here."

"Good point."

"Miss Alice walks the grounds at night," says Thatcher. "She wasn't a slave—she was a local daughter deemed not worthy of the boy she loved, a Middleton heir. She died an old maid in her thirties, and she still wears old-fashioned clothes."

I snort, not bothering to hide my skepticism.

"It's true," he says, hand on his heart.

"Aiiiiioooooooouuuuuuuu . . ."

A low, eerie wail emerges from one of the stables. Thatcher's face tightens into a grimace. That noise did *not* sound like it came from someone named "Miss Alice."

"Stay behind me," Thatcher orders, putting his arm out protectively but moving toward the third stable, where the cry seemed to have emanated from.

As we creep closer, two figures sprint out of the doorway, running like they've seen a . . . well, you know.

Thatcher doesn't even glance at the people running—he's focused on the stable. When we get to the entrance, he steps determinedly into the doorway, crossing his arms over his chest and blocking the exit.

"Leo," he grinds out, his tone full of disapproval.

I peer around his shoulder and see a huge, muscled guy with tight-cropped blond hair and a bulging-vein-in-neck issue. He's holding a hay hook in his hand, but when he sees Thatcher, he lets it drop into the soft dirt at his feet.

He's in real clothes—jeans and a T-shirt without any shimmering metallic sheen like the other ghosts have—but it's clear that this *Leo* is a ghost. He doesn't seem calm or graceful like the other ghosts I've seen, though—his energy is off the charts, like he just got a pep talk from his football coach before a state championship game. His cheeks have a slight stubble, the white-blond kind that catches the light, and his eyes are a dark brown, deep set and trained on Thatcher.

"Just having a little fun, T," says Leo. "You remember fun, right?" He tilts his head in a mocking gesture.

"Leo, you know you shouldn't be—"

"Oh, please," Leo interrupts Thatcher. "They were a couple of teenagers making out in the barn. I gave them a scare, and now they'll have a good story to tell their grandkids. No harm done."

I study the hay hook on the ground; its sharp blade is rusted but glinting menacingly in the moonlight.

"Did you get a look at them as they ran?" Leo asks me. "Were they friends of yours . . . Callie?"

My head snaps up. *He knows my name?*

I meet his eyes, staring back at him. I can tell that he's used to people being intimidated by him, but I've never been big on fear. Besides, what can he really do to hurt me? I'm dead.

"Stop it, Leo," says Thatcher.

"What?" Leo makes an innocent face. "I heard she has an amazing memory."

I'm taken aback. People—or . . . ghosts—are talking about me?

"And so much energy. God, it's practically pulsing off her." With a feral glint in his eyes, he rushes toward me—

Thatcher steps in front of me and Leo goes flying backward, collapsing onto the hay. A concussion of air explodes between him and Thatcher, and I can feel the vibrations throbbing around me.

Releasing dark laughter, Leo shoves himself to his feet. "I just need a little energy, T. Don't be so stingy with it." He shifts his gaze over to me. "You should let me be your Guide, Callie. I'll teach you things this guy never will."

"You're not a Guide, Leo," Thatcher says.

"Doesn't mean she couldn't learn from me."

He charges toward Thatcher. When he's close, another wave of power or energy or whatever it is ripples between them. Thatcher takes a step back, regains his balance, and remains standing. Leo hits the ground hard. He chuckles. "That would hurt if I were still alive." He scrambles back to his feet. "Come on, T, play fair. Turn off that I-shall-not-be-touched vibe you got going. Have you noticed that, Callie? This guy keeps so much distance between him and others, he might as well be on Mars. He's probably told you that we can't feel; we can't experience things like we did before. But that's just because he's afraid to feel anything."

"You should go," Thatcher says.

"Not until I knock you off your feet." He lowers himself into a tackling stance.

"Hey, are we having a party and I wasn't invited?" A raven-haired girl with dark skin and delicate features steps between Leo and Thatcher. Leo relaxes his stance.

She's small, petite, but something in her confident stance makes me think she isn't to be messed with. *And she's wearing clothes, too.* Her tight jeans outline muscular legs, and her tank top shows off her strong shoulders.

She glances at me briefly, and then her large brown eyes zero in on Thatcher, apparently her target all along. Her face is like a porcelain doll's—perfect rosebud lips and high cheekbones. The word *lovely* comes to mind. Those brown eyes look like they have glowing embers inside them—they flicker and burn. This girl, though obviously a ghost, looks *alive*—not like Ella or the others with their serene expressions.

"You two are not supposed to be here," Thatcher insists.

"You're not in charge of where we go," says Leo.

"Don't fight, boys," says the girl, smiling now. She fastens her gaze on me. "Callie, welcome to the other side. How's Thatcher treating you so far?"

"He's been great," I say, confused about who these two are and why animosity is thick in the air between Thatcher and Leo.

"Really?" she asks, flashing an even bigger grin. "He doesn't like that many ghosts, doesn't warm up to them, so take it as a compliment."

I can't tell if she's taking a jab at Thatcher or trying to put me at ease.

"Reena, please," says Thatcher, and I hear a twinge of hurt in his tone. A definite jab.

"Oh, Thatcher." Her voice lilts affectionately. "It's okay to make a new friend."

Leo lets out a loud laugh, and it sounds kind of mean. I move forward, feeling unexpectedly defensive for Thatcher.

"So attached already?" asks the girl, raising her eyebrows in surprise. "Don't worry, Callie—Leo and Thatcher are old friends." She smiles then, sincerely, and I'm drawn in to the light around her.

I smile back before I can help myself.

"I'm Reena," she says.

"Nice to meet you." My manners kick in automatically.

"You grew up in Charleston, too?" she asks.

"Born and raised, for a few generations now."

"Cool," she says. "I'm a transplant. Army brat."

"Oh, my dad's in the Navy," I say. "Well, he was. He teaches at the Citadel now."

"Awesome," says Reena. "My younger brother goes there."

"You have a younger brother in college?" She doesn't look older than me.

"Yeah," she answers, smiling. "Weird, huh? If I were alive, I'd be, like . . . twenty-eight!"

She and Leo break up laughing. "So old!" he shouts.

I back up a step, realizing that I'm talking to people who have been *dead* for, like . . . ten years? Will I be here that long? Thatcher said it was best to move on quickly—so why haven't Reena and Leo moved on? Why don't they glow? Why don't they look like Ella?

Reena locks her eyes onto my face and studies it so intently that I feel a little awkward.

"Have I got a zit on my nose or something?" I ask.

She grins, clearly not offended by my snarkiness. "You're funny. No, I can't figure out what it is, but you're not like the others."

"Her energy is off the charts," Leo says.

"Yeah, I can feel it, but it's more than that."

"We're leaving now," Thatcher says. "You should do the same."

"Has she been to her spot?" asks Reena, directing her question at Thatcher, stopping him in midstride.

"My what?" I ask.

"Let it go, Reena," says Thatcher, and it's more of an order than a suggestion.

I wonder what *it* refers to.

"Thatcher's a little protective of his charges," says Reena, still scrutinizing me as though I'm a sudoku puzzle that she can't quite complete.

"Was he your Guide?" I'm eager to learn more about this girl—and in the process maybe find out more about Thatcher. He obviously carries some weight around here.

"Something like that," she says.

"Are you a Guide?" For some reason, my question makes Reena and Leo break up in laughter.

"No, we both completed our haunting," says Reena.

Leo grins. "We avoided Solus another way."

And the way he says it, it sounds like *Soulless.*

"What do you mean?" I ask.

"Come on, Callie," Thatcher says, indicating the doorway. "No good will come of staying here."

"What's the rush?" Leo asks. "Afraid she'll learn the truth?"

"There are ways to extend your stay in the Prism, Callie," Reena cuts in quickly before Thatcher can respond to Leo's challenge. "Don't let Thatcher convince you that you can't have more time on Earth."

More time on Earth.

"Yeah," says Leo. "Not everyone wants to move on."

"I thought Solus was like Heaven," I say, looking to Thatcher.

"It is," says Thatcher. "There's an order to things, and there are rules that some people refuse to accept."

He glares pointedly at Reena, and it strikes me that she and I might have some things in common.

"You used to be more exciting when you didn't mind living outside the lines," says Reena. Then she turns to me. "It's no fun to follow the rules." She grins. "When you get bored of his restrictions, come find me."

Thatcher clenches his jaw as he stares hard at Reena.

"Time to go," he says through tight lips.

"We were just leaving." Leo smiles, and the flash of his big white teeth is almost blinding. He moves forward and fake-jabs at Thatcher, who flinches a little. Leo's laugh echoes eerily up to the rafters.

He motions for Reena to follow him, and they turn to walk out of the barn. With his back to me, I see that Leo's moon tattoo is dark and jagged, not like the smooth glowing green crescent I've seen on the other ghosts. I look quickly at Reena, but her hair is covering her neck. She gives us a small wave before they both exit through the large wooden double doors.

I expected them to create a portal, but they just walked into the night like normal living people.

When I'm sure they're gone, I ask, "Who were they? How do they know who I am?"

"Forget them," says Thatcher, avoiding my questions. "They just want to cause trouble."

"Why did they look more like living people? They were in regular clothes, without this—"

"We're all in regular clothes." Thatcher's voice is clipped, impatient. His eyes look more gray than blue now. "The shimmering aura means you're haunting, that you're on the path to Solus."

"If they finished their haunting, why are they still here?" I ask.

"They've broken the rules," he says. "They can't move on from the Prism because of their obsession with being on Earth."

"We can stay in the Prism?"

"Not indefinitely," he says, putting his hand on his forehead like his brain hurts. "The Prism is just a gateway to Solus, where we're all meant to be."

His skin is growing pale. It almost looks like he's fading away.

"What's wrong?" I ask.

"My energy is low," he says. "Leo's aggression drained me. We have to get . . ." His voice trails away like he no longer has the strength to push out the words.

I don't want to leave Earth, not now, but he appears sick and exhausted. . . . I hesitate for a moment, but when he creates the portal, he is barely able to lift his arm in order to make it large enough, and his weakness scares me a little. I stop arguing. I don't know how else to help him. I'm assuming everything I learned in the first-aid class I took is pretty useless here.

We step into the portal and are thrust through a speeding tunnel; I've already tuned out the sensation of movement that comes with this method of transportation. My mind is churning—I'm wondering how much time I can spend with my father, with Nick, with Carson, before I have to move on. Maybe I can stay with them on Earth. I'm thinking about Reena, hoping I'll see her again. She said something that resonated with me: It's no fun to follow the rules.

Seven

BACK IN THE PRISM, Thatcher appears to have recovered somewhat. He looks more like his no-nonsense, let's-get-this-done self.

"If you stay on Earth for too long, your energy will fade," he explains, now that his voice is back. "Earth is not a natural place for the soul to exist without a body, so it takes a lot of energy for us to be there. After a short amount of time away, we always need to return to the Prism—it's our energy base."

We walk for a few minutes through the mist. Nothing is getting any clearer—I can't see more than five feet in front of my face—but Thatcher moves with a purpose, like he's heading somewhere specific.

We stay silent, and I notice that I'm experiencing things differently here than I do on Earth. In the Prism, there's a lightness—it almost feels like I haven't eaten for a while. My whole being has a slight hum running through it. I become conscious of the fact that my sight and hearing are crisp, but my body feels like it's underwater—blurred.

My thoughts are buzzing with everything that's happened since the accident. My entire world has shifted—it's been lost, found, and reshaped. This mysterious place with fog and mist and grayness isn't my home. I want to be on Earth, to stay there as long as I can. Thatcher made it seem like that wasn't a good choice— or even an option—while Reena indicated that there was a way. And Ella Hartley was at the pier, walking alongside her family like everything was almost happy, nearly okay. That's what I want for the people I love, too.

I flash to Nick's sadness, the way he crumpled onto the window seat in my room, and I wince at the memory. His pain was so visceral—I have to find a way to ease it. Is that really what Thatcher will teach me to do?

Thatcher. I take in his profile, strong and sure. He's merely inches away from me, and I realize that he hasn't once brushed up against me or led me with a touch. I know if I—or anyone—rush toward him, it creates that undulating wave that repels, but what about a subtle approach?

I lean sideways in his direction slightly and his body moves away from me in a fluid motion, almost like we're opposing magnets. I try again, stretching my fingers toward his, but his hand moves in the other direction, and it looks involuntary, like we're meant to maintain a certain measured distance between us. I'm not even sure he's aware of my reaching for him.

Just as I'm about to ask him about it, we arrive at a blue door.

"Each of us has a prism, a sanctuary," Thatcher says. "This is yours. Open it."

When I turn the silver knob, the door swings inward, and I step into my room. It's not really my room, at least not as it exists now—there's no life-interrupted quality to it like my real room had, with the lemonade and the unmade bed. This room looks as if it's from my childhood, a past version of my room, and my phantom heart suffers a hit—*thump*—as I take in my desk, my bed, my window seat, my posters, my closet, my shelves. *Mine.*

Everything shimmers just a little bit, like it might disappear if I touch it.

Thatcher is standing just outside the doorway. His lips are parted slightly as he examines my space, but he's careful not to lean over the threshold even as his eyes fill with wonder.

"If you're so interested, you should just come in," I say.

He doesn't move, but he presses his lips into a firm line and quickly masks his awe. "You shouldn't invite ghosts into your prism," he chides as though I should have known. "It's your personal space."

I tilt my head, searching his face. Why does he shut down his feelings? Why does he avoid sharing too much with me?

"I've been through a lot today," I remind him. "And you're the one who's been beside me for all of it. Don't tell me you're leaving me now." I reach out to take his hand, but he pulls away from my touch, as though it could harm him, destroy him even.

I look down, a little hurt.

"Callie, I . . ." When I lift my gaze to his, he tries to smile as he cautiously steps into the room. Immediately, he gasps. The sun-spots—the ones that gather to form a portal—dance across his body, lighting up like a thousand fireflies all around him. I watch him, captivated, as he stands still and straight until the glow starts to fade.

"What was that?" I ask, almost breathless at the sight of him now. He looks lit from within.

But he tries to brush it off, turning to the window so I can't see his face as he answers. "The energy in your prism is very strong. When I entered, it was shared with me."

"Well, you're welcome!" I say, trying to lighten things a little. I go to stand next to him at the window, but when I approach, he moves to the side, putting a foot between us.

"Got it," I say, turning to my bed across the room.

"No, I didn't mean . . . ," he starts. But then he says, "Never mind."

"What?" I ask as I sit on the bed.

"Touching is discouraged," he says quietly.

"Why?"

"There's an energy exchange when ghosts touch. Like when I entered your prism. I've taken some of your energy already, just by being here."

"But if we touched, then wouldn't you be sharing some with me, too?" I ask.

"Yes, in theory. But—"

I shake my head, cutting him off. "It's okay," I say, suddenly feeling self-conscious that I'm sitting here trying to talk Thatcher into touching me. It's not a direction I meant to go in.

"Callie, it's not that I don't want to," he says, interpreting my interruption as disappointment. "I don't remember the last time I've shared even a casual handshake with someone. I miss it, sometimes."

I would think so. My heart aches for him.

"That makes me sad. Carson used to say that touch was the best healing people could give to each other."

Thatcher crosses his arms over his chest and nods. "It can be, yes."

"I went through a phase after my mom died where I didn't want to be touched," I confide in him. "But Carson would not tolerate it— she would wrap her arms around me and hold tight until I stopped trying to fight her off."

I smile at the memory, but when I glance at Thatcher, he looks bewildered.

"Don't worry, I won't do that to you," I say.

"You wouldn't be able to," says Thatcher. "Touching only happens if both ghosts are open to it."

"Is that why I've felt this magnetic opposition between us sometimes, how you stopped me from reaching Nick and Leo couldn't make contact with you?"

"Right. Your energy is personal—you need it for haunting—and it isn't to be shared. To that end, Callie, you shouldn't invite anyone else into your prism."

"What? So no prism-warming party?" I ask, teasing him a little.

I can tell that he doesn't know whether or not to take me seriously. Finally he says, "No parties."

"No jokes either," I say under my breath.

I move over to my green Pottery Barn antique-look desk and pick up a photo frame that holds a picture of me and Carson from Halloween about ten years ago—we're both wearing bumblebee costumes. Mine's orange, hers is blue. The frame is solid in my hand; it's really here. Mama took the picture—it was the last Halloween she had with us.

"Who set up this room?" I ask, wondering if it might have been, if it could have been—

"You did."

I feel silly for thinking Mama might have done it. I don't want to accept that she's not here waiting for me. I haven't been to church regularly, but I do know that the idea of a Heaven where your family members wait for you to join them has been in my head since I was a kid. It's heartbreaking to know that's not how it works. It doesn't seem fair.

Suddenly a thought occurs to me. "Did I miss my funeral?"

"What?" Thatcher blinks in surprise.

"My funeral," I repeat. "If it hasn't happened, can we—"

"Not possible," says Thatcher. "Time here feels very slow, but it actually moves quite quickly in Earth terms. Your accident was over two weeks ago."

"Two weeks? That can't be possible. I just got here."

"It's possible. We're in a different dimension. The time-space continuum—"

"Save the physics lesson." I sigh. "So my funeral already happened."

I look down at my hands and wonder if Dad spoke, if Carson said anything. If Nick wore the dark blue suit he bought for last year's formal.

Morbidly, I also wonder if Dad had an open casket for me—if my body was . . . intact.

I suddenly realize that I haven't thought of the other driver, and guilt rushes through me for being so selfish. "Was anyone else hurt?"

"No. Only you."

"Oh." *That's good.* How could I have been so self-involved that I didn't think to ask that until now? Is the Prism changing me? Dulling my humanity somehow? I almost can't believe I'm able to go a moment without weeping. Am I transforming into one of the calm and placid ghosts? Do I want to?

And then I wonder: How does Thatcher know so much about me?

"It seems like you know more about my death than I do," I say.

He nods. "The Guides know the circumstances of souls who come into the Prism. It helps us to aid them with the haunting process."

"It was Route Fifty-two, right?" I ask him.

"Yes, but going back there isn't an option. Dwelling on the end won't help your loved ones, or you, move forward."

I didn't ask to go back there, I think. So why is he so insistent that I not go?

"What was your end?" I ask him.

"An accident," he says. "Like yours." He doesn't flinch. But I've already seen the pain that blurs the edges of his controlled persona, the softness that lies underneath.

I gaze at his face, hard and resolute. I study the square line of his jaw. There's the slightest bit of stubble around the edge of it, like he hasn't shaved in a day or two. *I wonder if his face is frozen in time, exactly the way it was on the day he died.* I have the urge to reach up and touch it—I can imagine its soft bristle on my fingertips. I haven't touched anyone, even for a second, since I've been in the Prism, and now that Thatcher's told me it's "discouraged," I feel even more like I need to do it. Just a quick touch, his strong arms coming around me, bringing me in against his solid chest.

As though he knows the direction of my thoughts, he breaks his gaze from mine and clears his throat soundly.

"You'll be comfortable here," he says in a businesslike tone. He looks around again, like he's a real estate agent showing me the property. "So anyway, this is your prism, and you create what that is. Some people's prisms may be totally devoid of memories, but it's all about what you're focused on, and what's best to help you transition."

I take in a deep breath, acutely aware of the absence of sensation: no scent, no air rushing through the passages, no need to exhale because I'm not actually filling my lungs. A momentary panic shoots through me, as though I could suffocate.

"Are you okay?" Thatcher asks, taking a step toward me.

I nod quickly, try to swallow. No saliva. Crap. "Yeah, I'm just suddenly really noticing what's not there. I feel like I'm dying all over again."

He moves nearer. "Look at me, Callie. Don't center your thoughts on what's not there. Concentrate on what you can see."

What I see are his eyes, such a deep blue, like the view of the middle of the ocean from a ship my dad and I once went on. I couldn't see into the depths of the water, but I knew so much was there. Thatcher's like that. A calm surface, but buried beneath it is more than I can ever imagine.

"You can't die here," he says, his voice even, soothing, drawing me away from the panic. "No more pain."

"No more pleasure," I stammer.

"Not true. There are some physical sensations, not true physical sensations, but there are pleasant experiences. Right now, though, notice that your sight and hearing are so much more attuned. You still have them. Your soul can feel electrical impulses. When you need to feel that, rub your thumbs over your fingers." He holds his hand up to demonstrate.

His hands are large, strong, the kind where the muscles and tendons seem flexed even when they're relaxed. I follow his orders, circling my thumbs over my fingers, feeling myself becoming more centered.

I find myself swallowing again, even though there's no saliva, nothing to swallow. But it's not frightening. It's just what it is—or what it's not.

"Let yourself absorb the energy of your prism." His voice is almost hypnotic. "Just relax. Imagine you're floating on gentle waves, balloons holding you up, moving you with the soft wind."

I nod. "I'm okay now." But I still need his voice. "Tell me about this place."

"I like to think of the Prism as a honeycomb, like bees make. Each of us has our own chamber, or room, or our *prism* . . . and all the prisms make up the big world of Prism with a capital *P*. Does that make sense?"

"I think so," I murmur, back to being myself.

"Good," he says, backing away slowly as though I'm a skittish cat he doesn't want to frighten. "So this is your personal prism, your resting place."

"My final resting place?" I joke, trying to get us both back to where we were before I made a fool of myself.

He smiles indulgently, and I appreciate that. "Why don't you relax here for a while?"

"Relax?" I ask. "What am I supposed to do without the internet?"

"Nothing," he says. "That's the beauty of it. Sit, connect with your conscious mind, work through some of your memories. That's the first level."

"The first level of what?" I ask.

"The first level of the soul. With most who arrive here, the memories come when they are ready to be dealt with. Since you have all of yours, you can pick the ones you want to focus on, like a kaleidoscope."

I shake my head—this is getting too weird for me, and I don't need the pressure of connecting with my soul.

"I'll be back after a while, Callie."

"You're leaving me alone?" I'm suddenly cold at the thought of Thatcher leaving. I don't want to be alone with my thoughts, dwelling on my death. "Please don't go."

"You'll be fine. Just focus on what is instead of what's not. You're safe here."

"Safe? Safe from what?" I ask.

"It's just an expression."

"What about that Leo guy?"

He stiffens. "He can't bother you here. Just remember not to invite anyone in."

I glance frantically around my prism. "I'm not ready to be alone yet."

"But everything here is designed to bring you comfort."

I rub my hands up and down my arms. "It's not working. I know you're tired, that you need to be reenergized or whatever, but can't you do that here? You can rest on the bed. You don't even have to talk to me. I just don't want to be by myself. Not yet."

He studies me intently. Compassion flickers in his eyes. His gaze darts to the bed, to the chair, to me. "You can have the bed."

In long strides, he crosses over to the chair and settles into it.

Relief swamps me, because he's staying. The thought of being alone filled me with such dread. What if I had another panic attack? I never had them when I was alive. How strange to have one when I'm dead.

I wrap my arms around my body as I walk around my room, a little too antsy just yet to rest. *I wish Mama were here.* It's a thought I had a thousand times while I was alive. I'm sure everyone who loses a mother feels that way. But losing a mother and having a father who pushes away grief and tamps down his own feelings feels especially lonely sometimes.

When I was alive and loneliness hit, I found my next adventure, anything from trying to do a skateboard jump off the roof at age seven (minor cuts and bruises) to my last exhilarating moment, speeding along the highway (which didn't end so well).

But here? I have no idea how to chase away the empty.

A mirror hangs on the back of my door, and I pivot around in front of it, taking in my image. I look alive—I can't even see the shimmering robe in this mirror, just my last outfit—white shorts, boatneck T. I lean in closer to inspect my neck, but I don't see a moon mark.

"You can't see it here," Thatcher reminds me.

"I thought maybe I was an exception."

"Apparently so when it comes to a lot of things, but not that."

I glance over at him. He doesn't seem irritated or upset. He seems to just be waiting. "Will this hurt ever go away?"

"Eventually. Try to focus on your memories."

I take in each detail of this space, letting my eyes travel over the curve of my dresser drawers and the slight nick near the bottom where I ran into it roller-skating around my room in second grade, the collection of neglected but not yet donated stuffed animals in a corner chair, the soft draping of my sheer yellow curtains brushing the window seat.

As I absorb each inch of my prism, the hollow feeling in my stomach starts to fade.

This place is cozy, this place is mine—it knows me. I realize there are even items from different time periods on display. My bulletin board features the horse jumping ribbon I won in first grade—the one Dad let me take to school for show-and-tell three times, just so I could talk about how I urged the spotted pony Double Take over the highest fence on the course. I finger the purple satin, marveling at how real it feels. It can't be actually here, right? Does this place truly exist, like in a way that would hold up in science class?

I sit down on the bed, which feels exactly like my bed at home—the perfect combination of soft and firm—and I struggle to get in touch with the inner peace that ghosts are apparently supposed to have. Lying back, I let my head touch the pillow as I roll over on one side. I draw solace from Thatcher's presence. He's so tall, broad, strong. I bet every girl wanted to be his when he was alive. And now—

"Can we do anything on Earth except haunt? Can we sneak into a movie—"

"No. We have to remain focused on our purpose."

"Right, our purpose."

"Draw on your memories—"

"They just make me sad. To know all that's gone."

He leans forward, planting his elbows on his thighs, his eyes earnest, the blue darkening into sapphire. "If you could only hold on to one memory forever, which would it be?"

"Is that how it works? I can only keep one?"

He slowly shakes his head. "No, it's just an exercise to help you focus. But wouldn't you choose a good memory, one that makes you feel loved?"

"I have so many of those."

"Pick one. Concentrate on it. Share it with me," Thatcher urges solemnly, his voice hypnotic.

To pick only one seems an impossible task. But I give my mind the freedom to explore all the possibilities. A jumble of memories rushes through my mind, and it's almost like I'm inside each memory—hearing, seeing, smelling, feeling the moments. I'm being pummeled with the past, but I can't stop thinking of more and more—it's addictive to be with Nick again, and that's what it feels like, like I'm really *with* him for the time it takes to recall a memory.

"After the spring dance, I had a curfew and Nick didn't," I begin. "My dad made sure I was home by midnight, but after I said good night to him, Nick came up to my room . . ."

"Is the coast clear?" he asked, whispering in the darkness.

"Shhh." I pushed back my covers and met Nick at the window in my pajamas. He was still wearing his suit.

"You changed," he said.

"You're overdressed," I said, pulling him close and loosening his tie.

"May I have this dance?" he asked, stepping back and offering me his hand.

I took it, and he led me to a square of moonlight that spilled onto the little yellow rug near my bed.

I tried to get him to take off his suit that night, to crawl under the covers with me. But he said, "Tonight is about romance," and we held each other, swaying to the quiet songs my iPod shuffled until two a.m.

A fresh surge of grief hits my chest. I just re*lived* that moment. Was that my unconscious mind taking over? A tear forms in my eye. Why did I always push things away like that? Why didn't I savor that moment in the moonlight? Why did I need it to be *more*?

"That was intense," I whisper. "I could see, hear, smell, touch . . . everything. Like it was real again."

"I know. I could sense it . . . almost like I was there as you painted the images. Your memories are so powerful."

We're both silent for a minute.

Then he says, "You really miss him, don't you?"

"*Yes*. Isn't that normal? Didn't you lose a girl you loved when you died?"

Sadness equal to mine seems to consume him. I watch his throat muscles work. If he were alive, he'd be swallowing. "I lost her later."

Before I can say anything, he shoves himself to his feet, and I know he's regretting that he opened a small portal into his soul, revealed a hint of vulnerability, shared a portion of his life. I have an urge to wrap my arms around him and reassure him that everything will be all right.

"We've rested enough," he says succinctly. "We should probably return to haunting now."

In spite of the questions nagging me, I swing my legs over the bed and stand up. I point down to my desk, at the photo of me and Carson.

"I want to see her," I say, and to my surprise, he nods agreeably.

But when we rush through the portal that Thatcher draws, we don't emerge in Carson's room or her backyard or even her car.

We land in a graveyard.

Eight

THE SKY IS BLACK, but the yellow glow of a streetlamp peeks through the Spanish moss that hangs from the giant live oaks over the crumbling tombstones. This is a huge cemetery—we're in Historic Charleston. A crowd of people are gathered around a man in old-timey clothes who's holding an oil lamp above his head.

He rambles on about Charleston's paranormal history, talking about Boo Hags, creatures who "ride" their victims by slipping into their skin and walking around wearing their bodies. "It's best not to fight a Boo Hag," says the guide. "They won't kill ya unless you struggle—they may want to come back again for another ride later, see?"

"At least we know Boo Hags and possession aren't real," I say to Thatcher, like we're a couple sharing a private joke. His jaw twitches but he doesn't respond; he just stares straight ahead into the night.

The tour group is closed in tight around the guide, but a few other figures are hanging back a little bit.

I recognize Ryan, one of the Guides who met me when I first got to the Prism. He's with a girl who's about our age, and both of them have the glow and the moon mark. When Ryan sees me wave, they walk over to us.

"Hello, Callie, Thatcher," he says, smiling. "This is Genevieve—she joined us this week."

Genevieve has wide eyes and one of those mouths that relax into a frown.

Thatcher does little more than give her a nod in welcome. Nick, on the other hand, would have been totally gracious and known her entire life story in two minutes flat. He would have had her laughing in three.

I study this person who maybe can relate to what I'm feeling a little bit—the sweeping sense of devastation I'm dealing with.

"Hey," I say. "I'm so sorry for your loss. Or, um, the loss of you . . . or . . ." *What does a person say in this situation?*

"Hi." Ignoring my sympathetic gaffe, she rests her eyes on Thatcher, who's no longer looking in our direction. He and Ryan have moved away from us and seem to be engaged in a serious discussion.

I catch only a few of Ryan's words: "—an eye out for possible trouble."

"They won't do anything if we're here."

"They're getting bolder. Sarah had an encounter . . ." His voice goes so low that even straining, I can't make out what he's saying.

Thatcher swears harshly. Is that sort of language allowed in the afterlife?

"Is he your Guide?" Genevieve whispers to me.

"Yeah," I say.

"Oh." And I hear her wistful tone, like she's thinking I'm so lucky.

I don't know why, but I feel a sense of ownership over the strong shape of Thatcher's shoulders, the way his lips are parted slightly, his eyes narrowed as he scans the area like his stance alone can thwart any danger.

Stepping back over to us, Ryan smiles at me, and if ghosts could blush, I would.

"Genevieve," says Ryan, extending his hand in an inviting gesture. "Your mom . . ."

With a sigh, Genevieve turns back to the tour, and I can almost feel her energy level ebb. "My mom . . ."

I eye Genevieve warily. When I returned to Earth and saw Nick the first time, nothing in the world could have kept me from reaching out to him. Is she so distracted by Thatcher that she forgot her haunting?

"You're here to see your mom?" I ask.

"Yes." She looks at me with calm eyes. "She's lovely, but so sad." She turns to Ryan. "We'll help her, right?"

Ryan nods, and the two of them move away without a word and head closer to Genevieve's mom.

"Is everything all right?" I ask Thatcher.

"All under control."

I don't think he'd admit it if it weren't.

"Why does Genevieve seem so oblivious?" I ask.

He appears slightly guilty, like the answer is somehow his fault. "That's the normal state for someone who is new to the Prism."

I can understand how it would make the transition easier. "I guess that's why Ryan freaked out about my emotional outburst."

He gives me a wry grin. "Yeah." As though he expects more questions, he nods toward the group. "Pay attention."

Lantern Guy is talking more loudly now, shouting to be heard by the back row of tourists. "Your cameras will capture orbs of light—those are ghosts, and sometimes you can catch as many as ten at a time in a photograph." The tourists take out their Canons and start snapping away. The flashes point toward us, and I put my hand in front of my face to block all the lights.

"Old wives' tale," says Thatcher, leaning in toward me. He's relaxed again, in Guide mode. "Those are just lens flares they're getting."

"So we won't . . . show up?" I ask.

"No," he says. "They have no idea we're here."

"Tragic."

"What?"

"Well, these people are in the presence of real ghosts, and they're going to fall for Lantern Guy's tricks."

Thatcher doesn't reply, but he appears amused.

The flashes stop as the guide starts talking again. "There's been more paranormal activity this summer than ever before." He lowers his voice conspiratorially, like he's letting this whole tour group in on a big secret.

Ping-ping.

Searching in the area of the unexpected sound, I see a couple of small stones bouncing off a particularly haggard-looking tombstone. When I follow them to their source, I spot Leo. He's with another guy—a tall, lanky type. They're sitting on the roof of an ornate Gothic mausoleum, laughing as they toss stones in the air.

The way they're glowing in the dark night, against the aging, jagged stone, they look lit up with a spotlight, like performers in a show. And I guess they are. Each time a rock hits the gravestone, the tourists jump, but I can tell they're all having fun seeing this. It's what they came for.

Thatcher's presence is closer than ever, over my shoulder, and when I turn slightly, his face is inches from mine. I can see the sweep of his long eyelashes over his cheeks when he blinks. If he were alive, I'd be able to inhale his scent. He strikes me as a classic Ivory soap kind of guy. He's so intense, and while on one level his seriousness irritates me, on another his dependability is incredibly attractive.

"Let's go," he says quickly.

I step away. "Not yet." I eye him carefully. "This is interesting. They're moving things—people can see that they're here."

Thatcher shakes his head. "They shouldn't be here."

"Those little rocks aren't going to hurt anyone. Show me how to do that. I want to throw a stone."

He frowns. "No, Callie, you cannot *throw a stone*." He darts a quick glance up at Leo and the other guy with disdain before settling his gaze back on me. "It takes a lot of energy to move things—they can only do it because they're sharing energy, which can have unintended consequences. And for what? They have absolutely nothing meaningful to do here. They're just performing parlor tricks!"

"Wow, you're really mad."

Thatcher inhales, no doubt a habit from when he was alive. "Forget them. We're here to help your loved ones grieve, not to act like circus monkeys."

"Sorry," I mumble. "I just thought it might be fun."

"It's not *fun* to mess with the living. It's dangerous." He points up at Leo and the skinny guy. "*They* are dangerous."

Leo is holding on to a tree branch, jostling it in the air. "There's no wind," the tour guide loud-whispers. "And yet it moves. . . ." The people on the ghost tour are oohing and aahing, snapping photos and chattering energetically about this being the best ghost tour ever.

I shrug, imagining how rapidly my heart would be beating if I were on the tour and didn't know the truth—the wild adrenaline rush of the possibility of ghosts. Even though I didn't believe in ghosts, these guys could spook me. Or more likely I'd have been convinced it was all fake and talked Nick into hanging back so we could investigate and figure out how it worked. "It looks totally harmless to me. It's just giving the people a thrill."

"Creating thrills is not our purpose."

And then, as quickly as they appeared, Leo and his friend create a portal of glowing light and vanish through it.

Thatcher sighs, visibly relieved, and I decide to save the rest of my questions for later, maybe for Leo himself.

"She's what we're here for," Thatcher says.

I crane my neck to see where he's pointing. The tour guide is saying something about a woman named Theodosia Burr Alston, and that's when I spy Carson's glossy curls as she stands up from where she was sitting on a bench in the front of the crowd.

She brushes her hair out of her face, revealing that her normally sparkling eyes are tired. She has dark circles and she isn't wearing any makeup, which is rare for Carson, especially when she's out. Her usually smiling mouth is clenched in a tight line, and her sadness is so unfamiliar that my heart cracks open some more at the sight of it. She should be laughing, singing, dancing around like she always does, even in the face of darkness. But losing a best friend might be enough to break the brightest spirit I've ever known. I can't let that happen.

I want to rush up and squeeze her, but I know enough now to realize that won't work. I hang back, studying her more and thinking that she looks better than Nick did, at least, like she might be dealing with things in signature Carson fashion—moving forward, always.

But then I remember where we are.

"What's she doing on a ghost tour?" I ask.

"Looking for answers," he says. "But she knows it's a scam."

"You can tell?"

"I can read people." I look at him closely, wondering if that's what Thatcher's pain is—that he sees the sadness of the Living as he helps other ghosts haunt. How does someone apply for the job? And why would they? I think it would be don't-want-to-get-out-of-bed depressing day after day. It would take someone with a certain temperament, a special gift. While he holds himself aloof, I have to admit that I believe he is truly trying to help me—even if I don't appreciate ninety-nine percent of the lessons.

"What?" asks Thatcher, obviously uncomfortable with my scrutiny.

"Nothing."

When I turn back to Carson, I see the bored disappointment carved in her stony expression. "You're right. She's not buying this."

She reaches out her hand and pulls someone up beside her. His profile is reflected in the moonlight.

"Nick," I whisper.

His head is down, shoulders slumped. The weight of what's happened is sitting on his back and taking its toll. The darkness casts shadows over his face, making him impossible to read. I can't see his eyes; they're half closed and he won't pick up his head—it's like he's broken. I notice his fingers moving back and forth, back and forth, over the smooth amber heart he took from my room.

I can't believe he came—he's never thought much of Carson's interest in this stuff.

"Stay with me," Thatcher orders, and I'm aware of him eyeing my profile. He's afraid I'm going to run up to Nick again, but I follow his instructions this time.

We walk with the tour group through the graveyard. As we listen to more stories about various people buried here, we climb a hill to a specific gravestone that's supposedly a hot spot for paranormal activity. But Leo and his friend aren't around, so there's no action.

"Boo!"

Startled, I jump and spin around. Leo is standing there, grinning like the Cheshire cat. "Did you like the show?" he asks.

Before I can answer, Thatcher growls, "Get out of here, Leo."

"Aren't you tired of hanging around with this guy yet?" Leo asks me, totally ignoring Thatcher. "I can teach you so much."

"There's nothing you can teach her that she needs to know."

Leo glares at Thatcher. "Shouldn't she at least know her options, make her own decisions?"

"What options?" I ask.

"Ah, there's so much. Where to begin? With an encore, perhaps?" He dances a short distance away, as though he believes Thatcher is going to try to stop him. "Look at these suckers, Callie, all wanting the ghost experience. I could give them something they'd never forget."

"Leave them alone, Leo," Thatcher commands.

Leo steps toward me, holds his hands out imploringly. "But my partner in crime took off, and I'm a little low on energy. Want to give me some?"

Thatcher slides in between us. "She's not giving you anything."

"He's not trying to protect you, Callie. He's trying to deceive you, to make sure you never learn the truth about your powers. That's the way it is with the Guides. They want you to follow them like mindless sheep to *Soulless*. He knows if you knew everything I know, you'd never accept what he's offering."

"There's no peace to be found in your way," Thatcher says.

Leo throws his head back and stretches his arms toward the stars. "Who needs peace when we can have everything?"

He runs to the edge of the crowd and crouches. When Lantern Guy starts leading them away, Leo picks up a fallen tree branch just enough that someone trips over it, staggers, and falls. Leo's laughter, almost maniacal, echoes around us. He runs on through the crowd and disappears.

"See?" Thatcher says. "He's dangerous."

Okay, I have to admit that tripping someone isn't very nice, but still—

"He picked up a tree branch." Which weighs a lot more than a little pebble. What are his limitations? I don't ask, because I know Thatcher won't tell me. I don't think he's trying to keep anything from me, but I don't think he's telling me everything either.

"Forget about him, Callie," Thatcher says, as though he knows the direction my thoughts are traveling.

He's right. I have more important things to worry over. Nick and Carson. I watch them trailing along behind the group as Lantern Guy leads everyone back to Church Street and the tour's main office.

Carson and Nick hang back while the other members of the group thank the guide before leaving. I see Genevieve and Ryan trail after a woman who must be her mother. Nick stands off to the side with his arms crossed, still with that heavy sadness, but also annoyed and impatient. His hair is limp and dull—not like it was when I saw him just a short time ago. It doesn't look like he's washed it in *days*.

"How much time has passed since I saw him?" I ask.

"A couple of days."

"Shouldn't I be with him most of the time?"

"We can't bombard them with our presence. It drains our energy and isn't good for them."

"Yeah, well, it doesn't look like time without me has been good for him either."

After everyone else has gone, Carson pulls Lantern Guy aside. "I'm looking for something more," she says.

"What do you mean?" he asks.

"I know the ghost stories, I know the flashbulb trick . . . but I want to know, is there any *real* way to connect with someone who may be on the other side? Like, if you think you might be able to bring them back?"

Thatcher steps away from the conversation. I wonder if he doesn't want to hear the hogwash that old man is probably going to spout, but I'm intrigued by Carson's question. I lean in closer because Lantern Guy looks uncomfortable, like Carson is pushing him to reveal something vitally important.

But then he just says, "Lighten up, missy. It's a ghost tour, not a horror movie."

Carson frowns at him. She trudges over to Nick, grabs his arm, and drags him down the street toward her car.

I catch up to Thatcher, and we fall into step behind them.

"I told you," Nick says, his voice listless. "This is all just stupid BS."

"It was worth a try," says Carson determinedly. "Next we can get out the Ouija board, and if that doesn't work, we'll have to attempt a séance—"

"Carson," says Nick, opening the passenger-side door of her VW Bug. "I came with you tonight to be a good friend, but you sound like a crazy person."

They both slide into the car and Thatcher and I join them, slipping into the backseat quickly through their open doors. I almost feel guilty for eavesdropping, and I say so, but Thatcher says, "We're not eavesdropping; we're *haunting*."

"Feels the same to me."

"It won't once you're doing it properly, Callie."

They sit in the car for a minute, letting Nick's insult hang in the air.

"Don't you want her back?" asks Carson.

A heavy silence descends as Nick stares at the dashboard. I tense up. His answer is suddenly important and I don't know why. Before this moment I was so sure what his answer would be, but now I'm not so certain.

"Of course," he says.

I relax.

"Then let's try. If we believe she's still reachable, we can call on her spirit to—"

"To what?" says Nick, his voice tinged with anger. "To meet us in a cemetery during a ridiculous ghost tour? To show up in a photograph as a lens flare?"

My gaze drops to the floorboard as his comment hits me—I *was* there. I would be in a photograph, if I could be, if the trick were true. *I wish they could see me.*

"Nick Fisher, you stop it!" Carson demands, and I recognize her tone. It's the one she uses when I'm feeling sorry for myself and she wants me to just get up and *fix* whatever it is that's bothering me. It's a Carson signature. And she'd probably use it on me right this minute if she knew how I was dealing with death—not very well. God, I miss her.

"We're going to get Callie back," she continues. "I promise, she'll be in the stands with me cheering for your first soccer game of the season."

Oh my God, Carson's gone crazy. She actually thinks she can bring me back from the dead. I feel a pang of intense longing, because I wish she could. I wish she possessed such power.

"Forget it," Nick yells. His hair is in his face again—I can't see his eyes. He slams the dashboard with a heavy fist, and I jump at his force. He's not like this. Even when we fought—usually over some trivial something that we never could recall later—we argued heatedly, but we never yelled. "She's gone. I wish people would just accept it and move on."

Move on? They can't because I'm not doing my part. They're stuck because I'm a failure at haunting.

"You love her!" Carson exclaims. "She's your girlfriend and you believe you've lost her so you're not thinking clearly—"

"She *was* my girlfriend," says Nick. His face looks tired, drawn. "Carson, she's *gone.*"

"I *just* died!" I shout, leaning into the front seat and talking in between them. All right, it's been a little over two weeks, but still, grief sweeps through me. Didn't I matter more than that? I know I have no right to feel that way. I look imploringly at Thatcher.

"He doesn't need me. He's already moved on. I know I should be happy—"

"He hasn't moved on," Thatcher cuts in. *"Listen."*

I cross my arms and sit back, frustrated that he's not more sympathetic, that he's not helping me deal with all these rioting emotions. I want Nick to move on, but at the same time, it hurts.

Carson's still protesting, but Nick interrupts her.

"Letting her go is the best thing," he says. "I don't need more of a guilt trip from you than I'm already giving myself. I know it was my fault."

"Nick, you're not to blame," she says.

"Please, Cars," he says, running his hand through his limp hair. "Just drive me home."

She frowns but turns the key in the ignition and heads out.

It's superquiet in the Bug—I can't remember a time when there's been such silence in this car. Usually Carson and I roll down the windows and blast the radio. Sometimes when we do that—when the wind hits my face and the scenery rushes by and the song is the perfect one for the moment, with the perfect rhythm and lyrics that push me to want more, to live more—it can feel like I'm flying. We would scream out the words, smiling and loving those frozen pieces of time, never knowing that we wouldn't get enough of them.

Carson pulls up to the curb in front of Nick's house, and he leans his head back against the seat, his eyes closing.

"I miss her laugh," Carson says solemnly. "What about you, Nick? What do you miss the most?"

"Don't do this, Carson."

"Come on, Nick. Just tell me. Her bright red glittery toenails or the way she pulls her hair back or—"

"Her spirit, the way she's not afraid of anything. Wasn't afraid of anything."

Very unobtrusively, extremely slowly so as not to draw attention to myself, so Thatcher won't stop me, I slip my hand farthest from him around the front seat and touch Nick—or at least I think I'm touching him. I can't feel anything. But I desperately want him to know I'm here, to sense my presence, to be comforted by my love.

"She's talked about marrying you, you know," says Carson quietly. "She's that in love."

In any other situation I'd be mad at Carson for revealing what I told her in confidence, but right now, I'm glad he knows how I feel. *Felt.* I never really told him.

I sense Thatcher's eyes on me, but I don't meet them. I'm too focused on Nick. He doesn't say anything, doesn't open his eyes, and a tear rolls down his cheek.

"It's too late, Carson," he rasps. "Can't you understand that?"

Without another word, Nick gets out and slams the door shut.

My heart is breaking for his anguish. "He's confused," I say to Thatcher.

"Yes."

"He's grieving."

"True."

But having my thoughts affirmed doesn't make me feel much better.

Carson pulls away from his house, but she stops a few doors

down and parks on the street. She flips on the radio, leans her head against the steering wheel, and breathes deeply.

"What's she doing?" I ask.

"I think she's trying not to cry," says Thatcher, talking over the classic country DJ's thick twang.

"Carson," I say, leaning into the front seat again. "Don't be too hard on Nick. I'm here; I'm going to help you—"

"She can't hear—" starts Thatcher.

"I know," I interrupt, annoyed. "I *get* that she can't hear me. But I'm here; I want to talk to her. And maybe deep down, she *can* hear. I know she'd get the idea if I could just do something, like honk her horn or make the turn signal blink or something. I don't understand why—"

"That's not how it works," he says. "It's your presence that helps her. Remember how I told you about the first level of the soul, the conscious part where memories live?"

I nod slowly, still skeptical.

"We're trying to get beyond that, to reach Carson's *unconscious* sense of you. That's the second level of the soul. And just by being here, sharing her space, we'll do it."

"Well, it couldn't hurt to really show her I'm here, could it?" I ask.

"That's the spirit, Callie." A deep voice booms in from outside the car, and when I snap my head around, Leo is grinning through the passenger window.

"Get out of here," growls Thatcher, his tone low but firm.

Leo slips into the front seat, his figure moving through the car door as if it isn't there. He's inches from my best friend, and for some reason he makes me nervous. At least he doesn't have a hay hook in his hand. *But what's he doing?*

"All you have to do is concentrate, Callie," says Leo, twisting around in his seat to look at me. "Energy radiates off you. You have more power than you realize, than this guy will ever tell you."

"Don't listen to him, Callie," Thatcher says. "You don't understand the harm you can inflict."

I glance over at Carson. She's still sitting with her head down on the wheel. She doesn't sense any of us, but I wish she did.

"Can you show me how to touch something real?" I ask Leo. "Like you were doing with the rocks?"

With a smile, he reaches for my shoulder. I feel a slight shock skitter through me where his fingers are, like when you grab a door handle after shuffling around on the carpet. He puts his other hand on the radio button. "You mean like this?" he asks.

The station changes.

"Holy shit!" I shout, excited. "How did you do that?"

Before he can answer, Carson lifts her head, and then I hear the song. It's one that Carson and I loved in a jokey way, because it contains this lyric that says, "Call me Mr. Flintstone, I can make your bed rock." We found that hilarious. Slowly, a smile spreads across her tear-streaked face.

"Callie?" she whispers.

"Yes!" I shout. "I'm here!"

I turn back to Thatcher, and his quiet rage at Leo's presence is palpable. "She senses me," I say.

"She knows you're here, Callie," Leo assures me.

"No," says Thatcher. His face is tight and aggravated. "She doesn't. You're making a superficial connection right now. This isn't a game—we're trying to connect with her in a deeper way, on a soul level."

Leo rolls his eyes. "Good luck with this guy," he says to me. Then he leans over to Thatcher and whispers, "Relaaaax," before he slips out of the car and into the night.

Carson starts up the engine again and we drive toward her house.

"Show me how to do that," I say to Thatcher.

"What? Touch the button on the radio?"

"Yes!" I say. "Something! When will I be able to connect for real?"

"You are on your way to connecting for real. Your energy soothes them on an unconscious level. That's the second level of the soul—it's beyond the conscious—and it helps them know that you're okay. If you keep getting frustrated and upset, they'll feel that, too. And it won't have the desired effect."

I fold my arms over my chest. "So I should smother my emotions?" I ask. "Like you do?"

Thatcher looks me right in the eyes. "My feelings are not your concern."

"So you admit that you *have* feelings. Well, *there's* a step forward." I know I'm being mean, but he's telling me I have to let my entire world go, like throwing out a used napkin or something.

Thatcher's jaw clenches as he faces forward. The streetlights cast sporadic streams of light over his handsome features as we drive—we're almost back in my neighborhood—but his expression doesn't change. Regretfully, I think I might have hurt him.

After a moment, he stares at me intently, the blue-gray of his eyes almost swirling. "I care more than you will ever understand," he says, his voice a loud whisper. "Being a Guide isn't a privilege— it's a punishment. It means that I couldn't help someone move on. That someone is still suffering because of my death. And it's the heaviest burden any ghost has to carry."

Oh my God. I don't know what to say. A punishment? I've been wondering why anyone would do this willingly. "Someone in your family?" I ask him. "Someone never got over losing you?"

He nods quickly. What he's dealing with seems like one of the most awful things anyone could experience. "I find comfort in helping other ghosts move on," he says. "But I'm trapped in the Prism for now."

Thatcher holds my gaze. I see his pain, his torment. My heart aches for him. I wonder what it would be like if, after years, Carson didn't get over my death. If she remained perpetually grieving.

"How do I help them move on?" I ask.

"I told you that memories inhabit the first level of the soul. The unconscious is the second level, and that's what we're trying to connect with now. But Carson and Nick, and your father, won't fully release you until we haunt the third level of the soul."

I wonder again when we'll go to my father, but I'm afraid to ask, afraid to see him and acknowledge the state he's in. Facing Nick is hard enough. My father must be devastated.

"What's the third level?" I ask.

"The heart."

"The heart," I echo. And I wonder when Mama reached that stage with me. Was it when I was twelve? On the day I went to her grave without my father and lay on the grass in front of her stone in the warm sun, trying to gather everything I remembered about her and hold it close to me as tears ran down my face? I felt a release that day.

"I remember so much," I whisper into the darkness of Carson's backseat.

Thatcher nods. "I know."

"But you . . . ," I start. "You remember your life, too?"

"All the Guides do," he says. "We failed at our haunting, and the obliviousness of dying, the amnesia of the initial entry into the Prism that protects most ghosts, has worn off. So yes, we remember."

"That's harsh." I ache for Thatcher and the Guides, and for myself, sad that we have to suffer. But I'm also glad that beings like us are in the Prism, that everyone's not all calm and unemotional like most of the ghosts I've seen.

"So why do I remember everything?" I ask, worried that I've already somehow failed at haunting, too.

"You're a special case, Callie. But you have to let go of some of your questions. Solus is the answer to all things, but you can only get there if you find peace—and help your loved ones find peace—in the present. Try not to fear the unknown."

"You sound like you're reading something from a textbook," I say.

"I've said it a few times, to a few ghosts."

"Slowpoke!" Carson chides the car in front of her in her signature I-never-curse way, and I laugh.

"Thatcher," I say, staring at my friend as she drives. "I don't want them to forget me."

"They won't. You didn't forget your mom, right?"

I shake my head no.

"As hard as it is to accept, it's *good* for them to let you go."

Carson has a slight smile on her face. I want to believe that just my presence, just my being here and somehow connecting with her unconscious, put it there. But she's not feeling comforted because we're sitting in this backseat giving her good vibes. She's smiling because Leo changed the radio station and she experienced a tangible connection to me. No matter what Thatcher says, that's undeniable. I want to connect like *that*.

"Can't I help them let go in my own way?" I ask him. "I think if I could move something or show them that I'm really here—"

"Playing with energy like that is dangerous, Callie—it can drain the Prism of its reserves." Thatcher's voice is back to being serious, firm—I despise how quickly he can put up a wall. "We are not supposed to connect to Earth in that way—we're souls now, not humans."

Internally, I roll my eyes at what we're "not supposed" to do. Externally, I stay quiet and turn to the window to watch the houses in my neighborhood pass by. When we pull up in Carson's driveway, I look down the street at my own house. The light in my father's study is on.

My heart sinks as I stare at Dad's window. How many nights did he stay up late working while I texted with Carson or went online to plan my next stunt: bungee jumping, river rafting, finding the tallest, fastest roller coaster? Why did I never knock on my father's door to say good night? Or snuggle against him while he watched a military documentary, or tell him I loved him?

I sigh. When I was alive, I was so busy chasing a rush that I didn't let myself experience the parts of life that I miss the most now. Since I died, I haven't once wished I could get back into a car and speed down the docks. But I'd give anything to hug my father again.

As I watch Dad's shadow move across the drawn curtains, I promise myself that I'll show him I'm here—I'll prove it to even his scientific mind. I may have died, but I'm not gone, so I have no intention of "letting go." Not if it means never telling the people I love what they truly mean to me.

It's clear after tonight that Thatcher isn't going to help me to connect that way. And now someone else's words echo back to me: "When you get bored of his restrictions, come find me."

Nine

WHEN THATCHER LEAVES ME in my prism and orders me to "rest," I try to figure out how I can find Reena.

I could go back to Middleton Place, but I have no idea how to return to Earth, so I close my eyes and call out to Reena in my mind. Carson was big on telepathy, meaning she was always trying to get me to guess what number she was thinking of. It worked, like, twice, and she was convinced we were cosmically in sync. I laughed it off—especially since I guessed the number wrong ninety percent of the time.

The thing is, since I died, nothing seems impossible. Who knows? Maybe I can summon Reena. It's worth a shot.

I spend ten minutes sitting cross-legged on my bed with my fingers in little "okay symbols" like I've seen people do in yoga class. I half expect Reena to pop into my room out of thin air.

But . . . nothing.

Finally losing interest, I flop backward and stare at the ceiling. I want to call up a memory, let my mind go to Nick, but Thatcher intrudes. Solus means so much to him, and yet it's denied to him—all because someone wouldn't let him go. But is that really a failure on his part? I think it could be something positive. . . . Someone loved him so much that they didn't want to give him up. Don't we all want that kind of lasting commitment?

Still, it hurts Thatcher to be trapped here.

And I wonder about the love he lost after he died. Was it someone he was guiding? Did he fall for her, then have to watch her move on to Solus while he stayed behind? Is that why he keeps his distance? To make sure he never goes through that anguish again?

A rap on my door stops my careening thoughts.

Ghosts knock?

"Callie?"

It's a girl's voice, muted by the barrier between us. I open the door, and there is Reena, her dark hair swirling around her face like she's in a shampoo commercial for extra shine. Her eyes still have a fire in them, though they look less wild and more like a soft shade of brown now that I see them up close.

"Reena." My melancholy is replaced with the excitement of maybe having summoned her. "Did I, um . . . call you here?" I ask, sounding stupid even to myself.

She laughs. "No. That's not a power we have. I came to find you. I wanted to talk."

"Oh, okay." I'm disappointed to discover that I don't have

magical psychic powers. So far, death isn't impressing me with the benefits it provides.

"Why? Were you looking for me?" she asks.

I feel like an absolute idiot. "Sort of. I mean, I was hoping I'd see you again."

"Good," she says. "Listen, I'm sorry if I came off as rude before. Leo's one of my best friends, and he and Thatcher don't get along that well, so I'm a peacekeeper."

I grin at her. "You must be busy with that."

"I don't mind. Keeps me out of trouble, most of the time."

I like her loyalty, and I feel a connection to her—sometimes only a girl can understand another girl. Right now, I really need someone who understands me.

"Do you want to come in?" I ask, my curiosity about Reena overriding Thatcher's edict that I not invite anyone in. After all, he was here. It can't be that bad to share your space. "I'm supposed to be 'resting,' but I don't think I know how to do that yet."

"Sure." Reena bounds into the room. And even though she's probably, like, five feet, two inches, she fills the space with her presence, just like Carson does. Did. Does. *How am I supposed to think of my best friend now?*

"Resting is overrated," says Reena, looking around the room. She seems to light up slowly, like when you push the Brightness button on your computer screen. She smiles at me, and the word *megawatt* comes to mind. Throwing her arms up and her head back, she spins around. "Great energy! Your prism is so much like real life."

"It's my old room. I mean, almost."

"Wow." Reena points to the cluster of framed photos on the desk. "You have so many pictures."

"Carson and Nick," I say, watching her gaze land on a shot of the three of us at the state fair last year. "My best friend and my boyfriend. I guess whatever subconscious or soul thing conjures this room thought I needed them."

"Tell me about *her*," says Reena, pulling her hair up into a ponytail as she points at a photo of Carson.

"What do you want to know?" I ask.

"Everything. She's your best friend?"

"Since forever." I'm grateful that someone wants to listen to me. I close my eyes so I can hear Carson. "She laughs all the time." I can't help but smile at the memory. "Sometimes in short little bursts that she tries to catch with her hand, like if we're in class or church or somewhere she can't let it out, and sometimes in big, long hoots where she has to gasp for air. But she never fake-laughs—it's always this genuine joy that just comes out of her, almost like she can't control it."

I open my eyes to find Reena studying me intently, as though I intrigue her. "She sounds awesome," she says. "What else do you remember?"

"Well . . . Carson's nice to everybody—even people who are completely annoying—because she really does believe in that old saying about catching more flies with honey. We're different that way; she just has this positive energy.

"And speaking of energy, she's really in tune with ghosts and paranormal stuff. She's had a Ouija board since we were eight years old, and she's even tried to get me to do séances and stuff like that."

"Fascinating," says Reena, and she doesn't sound sarcastic—she's really interested. "Your memories are so detailed, so sharp."

"I know," I say. "Thatcher says most ghosts forget things when they get here."

"Not me," says Reena. "I remember everything, too, just like you. I was a cheerleader, if you can believe that."

I grin at her. "Yeah, you struck me as the cheerleader type."

"Do not stereotype. We were good!" She flops down onto my bed. "Our squad was really athletic—we did lots of tumbling and all that stuff."

"Cool," I say, glad to be hearing about a life instead of a death.

"I was top of the pyramid," says Reena, holding her arms out straight and making cheerleader fists. "And I only fell once!"

I look at her curiously, wondering . . .

"Oh, no!" she says. "That's not how I died." She gives me that megawatt smile again, and I laugh.

"Phew," I say, although I'm not sure why I'm relieved. She *did* die, after all.

She pops up from the bed and circles around the room again. "This is really cool. Usually it's just family around these parts, if there's anything personal at all. There has to be a lot of love for a friend to make it into someone's prism."

"Carson and Nick are my family." I realize that I probably should have said "were," but I just can't. "Them and my dad."

"So they're the ones you have to haunt," she says, sitting on the window seat and letting her feet dangle over the edge.

"Yeah, I haven't really gotten to do much besides watch them yet, but Thatcher says just being with them is part of it?"

My voice goes up into a question because I wonder how Reena feels about this—if she really thinks that haunting shouldn't involve actually proving that we're there.

"Thatcher." Reena looks up at my ceiling where the glow-in-the-dark stars that are in my real room are also placed. "How do you like him so far?"

"He's . . ." I wonder how much to tell her, and how much she knows. I want to say that he's mysterious, he's hurting, he's hiding something. But I can't help but feel that revealing any of that would be a betrayal of him. "He's a little evasive about my questions."

"Does he say things like 'There's an order to things' and 'You have to be patient'?" she asks, her intonation dropping to imitate Thatcher perfectly.

"Yes!" I sit down on the bed and draw my legs up beneath me. "So far it's all about *being with* everyone, but not really interacting."

"He hasn't let you make any real connections yet?" she asks.

I shake my head no. "Leo was there the other night—he did something amazing with the radio, but Thatcher told me that wasn't what we're supposed to do." I feel a twinge of guilt for being so dismissive of Thatcher. I know he's trying to help, but his process just isn't working for me. It's boring and slow.

"Shocker," Reena says, stretching out on the window seat and leaning against the wall. Her muscular legs stretch out all the way, but they don't reach the end of the seat—she's petite like Carson. "He's totally no fun. You want to be able to show your friends you're there, right?"

"Right."

"Yeah, I mean, let's get some candles floating around the room!"

I stare at her.

"I'm joking," she says, breaking into a laugh. "But seriously, the letting-them-know-you're-there thing? I can help with that."

"That'd be great." I smile at her. It's nice to have Reena here. She's funny and straightforward and willing to help. "Can I ask you something?"

"Of course," she says.

"When you hang out with your family now, is it really hard?"

Her smile doesn't fade. "I'm done with my haunting." Then she turns away from me and looks out the window into the gray mist.

I stare at the back of her neck. I shouldn't be able to see anything, but there's a quarter-sized black spot with jagged edges. Her green moon is gone, like Leo's was—it's just a dark, messy circle.

"So everyone in your family has moved on from your death?" I ask, eager to find out more. "But you haven't merged with Solus. . . ."

Reena smiles at me. "You're piecing it all together even though Thatcher hasn't told you anything. I like that. You're smart."

"Thanks."

"And you're right," she says. "I haven't merged. I never will, actually. I can stay in the Prism, and on Earth, forever."

Forever. I remember her saying there were ways to have more time on Earth. But forever? "How?"

Reena's smile fades. "It's complicated. But it's not impossible. And whatever you do, don't talk to Thatcher about it. He's all about merging—*graduating* to Solus. Shouldn't death free us from having to do things we don't want to do?"

When I search her face, I can tell that she's conflicted. She's pretending to be happy, but I saw it—I saw the sadness.

Reena brightens again quickly. "It's wonderful to be able to see the people you love living their lives—now I never have to leave them."

I look over at my photographs and wonder if they're all I have left of the people I love now. Just images, observations, never a real connection. Even if I help them heal, they'll never really know I was there. They'll just move on . . . without me. I feel a tear trickle down my cheek and I avert my face, wiping it away so Reena won't see.

But she's staring at me intently.

"Do you like the water?" she asks, and I'm grateful that she's not calling attention to my emotional moment.

"Of course," I say.

Reena grins. "Wanna take a walk?"

I glance at the door, hesitating for just a second. Then I say, "Let's go."

Reena creates a portal and we step out into a beach scene—with waves and sailboats and seagulls. The sun is low in the sky, casting an orange-pink glow as it sets, and the sand at my feet is soft and loose, with dozens of footprints. A small dock is about thirty feet out, and two kids are doing fancy jumps and dives off the edge. I spot the remnants of a sand castle at the water's edge.

"Are we at—"

"Folly Beach," says Reena, finishing my sentence.

"Nice."

The flat white sand stretches for a few miles, and the pier is in the distance. Walking by, a man with the green moon tattoo—in a near-full phase—nods his head at us. He's strolling next to a woman without the mark, without the glow, and she almost disappears beside the radiance of his glistening figure. I can tell that he's older by his salt-and-pepper hair, but his face is fresh and dewy, shining like that of a guy in a shaving ad after he splashes water on his face. Then a girl on my left catches my eye—she's stretched out in the sand, almost like she's taking in the sun. She has a drizzle of freckles on her creamy skin, visible through her cloaklike shimmer, and it looks like her red hair has a neon light underneath it. Sitting up, she watches as the guy who was next to her stands and walks into the water—he's got a great body and a cute face, but there's no light around him. *He's alive*, I think. The girl looks up at us, though, and her green eyes are calm and serene, like she's in a trance.

As Reena and I stroll, a sense of serenity begins to steal over me, and I start to relax. The gurgle of the water lapping softly on the sand, the happy shrieks of kids as they jump off the dock, the soft strains of music from car stereos in the parking lot behind us— it all feels so . . . normal.

"Did you come here a lot when you were alive?" I ask, and I realize I'm getting used to saying things like that.

"Yeah." Reena stares into the fading sun. "There are always good bonfires—"

"At the pit by the east entrance," I interrupt.

"Right!" she says, laughing.

"I forgot you were a local."

She nods. "All the ghosts you see are—or at least they died around Charleston. The Prism is divided up by location of death."

"Oh," I say, thinking about the stretch of highway where I met my fate.

"For me it was the upper Wando River," she says.

"Oh, no." Sympathy swamps me. "You drowned."

She bobs her head, and her eyes get a faraway look in them, like she's remembering the terror of not being able to find air.

"I was in a car accident," I say, trying to distract her with my own story. I don't want her to get upset. "I was on Route Fifty-two, heading to my boyfriend's house. He called my cell and I answered. I'm not even sure how it happened. It was so fast . . . and then I was in the Prism; it was all over."

"Sometimes knowing what happened can be good," says Reena.

"Closure," I say.

Reena nods solemnly. "Sorry to bring up something so grim."

"It's okay." But I brush away the mental image of my crumpled car. I don't want to dwell on that right now.

"Want to check out the pit?" she asks. "See if there's anything going on tonight?"

"Sure." I know that part of me is pretending that I'm just here with my friend, heading to a bonfire. It's a relief to pretend, just for a moment.

"Where's Leo tonight?" I ask as we walk.

"Doing his own thing."

"Oh." I'm still unclear on how I feel about Leo—he seemed like kind of a bully in the barn, but then he tried to help me let Carson know that I was there.

As if Reena reads my thoughts, she says, "Leo's a good guy. He's a little . . ." She pauses and looks ahead, across the sand. "Troubled," she finishes.

I nod like I understand, but the truth is that I'm not sure I do. What I do know is that I'm way more comfortable with her. She gets me in a way that Thatcher doesn't.

"Dying young can do that to people," says Reena.

And then I look up at her and say, "Tell me about it."

She laughs. "Yeah, I guess I'm not telling you anything that you haven't figured out."

When we get to the edge of the beach, it's almost completely dark. A girl and a guy are standing by the fire pit—they both have the glow of ghosts, but they're in normal clothes, too, like Reena.

"Hey, you guys," says Reena. "Norris, Delia, this is Callie."

"Hey," I say, giving them a wave.

Norris I've seen before—he's the guy who was in the grave-yard with Leo during the ghost tour. He has an oval-shaped face and a sharp nose; everything about him looks stretched out—tall torso, long legs, and stick-straight brown hair. He has a blue hoodie pulled up over his head, but I can see that his eyes are bright and amused.

The girl, Delia, has those tight curls that always seem to frizz in the Charleston humidity, but hers shine like spun gold—they're round and thick and perfect. She collects them up into a bun as I smile at her, and she ties a knot into her hair to hold it in place.

That's when I see a black mark on her neck—like Leo and Reena have. It's just above the collar of her light cotton shirt.

I suddenly remember that I still have this aura around me—but their clothes show normally, without the cloaking glow. I look down at my body self-consciously.

"Don't worry," says Delia. "We all had that aura once."

"It's very eye-catching," says Norris with a wry smile.

"Why don't you guys have it?" I ask.

The three of them share a secretive look but they don't answer, and I decide not to press the issue. Reena just leads me closer to Norris and Delia, and we sit down with them on a fallen log bench. That's when I notice that there are other people here—of the non-glowing sort. *Living* people.

Three guys in T-shirts and shorts and with bare feet are hovering around the start of a fire. I recognize them from the soccer team—they're my year: Eli, Hunter, and Brian. They've got a giant blue cooler and Eli grabs three beers from it. He tosses two to Hunter and Brian, and when they open up the cans, they make that delicious metal pop sound.

I'll never open a can again, I think, knowing it's a silly thing to be sad about.

"I know them," I say to Reena.

"Fun," she says, her eyes glowing bright in the firelight. "Do you like them?"

"What do you mean?"

"Are they cool?" asks Delia, leaning across Reena's lap to get in on the conversation. "Are they *friends* of yours?"

"No," I say. "I mean, not really, but they're okay guys. They're on the soccer team. . . ."

I almost say "with my boyfriend, Nick," but I stop myself. I don't want to talk about anything that's going to bring me down, that's going to remind me of what I've lost when I'm trying so hard to pretend that nothing has really changed.

We're just a few feet away from Eli, Hunter, and Brian.

I look down at the log where I'm sitting and realize with some surprise that I'm not actually touching it. I'm doing that hover thing again, which I guess is what happens now. I'm *remembering* sitting, but not actually making contact with my seat. Weird. I notice my skin, how it isn't touched by the breeze that I know is coming off the water. The trees are moving back and forth, almost like a storm might roll in, but I don't feel the air. I lean forward a little bit to determine if I can sense the heat from the fire, but I don't. I wonder if I could walk right through it without a trace of a burn, and I guess I could. Being dead, not having a body to protect or even experience, is so new. Will I ever get used to my senses fading away?

"Y'all, I feel good," says Delia. She's sitting to my left, leaning back and looking up at the stars. "My energy is on point tonight."

"It's Callie," says Reena from my right. And I think about energy; maybe that's my new sense, my new way of feeling.

"Let me get in on that!" says Norris, pushing Delia gently so he can sit next to me.

She laughs and moves over.

I wonder for a moment if I'm like the fire, sharing my warmth.

Maybe I have more energy because I'm newly dead, and they've been gone for a while. I like the sense of togetherness I have here with these three.

"Do you feel it, Callie?" asks Reena.

"Feel what?"

"We're sharing energy," she says. "The four of us, I mean. Can you tell?"

"I feel something," I say, tuning in to the buzzing current that runs through me, has been running through me since I got here. "But it doesn't hurt or anything."

"No, it doesn't hurt," says Delia. "It's nice, actually. Thanks for sharing."

"No problem," I say, not sure what I'm doing but glad everyone's happy. I can hear the crickets going now, hiding in the forest as the waves rumble on the beach.

"God, I wish I could have a beer," says Norris, pantomiming drinking from a bottle.

"Do we ever eat?" I ask, and I can't believe this didn't occur to me sooner.

"No," says Delia. "It's the most incredible bummer."

"Stop, you guys," says Reena. "If we start talking about food, we'll want it. Don't think about it."

"Cheeseburger, cheeseburger, cheeseburger!" chants Norris.

Delia puts her fingers in her ears and sings, "Lalalalalala . . ."

It's too late for me, though. I'm already thinking about the blue-cheese burger from my favorite fancy diner at Hilton Head. I don't crave it, exactly—not like when I was alive and my mouth would start to water—but I *remember* it, the way it felt on my tongue and the way it slid down my throat.

"Oh, no," says Delia, looking at me with a distraught face.

"What?" I ask.

"I can tell you're remembering food," she says. "It's a slippery slope."

"Thatcher won't like it," says Reena ominously.

I meet her gaze, and it's almost as if she's challenging me to do something else that Thatcher won't like. Suddenly she cracks up into laughter, the dare gone. Maybe it was never there. Delia and Norris join in and I smile. "You guys!" I shout. "I got scared that thinking about food was dangerous or something."

"Only to your sanity," says Norris. "Just try to put it out of your mind until we figure out a way to get into a body and go for an ice cream."

"Ice cream . . . oh!" Delia flops down on the log dramatically.

I laugh and pull her up again, feeling a flash of heat that radiates out from where our hands touch to encompass all of me. She didn't move away, I notice—she's not like Thatcher. With Reena and Delia and Norris it feels like there are no walls up, no boundaries.

More than that, they see me. They hear me. When I'm haunting, even though I'm with the people I love most in the world, I'm invisible. Right now, I'm not.

We move on to discuss how great it is to be on the beach without getting sandy, since we're not physically touching it, and then I hear something from over by the fire that gets my attention.

"Dude, have you guys seen Carson Jenkins's *ass* lately?" Eli puts down his beer and gestures in a lewd way.

"Yeah," says Brian. "It's getting big, and I *like* it."

"Whatever, she's getting to be a porker," says Eli.

My mouth drops open.

"What?" asks Reena.

"They're talking about my best friend," I say.

Brian and Hunter are laughing.

"As if any of you have a *shot*!" I shout.

Reena looks at me and smiles. "They can't hear you," she says, and my mind replays Thatcher's words.

"I know," I say quietly.

"Still, we can't let him get away with that." She glances at Delia and says, "Back me up."

Then, suddenly, she's striding toward Eli. Delia and Norris are smiling gleefully, like they know exactly what Reena's doing.

Eli's skin is tan from the summer sun and his teeth are gleaming white. He tips his head back to take a sip of beer, and that's when Reena strikes. She closes her eyes and raises her hand like she's going to slap him across the face.

Instead she smacks the can, and it bolts out of Eli's hand and across the fire pit, landing with a thud at Hunter's feet.

"Dude, spaz, what was that?" Brian laughs.

Hunter shakes his head, picking up the almost-full can. "Don't waste this shit, Eli," he says. "My brother only got us one case."

Stunned, Eli stares at the hand that was holding the beer like it betrayed him. "I have no idea what the ef just happened," he says, opening the cooler again. "Thing flew out of my hand."

"Whatever, man, just don't mess around," says Hunter, staring lovingly at the can. "Liquid gold, baby."

Reena is back at my side, smiling.

"That was amazing," I say, getting excited. "You have to show me how you did that!"

"Oh, I'm just getting started."

"Huh?" I say, but she's already up and leaning over next to Eli's ear.

She whispers something that I don't hear, but it's obvious that Eli does. He whips his head around. "Who said that?"

"Said what, man?" asks Brian, lazily leaning back on a log.

"That's not funny, y'all," says Eli, looking back and forth from Brian to Hunter. His eyes are big and there's sweat beading on his forehead, though it's not a superhot night. The temperature dips low sometimes, even in the summer, and Brian is wearing a long-sleeved T-shirt, so tonight it must be around seventy degrees, which is frigid for Charleston.

Brian and Hunter are both laughing at Eli. "Dude, you're freaking out," says Hunter. "Did you smoke up before you got here or something?"

"No," says Eli. "My mom would kill me if she found my stash again. I'm dry. I just have these."

He takes a pack of cigarettes out of his pocket along with some matches, sheltering the flame as he lights up. I notice his hands are shaking. The firelight dances across his face and makes his expression flicker from light to shadow and back again.

Norris starts clapping, and his neighing laugh echoes over the beach.

Delia tosses her head back and howls a ghostly sound, like the one I heard at Middleton Place. I look at her a little warily, but she just smiles. "What use is it being a ghost if you can't have a little fun haunting?" she says.

My shoulders relax. She's right. And even if Thatcher thinks it's bad to do these kinds of tricks, I think it's pretty entertaining. I could use some fun in my, uh, life? Death?

Eli sits down. Using two fingers, Reena pulls the cigarette directly out of his mouth, flinging it into the fire.

"Jesus!" shouts Eli. "What the hell is going on?"

"You're being a complete freak!" says Brian as he and Hunter start to laugh again. "Did you just spit out a fresh cigarette?"

"No!" says Eli. "Someone took it out of my mouth. I'm telling you guys, there's something weird happening . . . it's like there's a—"

Just then, Reena grabs Eli's entire pack of cigarettes and throws it into the fire. Then she leans in to him again, and this time I hear her say, "Eli, those things will kill you."

His eyes wide, he frantically glances around. He grabs his bag and says, "I'm out. You guys find your own ride home."

Brian and Hunter start laughing again, but then they realize their ride is really leaving and they start calling after him. Eli's long gone, though—he bolted.

Reena comes back and sits with us again.

"That was epic," says Norris.

"Want to keep it going?" asks Delia, standing up and taking his hand. I see a stream of blue light pass between them. *Is that the energy we're sharing?*

"You guys go ahead," says Reena, lying back across the log. "I'm shot."

Delia and Norris wave to us and then jog down the path behind Brian and Hunter, who are struggling to catch up to Eli.

"What are they going to do?" I ask.

"Just have a little more fun," she says.

I smile. "That was great."

"Aw, shucks, it was nothing." She smiles at me.

"Eli's not going to forget it," I say.

"Well, he deserved it. Calling Carson fat. What an ass."

It's almost like now Reena's our friend, too. Even though Carson doesn't know her. Will never know her. *Stop thinking about sad stuff.*

"So can you show me how to do that?" I ask.

"Which part?"

"All of it," I say. "The whispering, the moving things . . ."

"Sure," she says, her doll face growing serious. "As long as you promise to use it for good and not evil."

"I promise," I say earnestly.

Reena laughs. "Callie, I'm kidding. I just used my ghost powers to knock beer around. I don't care what you do with it. I mean, we're dead. We need to be able to enjoy *some* perks."

"Like freaking out the jerks I went to school with," I say, smiling back. "I forgot that I wasn't talking to—"

"Thatcher," Reena and I say at the same time, breaking up into laughter together.

"He's okay," says Reena, slipping down onto the sand so that her back is against the log I'm on. "He's just really uptight."

"Yeah." I wonder if Reena sees what I see. That his controlled facade hides so much pain.

"You probably shouldn't mention that we hung out," she says. "He wouldn't like it."

"Why not?" I ask.

"We just see life—or I guess death—in different ways," she says.

"How?"

"He's all right with it; I'm not." Her face is serious now as she looks out into the darkness. The fire is dying, but the small flickers of light play on her cheeks, casting shapes under her glowing eyes.

I know that what she said isn't true. Thatcher isn't okay with death; he's tormented by having to stay in the Prism. But I'm not sure he reveals that to everyone, and I don't want to betray what I've sensed in him—the sadness he carries. "How could anyone be all right with death?" I ask.

"Right?" says Reena. "I mean, I'll admit it: I'm angry. I'm too young to be dead. And idiots like these guys . . ." She gestures toward the fire pit. "They don't appreciate what they have—they just act stupid all day."

Her voice is hard, her smile gone. A stab of regret pierces me as I realize that I didn't do much better than the soccer guys when

I was living my life. In my own way, I acted stupid all day, too—I didn't live the way I could have, if I'd only been more aware, and more grateful.

"That's why I like spending as much time as I can on Earth," she says. Her voice is heavy with longing. "I would give anything, *do anything*, to be alive again."

Shadows are dancing on her face, her eyes almost glowing with the desire to be alive. Her intensity sends a shiver racing through me. Then she relaxes and shrugs.

"So that's the difference between me and Thatcher," she says.

We sit there for a while longer, listening to the water, the final crackles of the fire, the wind in the trees at the edge of the beach.

Finally, I ask her again: "Can you show me how to move things?"

"Sure," she says, her voice quiet. "Here." She reaches out and holds my shoulder with one hand, and it buzzes where she's touching me. Then she picks up a stick in her other hand and holds its end in the flames. When it lights, she pulls it back, close to us.

"Fire is a good thing to practice with," she says. "Try to use your energy on this, get the flame to go out."

I stare at the flickering light, unsure of what to do.

"You're not here in the same way that you used to exist," says Reena, sensing my confusion. "You have to *feel* yourself blowing out the flame before you can actually do it—almost like you're imagining it happening first."

She bends over slightly, one hand still on my shoulder. Her pink lips round into an O shape, and she closes her eyes as she blows out a steady stream of air.

The fire on the stick goes out.

"Wow. Impressive."

"That's nothing." She holds the stick in the burning embers again, letting it catch. Then she brings it close to us. "Now you."

Closing my eyes, I remember birthday cake wishes—my fifth birthday in particular, when I had a Care Bears cake with trick candles that kept relighting as I tried to blow them out, which made Mama laugh and laugh. I remember Carson's last séance attempt, where the room was so filled with candles that I declared it a fire hazard and threatened to leave unless she let me extinguish all but one that we could keep our eyes on—it took me ten minutes, circling the room huffing and puffing, to get them out. I remember a night with Nick when he tried to be romantic by lighting a kiwi-scented candle that smelled more like something that had gone bad in the fridge.

And then, I blow. It doesn't quite feel like air is rushing from my mouth, more like there's a wish—a desire—that's transported through me. I open my eyes, and the fire that was on the stick is out, a thin trail of smoke coming from its tip.

"Ah!" I jump up and clap excitedly. "I did it!"

"Nice job," says Reena. Her voice is faint, and when I glance down at her I realize that she looks *exhausted*. Like she's just run a marathon or gotten over the flu or something. Her glow is waning and her eyes are dull; even her body seems slighter.

"Are you okay?" I ask.

"My energy is fading—we should go back to the Prison . . . uh, I mean the Prism. Can you create the portal? I'm tapped."

"Oh, I haven't done that yet."

"You haven't?"

I feel silly. "I mean, Thatcher always does it—he hasn't shown me how or anything so . . ."

Reena frowns. "You should know how to do this. Lots of new ghosts don't have the memories to be able to do this, but you do. Watch and learn."

She closes her eyes and slowly traces a door as she talks. "I'm creating this portal by picturing where I want us to go, but not just with my eyes. I use each sense—sight, taste, touch, sound, and smell —to determine where it will lead."

Reena pauses. "Like, remember when you were telling me all that stuff about Carson?"

I nod.

"You could use those thoughts to get to her. After you fill your mind with somewhere—or someone—you just outline the shape of the doorway with your hand, using the energy you've gathered through calling on your senses."

"Okay, but I'm confused. When you go to Earth, doesn't the portal decide where you end up?"

"No." Reena pauses in front of the doorway she created, which is rippling with light. "Who told you that?"

"Thatcher."

She twists her lips. "Maybe there are places he doesn't want you to go."

She stumbles a bit, and I grab her arm to steady her, another pulse of energy passing between us. She looks so tired that I'm afraid she might faint right here. But I need one more answer.

I frown. "Why did Thatcher tell me I don't have control over where I go?"

"So he would have it," says Reena, her voice barely audible.

Ten

REENA AND I STEP THROUGH the portals she's created. When I enter mine, I enter my prism room—and I'm not alone.

Thatcher's back is to me as he gazes out the window. It's weird to see him, this guy I've just met, standing in such an intimate space—my bedroom, or at least a replica of it—and waiting for me. His muscles seem tense and rigid. The soft edges of his hair are grazing his neck, and I take in the width of his broad shoulders. When he's still like this, and quiet, I can feel the power within him. The way he's standing—so protective, so watchful—almost makes me feel guilty. Almost.

And then he turns. "Why did you leave your prism?"

His eyes are flat with anger.

"I went out with a friend," I say, defensive.

"Out with a friend? This isn't high school." He crosses the room and stands next to me. "Didn't I tell you to stay here?"

"You did not," I say lightly, ignoring his imposing figure and flopping down casually on the bed. "You said to rest. I feel rested. I took a walk on the beach with Reena and I feel much—"

"You were with Reena?" he asks.

"Yes."

Thatcher leans over the bed. "Did you let her into your prism?"

"Thatcher, stop it," I say, my eyes widening. "You're scaring me."

"Did you?" he shouts, and the vibrations of his anger course through my skin.

"Yes," I say, defiantly. "Yes, I let her in."

He plows his hands through his hair. "You don't realize what you've done. Now she can come in anytime she wants."

"Just like you. Why do you hate her so much?"

"I don't hate her, but she's a complication. Spending time with her distracts you from your purpose."

"I only want a friend here."

"The Prism isn't a place for friends." I can tell by his tone that he's repeating a rule, and I'm not sure it's one he wants to follow.

"But Norris and Delia seem so nice," I say. "And Reena is hilarious—she's fun and open and interested in my life—"

I stop talking because I see that Thatcher is glowering at me.

"What did you tell them about your life?" he asks, looking around the room like he's searching for something.

"I don't know," I say. "Reena asked about Carson, and we went to Folly Beach. Why?"

Thatcher doesn't say anything for a minute; he just shakes

his head. When he looks at me, his face is tight and controlled. "I thought I explained that your prism is sacred. I told you not to open the door."

"But *you're* here!" I shout at him, tired of his chastising. "You came in while I was gone and you didn't even have the decency to wait outside. Is that what you mean by *sacred*?"

He bows his head, eyes to the floor. "You're right," he says. "I shouldn't have entered without your permission. I thought we were . . ." His voice trails off again as he looks up at me. "Never mind. I'm sorry."

But that's not what I want from him—I don't want him to apologize for feeling comfortable here.

"Thatcher, it's okay," I say. "I don't mind if you come in; that's my point. I want us to be friends, I just—"

Thatcher shakes his head. The depth of seriousness in his blue eyes silences me.

"I'm not your friend," he says slowly. "I'm your *Guide*. Death isn't a party, Callie."

I sense the line he's drawing in his mind, and I don't want him to shut me out.

Without responding, I stroll over to my desk and pick up the framed photo of me and Carson. The now-familiar grief stabs me as I look at our smiling faces. "I'm so alone. Don't you understand that . . . even a little?"

Thatcher stands up and walks toward me. He stops when he's a foot away, looking over my shoulder at the picture in my hand.

"You've surrounded yourself with memories," he says. "I know it must be very hard for you to try to let go, when they're here with you, all around you." He takes in my room, furnished with life, and as his gaze travels over my things, he softens, moving away from the declaration he just made.

"When I tell you to rest here, it's because being in the Prism, letting its energy flow into you, should help you connect with a deeper level of your soul—a level beyond your memories of Earth."

I put down the frame and turn toward him. "How did you get beyond your memories?"

"At first I didn't remember much," he says. "Just little flashes of my life, like a backyard birthday party, a football game . . . but it was like I was watching someone else's home movies. I didn't connect to the memories fully until later, when it became clear that my haunting was failing."

"And then what happened?" I ask.

He sits on my bed. "I came here with . . . friends. And they remembered some things. Together, we had a larger collective memory than most ghosts do. As the haunting dragged on, I remembered more and more. Each memory started to come with a wave of fresh pain. I knew I had died, I knew what that meant— emotionally knew it—and it was the most intense heartache I've ever felt."

I sit beside him, leaning in as close I can without repelling him. "So you're not as immune as the other ghosts. You do know how this feels."

"I know," he says, his voice softer, with a ragged edge, and I can hear how desperately he wishes that he didn't know. My heart goes out to him. I want to fold my hand around his, to squeeze, to re-assure him with a tender caress. Words fail me. I can never touch him the way I'd want to, living.

"Does that help you trust me?" he asks.

"What?"

"I need you to trust me," he says, and his eyes are sincere, wide open. "When I leave you to rest in your prism, I expect that's what you'll do. You need to connect with a deeper part of your soul—it's essential. I don't want you to have to exist as I do."

"Gosh, Thatcher, it almost sounds like you care about me."

"No, no, I . . . I just don't want you going off on your own or spending time with other ghosts."

I smile at him, feeling grateful that he shared all that with me.

"So you're saying we're exclusive?" I joke.

He frowns, and I wonder if a time will ever come when he can accept my teasing. "Just . . . please," he pleads, "do as I ask."

"Okay." I cross my arms over my chest. "I'll try."

"Thank you," says Thatcher. "So what did you and Reena . . . do?"

I shift my eyes away from him. "We walked on the beach. We talked." I don't want to tell him about running into the soccer guys; I don't think he'd approve of that part.

"Did she say anything about me?"

"Not really." He flinches but rights himself quickly, back to business.

"We should continue with your haunting," he says.

"You mean with my being in the same room as living people?" I ask, half joking, half impatient.

"Remember how you just said you'd trust me?" he says. "Sharing your peaceful energy with them is a much more advanced form of haunting than throwing rocks or changing the radio station—no matter what you may have heard from Reena. Let's just see where the day takes us, okay?"

He stands up and traces a portal.

"Where are we going?" I ask.

"Where we're needed," he says. And I wonder if he's controlling our destination, now that I know that it's possible.

When I walk through the portal, I look around, and my heart drops. *Nick's room.*

I don't see him anywhere—it's dark, the shades are drawn, and a dirty laundry pile is spilling over in the corner. There's a soiled shirt on top. I want to pick it up and breathe in Nick's scent. As soon as I imagine that, I can almost feel the soft fabric clinging to his sculpted back, under my hands.

On Nick's desk there's a half-eaten bowl of Cheerios. I have to bite my lip to keep from tearing up—it's so *Nick* to eat cereal in his room. It must seem silly to Thatcher, the fact that dirty dishes make me emotional. I fight to control my reaction.

The desktop screen saver flashes photos from last year—Nick and me tandem parasailing, me and Carson with the top down on the day she got her VW Bug, Nick and me screaming at the top of our lungs as the bungee-like Sling Shot propelled us toward the fluffy clouds. It was such a rush. I peer over at Thatcher—and our gazes collide. I want to drag him over to the computer, make him watch the slide show, and ask him, "How can you expect me to give all this up without a whimper?"

Then he looks away quickly, his attention drawn to the bed.

"He's asleep," he says.

I thought it was just a rumpled, unmade bed, but now I see that Nick *is* here. He's almost all the way under the comforter—just a tuft of brown curls is visible. My chest tightens painfully as grief wells up.

"It's good that he's asleep," says Thatcher, looking at my boyfriend like he's studying a science experiment. "The transitional moments between sleeping and waking are more vulnerable, more open for a connection."

"Oh, so that means—"

But Thatcher is already leaning toward Nick. Then the comforter rustles. When Nick sits up sleepily, I stagger back a step. His face is puffy, his eyes dark and drawn. He looks like he's been in a boxing ring with a prizefighter.

Every aspect of me—body, heart, soul—yearns to comfort him. I'm angry that I can't, that I have to watch him suffer like this. Being in the Prism is purgatory.

"Callie, stay calm," says Thatcher. "He's suffered a loss. It's natural for him to lose sleep and be upset. You're going to ease that."

I nod—this is for Nick. I would do anything to take away the pain reflected in his face.

"Did you wake him up?" I ask.

Thatcher nods.

"But you didn't touch him?"

"No—like I told you, our energy affects them. They can sense our presence on a subconscious level."

I push my hand forward, toward Nick. I can't help myself. I want to touch him, like Reena did with Eli.

Thatcher moves to block my reach. "The internal connection is more powerful."

"Knowing that I'm here will help him. Nick isn't Carson; he doesn't believe like she does—we should show him that I'm here first." *I just want to be able to feel Nick's skin again.*

"What we're trying to do is more than that," says Thatcher. "If you concentrate on being at peace, that's what you'll give to him."

"How am I supposed to *concentrate on being at peace*?" I fling his words back to him sarcastically because they sound ridiculous to me. When I'm a jumble of conflicting emotions, how can I be at peace?

"Close your eyes, Callie."

I huff a little bit, feeling stuck. "Fine." I do it. I close my eyes.

"Any emotion that you feel, let it go. Anything physical that enters your mind is purely your imagination, so let it go. You are a soul; you are a life force that's evolved beyond the body, beyond your skin and hair and eyes and lips. You are smooth, strong, gentle, everlasting now."

As he talks, his words run over my body and I can't help but feel something physical, despite him telling me to let that go. Because of his voice. *His voice.* It's like a velvet cloth draping over me and closing out the rest of the world with its soft, tender tone. He doesn't sound authoritative or impatient or frustrated.

His rhythm is effortless and full of grace. I almost feel like I'm falling asleep, but I open my eyes and I'm wide-awake, here in Nick's room. The blanket of Thatcher's voice, though, makes me feel thoughtless. Not in the sense of being uncaring, but in the sense that my brain isn't moving. I'm giving in to a sensation of . . . peace?

I watch Nick scan the room. His breathing is even, his face soft. He looks serene, still. Maybe it's working. His gaze moves in my direction, unseeing, but I imagine that he feels my presence. He always used to be able to sense that I was coming: even if I was just walking behind him in the hall at school, he'd turn and meet my eyes. Or if I was about to drive up to his house, he'd be waiting in the window. I can still see the shadow of his smile the last time we—

Suddenly the tone of a text on Nick's phone sounds. To me, it feels like glass is shattering, like the fragile hold that peace had on me, on us, is broken.

Nick picks up his phone and starts texting back, and more texts come in, rapid-fire style, as he responds with fast-moving fingers.

I look at Thatcher. His eyes are still closed.

"You stopped talking," I say.

"I never spoke."

"I heard you—the stuff about the life force, and my body."

Heat rushes into my cheeks.

"You were tuned in to an internal peace. I thought it, but I didn't say it out loud." He smiles. "You're learning." I think about when I tried to call to Reena and she came—that *must* have been more than coincidence.

"Jesus." Nick tosses the phone to the end of his bed, annoyed. Before I think twice, I lean over and read the parts of the text conversation that I can see. The person he's talking to is just the letter *H*.

Nick: because i didn't get a chance to

H: well i guess it doesn't matter now

Nick: Just

Nick: i can't talk about this ok?

H: It's been 3 weeks

That's the end of the conversation. Three weeks. "Three weeks since what?" I wonder aloud.

"Callie, the world of the Living isn't your concern anymore," says Thatcher. "I know your pain is hard to let go of, but didn't you feel the peace just now, the larger picture?"

I did, but hello . . . who is H? What are these texts? "Not now, Thatcher," I say, looking back at Nick. He's leaning against his headboard, staring into space. His face is tortured.

I look down at my feet so I don't have to see Nick's pain. That's when I spot an empty bottle of Jameson whiskey sticking out from under the bed.

Thatcher catches me eyeing it. "Desperate times . . ."

"That's not like Nick. He hardly even drinks at parties."

"Grief can do strange things to people." Thatcher grows somber, like he's talking not just about the change in Nick, but his own personal experience.

"What do the texts mean?" I ask, but he just shakes his head. "Was he talking about the time since I died? Three weeks?"

"That's not your focus," he says. "You can't get into their everyday lives. You're here for something bigger, and your energy needs to be calm. Get your feelings under control."

I hate this. Thatcher keeps telling me to even out my energy, to contain my feelings, but I can't. I don't know how to *not feel* what I feel. And what I feel is confusion about those texts, not to mention devastation at the sight of my boyfriend, who's drinking alone, mourning the loss of . . . me. It's so unfair that I'm here but he doesn't know it.

"Nick! Dinner!" Mrs. Fisher calls from downstairs, and after a beat, Nick snaps out of his spacey trance and heads down the stairs.

"Let's try with someone else," says Thatcher. "Maybe if it's not Nick, you'll be able to control your emotions a little more, hold the peace longer."

I hesitate for a second, staring at the phone. Instinctively, I reach out to touch the screen, recalling hours of texting Carson and flipping through apps. It scrolls up, and I can see more of the conversation. Just one more line.

"I touched it!" I say, jumping up and waving my arms. "I touched the phone!"

Thatcher folds his arms across his chest. "Yes, you did."

"Your enthusiasm seems less than genuine."

"Touching objects is not your goal. It has nothing, in fact, to do with what we're trying to accomplish."

Reena would be excited for me—she'd help me do even more.

I'm so happy about the touch that I almost forget why I reached for the phone screen in the first place. Almost. I read the top line.

H: Why didn't you do it before the accident?

Eleven

AS WE HURTLE THROUGH THE PORTAL, my mind races with questions: *Who is "H"? What was Nick supposed to do before the accident? Were they definitely talking about* my *accident?* Thatcher wants me to forget it—I can tell that he thinks seeing Carson will distract me. I know he wants me to sit and be calm, but no matter what he says, I'm going to touch something again, and get some answers.

We're standing in Carson's front yard. I can't feel the sun's rays the same way I did when I was alive. Instead I'm experiencing the fantasy of this type of day, an imagined warmth. It doesn't seem real because it isn't—my body isn't here. All sensation is a memory. But I can see the sultry heat in the wilting stems of the front-garden flowers. The sun is beating down in that harsh way that only Charleston in summer can withstand, when every glass of sweet tea is sweating like it's in a sauna and people move three times more slowly than they do in the winter.

Carson's VW Beetle is in the driveway of her bungalow-style house. Intense barking echoes in the distance.

"Come on," I say to Thatcher, glad to have him following *me* for once.

We walk along the side path to the backyard where Carson's puggle is sniffing around the lace-curtained doghouse.

"Georgia, girl!" I shout, wishing I could scoop her up in my arms.

She starts barking like crazy.

I squat next to her. She keeps barking in random directions, like she's trying to find me.

"Georgia, what on the green Earth are you doing?"

From the sliding glass door of her patio, Carson stares down at Georgia and shakes her head. She's wearing bright pink flip-flops, tiny jean shorts, and a white T. She's got a copy of *Their Eyes Were Watching God* in her right hand—it's on our summer reading list for English. I have the urge to rush up and hug her, to take her hand and get in the car to go for a drive, to tell her *everything* that's happening to me. I feel bottled up, stuck, without her to talk to.

I stand up, but Thatcher moves forward, cautioning me.

"I won't do anything," I reassure him. "I just want to be near her."

Georgia's still barking as I move closer, and Carson is shouting, "Hush, Georgia, hush!"

"Shhh . . . ," I whisper to the dog. Georgia stops and cocks her head—she's looking right at me.

Carson looks up, too, not at me, but past me into the backyard.

"I think the dog sees me," I say excitedly, moving closer to Carson.

"Callie, be careful," says Thatcher, and I ignore the caution in his tone. I'm determined to show her I'm here.

I reach forward for Carson's arm, sure that she'll feel my touch—she's so in tune with people's spirits; she's always believed. And since the night of the ghost tour, with our song coming on the radio, she's probably looking for me everywhere.

I imagine the softness of her cotton sleeve as my fingertips get closer and closer. . . . But just before I touch her, a jolt of heat rushes through me, stinging my hand, and Carson yelps in pain. She rubs her arm near where my hand was, where a faint red shadow lingers.

"Georgia, did you see . . . ," she starts. She gazes out into her yard, and her eyes reflect something that looks like wonder—or hope. Then her face clouds over and her mouth falls into a heart-broken line, like she's been hit with a fresh wave of hurt.

"Carson, I'm sorry," I say, reaching out to her again.

Suddenly I feel a pull, something sweeping me away . . . Thatcher. And then we're not at Carson's anymore. We're out on the Battery, a walking path on the water at the tip of Charleston's peninsula, under the palmettos that sway in the soft breeze.

"What just happened?" I ask.

"I had to get us out of there," he says, staring at me intensely.

"You were too worked up. Your energy wasn't controlled—it misfired, you *hurt* her, and you were about to do it *again*."

I lower my head instantly as a tear threatens to fall. "I didn't mean to. I was trying to show her I was there."

"I know. I know. But I've been trying to explain how that type of connection—the surface level—only makes them linger in sadness."

He runs his hand through his hair and looks out on the water, frowning. "Trying to prove that you're physically with them only leads to them holding on tighter. We're looking for a release. Superficial connections can make them sad—only a soulful connection brings peace."

I nod. I understand what he's saying, but it's such an abstract concept. Reaching out feels so much more natural to me.

"Are you hurt?" asks Thatcher.

I realize I'm cradling my hand, the one that touched Carson. I can still feel it throbbing with energy.

"Callie," says Thatcher softly. He looks at me carefully, his face more sympathetic than usual.

He moves his arm toward me, and I place my vibrating hand in his, knowing that in this instance, he is choosing touch, reaching for it. The moment our skin meets, I feel an undulating wave of pleasure wash through me. If I still breathed, it would steal my breath. It's cataclysmic, intense. A rush of emotion, affection, magnetic power encompasses me. Thatcher turns my hand over and traces the lines of my palm very slowly. As he does, the buzzing slows and then stops. His fingers are soft on my skin, and it's like he's drawing out the excess energy from an ocean and leaving a glassy lake in its place, still and serene.

I look up at him in wonder, and I take in his blue eyes—which are open and kind in this moment. "You have so much energy," he says, his voice almost wistful. "But it will fade, and then you'll be calmer, like the rest of the ghosts."

"Am I supposed to want that? To feel *less*?"

"Don't think of it that way. It's not feeling less; it's feeling *peace*."

I look at him skeptically.

"It's better," he reassures me. "Trust me. It makes it much easier to haunt. Most ghosts come to the Prism without their memories and with a natural sense of tranquillity because we're incomplete echoes of our former selves. Only merging with Solus makes us whole again."

"I don't like the idea of being an echo," I say.

"You're not one," says Thatcher, and I think I see a smile on his lips. "That's the problem."

"But I still don't understand why I'm not at peace like the other ghosts," I say.

Thatcher stares at me, his face growing serious again, but he doesn't reply. It almost seems like he's trying to will me to answer the question for myself.

"Maybe it's because I've spent my life trying to feel *more*," I mumble.

"What?" Thatcher tilts his head.

I shrug. "Nothing."

He looks away, and for a second I think he's going to put up a wall again, turn back into a Guide instead of a friend.

Instead he motions inland. "Do you know White Point Gardens?"

"Of course." He doesn't face me, but I can see the openness in his relaxed profile, and warmth consumes me as I fall into step beside him.

"I like to walk and talk," he says, and I understand, because I'm like that, too. Somehow, moving forward makes conversations a little lighter, a little easier.

We step through the manicured grounds, under dappled shade from the dozens of live oaks that seem to stretch out horizontally with long arms and leafy green fingers. In this park, there are war monuments—cannons and mortars from the Civil War—and we always used to take field trips here in elementary school to hear about "The War of Northern Aggression." Today, though, I look up into the trees and spot a heron nesting amid the Spanish moss, settling into a soft bed under the warm golden sun.

Thatcher stares straight ahead, and I wonder what he sees in White Point Gardens, what memories of his lie here.

"I had a little sister," he says quietly. "Wendy, like the girl from *Peter Pan*—my mom loved J. M. Barrie."

I stay silent for a moment, eager to learn more about Thatcher. We're almost friends . . . aren't we? So I go with it.

"Mama was a huge reader, too. I'm named after the housekeeper in *To Kill a Mockingbird*."

"I figured," says Thatcher.

"You did?" I realize as I say it that I hardly ever tell anyone that, but if I do I usually get a blank stare.

"Freshman English. I watched the movie instead of reading the book."

"You cheater."

"Reading took too long. I had better things to do."

I can relate. I smile at Thatcher. I want to know his story more than ever. "Wendy Darling. Go on."

"She was like that character, too." Warmth, like from a crackling fire on a cool morning, flows through his voice as he remembers her. "Even though she was six years younger than I was."

"You mean she took care of you?"

"She looked out for me. I wasn't always the most . . . cautious person."

"Really?" I ask, wondering what other unexpected things Thatcher and I might have in common. "You seem so . . . controlled."

"I changed. I wasn't this way when I was alive."

"Well, I guess not if you ended up dead," I say, jokingly. But that sounds awful, so I quickly add, "Sorry, I didn't mean—"

"It's okay; I've accepted it. And you're right. When I was alive, I wanted attention. I felt bored all the time. It was like I was waiting for something exciting to happen to me, but nothing ever did. I started doing stupid things, like driving with my headlights off at night and getting drunk whenever I could—just to feel more *there*. To feel like I existed. Does that make sense?"

"Yes." And then I look back over my shoulder, pointing toward the water, which is sparkling in the bright summer sun. "On the day that I died, I took my car for a spin on the pier."

Thatcher's eyes get wide. "Whoa." For a second he's not my Guide, but like a future friend I'm meeting for the first time. "What did you get up to?"

I smile with satisfaction and maybe even a little pride that my daredevil antics have impressed him. I shove away this little voice that is asking why it matters if he thinks highly of me. "Sixty. I didn't time it, but I'd guess it took less than five seconds."

He lets out a low whistle.

We turn back around and keep walking. "How did it make you feel?" he asks.

"Invincible."

"Alive," he says.

"Yes."

"Were you bored, too?" he asks. "Is that why you did it?"

"Not bored." I think about it for a minute, searching for the right word so he'll understand. "Empty."

"Empty?"

I rub my thumbs over the tips of my fingers, trying to generate sensation, but it's so faint. I wonder how much longer before I won't be able to feel them at all. It almost feels like I'm fading into nothingness. "I think so. After Mama died, it felt like I wasn't allowed to feel sad. I pushed that deep down."

"But you still wanted to feel *something*," says Thatcher.

I fold my arms across my chest protectively, but I nod.

"So you chased the thrill," he says.

I nod again. "Uh-huh."

"I understand," he says. "I really do."

"But you did it because you were bored," I point out.

"Well . . . partly." Then he smiles like he's remembering something nice. "Wendy used to wait up for me no matter how late it was when I got home. I'd see the crack of light from under her bedroom door—she'd turn it off as soon as she heard me in the bathroom getting ready for bed. I don't think she could sleep unless she knew I was home safe."

"She sounds sweet." I wonder what it's like to have a sibling. I always wanted one, but now that I'm dead, maybe it would just feel like an extra sadness.

"She was. She is, I guess. She always acted like a little adult. I think it's because she had a rare form of leukemia when she was four years old, and she spent a lot of time in the hospital."

"How awful. I know how hard it is when someone you love is sick. It sucks for everyone."

"That pretty much describes it, yeah. For a while, it's your entire focus. It consumes your life. The good news is that she recovered fully, but she kept this sense of purpose with her, this reverence for life." We slow down a bit. "At least, she did until I died."

"And then . . ."

Thatcher looks down at the ground and keeps walking. "And then something in her eyes went dark. I was gone—I was trying to haunt her, and my parents . . . but I couldn't reach her. I never did."

"Never?" I ask.

His face darkens. "Well . . . once," he says. "But it wasn't the right moment—"

He stops talking and I see his face shift, like he's closing off a memory before he continues. "I tried. I tried it all, just like you're doing. But that surface connection—the kind that comes off to them like tricks and ghost stories—it doesn't work. It can make things worse."

"Worse?"

But he doesn't explain. "She's the reason that I'm a Guide," he says. "Until she moves on and accepts my death, I can't merge."

"Oh." I lower my gaze to the ground, focusing on the ramifications of everything he's shared. *That* he shared at all. It creates this strong connection between us that I had thought was impossible. I knew someone hadn't gotten over Thatcher's death. But hearing the specifics, knowing about Wendy and his relationship with her, is devastating. All this time, I had deemed him a creature incapable of emotion.

But now I understand that he is—or at least he was—able to love deeply.

Lifting my gaze to his, I'm struck by the raw emotions swirling in the depths of his blue eyes: pain, turmoil, sadness.

"You're not an echo either," I assure him.

"I wish I were."

"No," I say, my voice so low it's almost a whisper. "Don't wish for that."

Instinctively, because I can't help myself, I reach for his face. When my fingers graze his jaw, a charged current runs through my hand and into my stomach, and from there it blossoms out into my fingers and toes, making me tremble and buzz. I move his head to the side and look at his green moon tattoo.

"It's almost full," I say.

"It's frozen. The moon cycles build to become full at a merging, but mine will stay that way until Wendy accepts my death."

"And when that happens, you'll be gone?" I ask, suddenly not wanting to lose him, now that we're becoming closer.

"*If* that happens," he says. "Then I'll go, yes."

I move my hand away from his face and drop it back to my side, but Thatcher catches my fingers in midair and the pleasure washes through me in rolling waves, like the ocean constantly lapping at the shore. I'm beginning to understand why touch is discouraged. It's so much more than physical. It's like completion.

"It's been years," he says, still holding on to me. "I've said good-bye to lots of ghosts—it's been cathartic to help them. But with you . . ."

When he pauses, our faces are just inches apart. If we were alive, I'd be able to feel his breath on my cheeks. As it is, my heart speeds up at his nearness—and although I know it must be a phantom feeling, it doesn't seem like the memory of my heart in this moment—it feels like it's really there, beating bloody red liquid life through my body. I feel drawn to Thatcher, like there's a magnet between us, an energy field that needs to connect—mine with his.

Suddenly a Frisbee flies past us, through us, and a dog races after it, deftly dodging the area where we stand even though I know it can't see us.

The action interrupts the pull I felt, and one face flashes through my mind: *Nick.*

I stumble backward. "I'm sorry," I say, shaking my head. "Can we just go back? I want to go back now."

Thatcher's face hardens as he steps away from me. "Of course."

He puts his hands in his pockets and shrugs his shoulders, and I can tell he's closing up to me again, like a shop putting down its blinds and locking the door.

Twelve

I'M STILL A LITTLE DAZED when Thatcher delivers me to my prism. When he orders me not to let anyone in, I promise I won't. I don't want him hanging around any longer than necessary.

I lie on my bed and stare at my ceiling. If it were dark in here, would I see the glow of the stars on my ceiling in my real room? It's a silly thing to focus on, but I'm trying really hard not to think about how close I came to kissing Thatcher, to just rising up on my toes and pressing my mouth to his. What does an after-death kiss feel like?

I love Nick, so what is this attraction that's drawing me to Thatcher? Is it because he's my all-knowing, all-powerful Guide? No, it's deeper than that. It's this connection, this loneliness in his soul that I want to befriend, this ache in mine that he soothes. It's this satisfaction that I feel when I calm the storm in his eyes. It's the strength in him tempered with compassion.

I can't imagine the sadness that would engulf me if he left the Prism before I did. What must it be like for him, knowing that each bit of progress I make is carrying me away from him? He said he's had lots of good-byes but I'm different. Will he grieve when I go? Will I miss him the way that I miss Nick?

It seems inconceivable, and my yearning to be with Nick suddenly overwhelms me. I miss him so much, but it's the Nick before I died who I long for. The Nick I've seen lately scares me—and saddens me. It's like he's pushing me away, pushing me toward Thatcher, even though he doesn't know Thatcher exists.

All these thoughts cause guilt to ratchet through me. I'm being unfair to Nick. He's grieving. I need to see him—alone. Those texts, the empty bottle . . . I'm worried about the downward spiral he's in. Something's not right. I know he believes it's his fault that I died, but I sense that something more is eating at him. I'm not sure that I want Thatcher to be around when I find out what it is.

I wonder if I can gather my thought energy to create a portal that will lead me to Nick, like Reena said it would. I close my eyes, ready to try to do this. And I fill myself with glimpses of my boyfriend. *Dark curls I can run my fingers through, a smile that makes my heart jump even from across the halls at school, the softest cheek with a bristle of stubble, brown eyes that light up when I walk into the room, the smell of Old Spice and peppermint Tic Tacs, curious lips that open with mine when we kiss . . .*

When I hold out my hand to trace the portal, it almost feels involuntary, like someone else is doing it for me. A doorway framed by glowing flecks of light appears. And before I can second-guess myself, I walk through.

I step out into the middle of East Bay Street, Charleston's Rainbow Row. The houses are painted all different pastels—pink, yellow, blue—and window boxes are filled with flowers. A slew of tourists are taking pictures. The colors are almost blinding in the bright sun, and I see a couple of ghosts milling around on the street, too—strolling slowly beside the Living with serene faces that are lit up with the Prism's glow.

At first I think my portal must not have worked—I meant to find Nick, not go sightseeing. But then I spot him sitting alone on a bench, and my heart leaps. Reena was telling me the truth. I *can* control where I go.

Nick is sitting across from the pink house, my favorite. I used to stare up into the five second-floor windows of this one every time I walked by after Mama died, wondering who was inside and what their lives were like. It seemed like a magical place where no one would ever let a mother go away.

When I felt close enough to Nick to share memories of Mama, I brought him here, too. Once I started telling him about her—the way she brushed her hair before bed, the way she dabbed on perfume in succession: neck, wrists, backs of knees—it was like a floodgate had opened and I couldn't stop telling him the tiniest details, like I was desperate for someone else to know these things about her. My memories had been bottled up for so long because Dad didn't want to discuss her, but Nick always listened and said just the right things to make me smile again. When I see his expression now—forlorn and empty—I want him to know that I'm still beside him.

His eyes are closed as he turns his face up to the blazing midday sun, and he's got his headphones on. I glance at the screen of his iPhone—Bon Iver. He's in full wallow mode. I notice that his right hand is closed around something, and I guess that it's the amber pendant he took from my room—his piece of me. I sit down next to him, wondering if I can make a connection on my own. I'm not going to do anything crazy, like try to make a magnolia blossom float in front of Nick's face or anything. But I'm also not going to just sit on this bench next to him sharing energy. I want him to really know I'm here.

I start to rub my hands together, trying to pool some of my energy. My palms warm, and then I separate them and hold them slightly apart. I can still feel the heat emanating from them. Then I pause and wait for a moment before I reach up to lightly touch the edge of Nick's earbud. I want him to unplug so that all of his senses will be open to knowing I'm here.

My hand moves closer, closer . . . but before my finger grazes him, Nick opens his eyes and pulls out the earbud closest to me. He looks down at his iPod and stops the music.

He's aware of my presence.

"Nick," I say softly.

He looks around, looking right through me, and even though he doesn't see me, I can tell that he senses something.

He takes out the other earbud and slowly puts his left hand—the one in between us—onto the bench. His palm opens slightly.

An invitation.

I rub my hands together again, wanting to gather more energy and make sure this connection works. When I feel a tingle, I gently reach my hand down and place it over his, lacing our fingers together—the way we always held hands.

His fingers curl up automatically, weaving through mine. And I can feel it. I think I can feel his touch. *Can he feel mine?*

He's staring straight ahead, his eyes wide open like he can't quite believe what's happening—his hand is holding mine. I want to lean into him, but I'm afraid. I think of the mark I left on Carson—if I get too excited or eager, could my energy hurt Nick, too?

So I sit there, still, trying to be content with this light touch. A thousand thoughts rush at me—*I will never hold Nick again, This is one of the last touches we'll ever share, Does he know that this is me trying to help him say good-bye?*—but I bat them all away, worried that if I let my emotions take over, I'll lose this moment.

Then I hear Nick whispering softly to himself. And I realize that he's whispering to me.

"I'm so sorry, Callie," he says, his lower lip starting to tremble. He opens his right hand a little and I see the amber heart there. He fingers it gently as he speaks. "Your father blames me; everyone does. I do. It was my fault. I tried to tell you; I was going to . . ." His voice falters then, but I want to hear what he has to say. Still, I fight not to panic; I focus on staying calm. I'm holding his hand—maybe there's a way to connect physically *and* bring some peace to the Living. Maybe Thatcher doesn't know that the haunting methods can coexist. *The connection is working.*

Then Nick looks down at our hands, and I wonder what he feels. His fingers are curled around mine—but what does it look like if he can't see me?

A rueful chuckle escapes his lips, and the noise doesn't sound like his laugh. It sounds bitter, hard. He picks up his hand and it passes right through mine. He shakes it like he's flinging off soreness or brushing away a bad thought.

"I must be crazy," he says under his breath, shoving the amber heart back into his pocket with a disgusted sigh.

No! I want to scream and flail and cry out. *I'm here!* I will him to look at me, to see me, but he's leaning away from me now, an angry frown on his face.

His phone rings—*Carson*. He hits the Ignore button.

"Nick, please," I say.

My throat clenches as I watch Nick open his backpack and pull out a half-empty bottle of Jameson. He unscrews the top and takes a long pull. Then he wipes his sleeve over his mouth and puts the bottle back in his bag, zipping it shut.

This isn't you.

I shut my eyes tight, not wanting to see what's happening. Did my touch make it worse? When I look up again, Nick stands and walks away from the bench—away from me—without glancing back.

Why would he? His girlfriend's not here. I'm just a ghost who made him think he's gone mad.

As he climbs into his car, I realize that his grief isn't just paralyzing him—it's *dangerous*. Doesn't he remember how much he has to live for?

He pulls out from the curb and I watch him drive away. I couldn't stop him if I tried—I'm helpless. I slump onto the bench, unsure of myself. What have I learned to do? Sit peacefully, blow out a lit stick, trick my boyfriend into holding a hand that isn't there?

Tears well up. I've made things worse. I'm going to be like Thatcher. A failure. Those I love are never going to move on. I'm causing Carson and Nick more pain each time I see them. What will I do to my father? I'm afraid to face him.

Suddenly a buzz electrifies my shoulder, and a wave of sensation like being yanked beneath an ocean swell and losing my balance washes through me.

Bolting off the bench, fighting off a spurt of dizziness, I spin around.

I'm not alone.

I shiver as Leo grins at me, his eyes glowing.

Thirteen)

I BACK UP A STEP. "You're not supposed to touch me without permission."

He holds up his palms in a surrender gesture. "Sorry. I just needed a little energy boost."

Maybe I didn't repel him because all my defenses were down, or maybe it has something to do with the black mark on his neck. I get the sense that not all the rules of the Prism apply to him. "Are you stalking me?" He was at the graveyard and in Carson's car. Now here.

"You're paranoid."

"Doesn't mean I'm not right."

Shrugging, he sits on the bench, stretches his arms along the back and his long legs in front of him. "I'm waiting for someone."

Is it just coincidence that he's waiting where I happen to be?

"Where's Thatcher?" he asks.

Guilt swamps me, along with a sense of disloyalty.

Leo chuckles. "He doesn't know about your little private excursions, does he? He will not be happy."

Don't I know that.

"I have to go." But I'm suddenly self-conscious about him watching me create a portal.

"What's the rush? You should stay. It's always more exciting when Thatcher isn't around. He is such a total downer since he died."

I'm taken aback. "You knew him when he was alive?"

"Oh, yeah." He interlaces his fingers together, makes a double fist. "We were close."

Before I can ask him what happened, Reena appears down the street. When I turn toward her, she waves. "Hey!"

Behind her are Delia and Norris.

"About time," Leo says, shoving himself off the bench.

"Sorry. We got caught up in something." She smiles at me. "So glad you're here, Callie. You can hang with us."

"I don't know. I've been gone for a while."

"Are you feeling tired?"

"No, but—"

"Then play with us."

A thousand alarm bells go off in my head. I know Thatcher wouldn't like this, but my curiosity has always overwhelmed my caution. Besides, I know these ghosts.

"I guess I could stay a little while longer." Not to mention I welcome a distraction from my inability to make any progress with

Nick. Maybe hanging around with Reena will teach me something that will help.

"Great. So what's up?" Reena asks, smiling fully now.

So many things.

"Not much," I say. "Still dead."

Norris and Delia laugh enthusiastically. "I like you, Callie," says Delia. "Just being around you, I feel amazing."

"Callie's found what Ponce de León never could," says Norris, and I'm not sure what he means, but he's smiling, so it must be good.

"How are things going with your haunting?" prods Reena.

Her face is cheerful, curious. The warm glow in her eyes says that I can trust her, that I can talk to her.

"I don't know," I say. "I mean, I'm trying. I just feel kind of . . ."

"Down?" asks Reena.

"Yeah. Something like that."

She reaches into her pocket for a hair tie and pulls her long black locks into a quick ponytail.

"Why don't we all go have a little fun?" she suggests. "I can show you how to interact a little more. You want to connect with those you love, don't you?"

"Yeah, but—"

"Thatcher has her brainwashed," Leo sneers.

"No, he doesn't," I say in my—and his—defense.

"But he's trying to convince you to stick with the whole soul-touching thing, right?" He leans toward me. "Who are you gonna believe? Those who completed their hauntings? Or the guy who failed at his?"

Although Thatcher did fail, he must have learned something from his experience or he wouldn't be a Guide. Leo's dislike of Thatcher has me not wanting to be anywhere near Leo. I still don't trust him. "You guys go on, have fun. I really need to get back."

Reena steps nearer to me. "Look, Callie, where's the harm in at least learning how to do it? It's like all the facts you learn for a history exam. They're not all on the test, but you're prepared if they are. Everyone's experience in the Prism is different." She comes a little closer and lowers her voice, like we're sharing something she doesn't want the others to know. "You already know that Thatcher hasn't told you everything—like the truth about the portals. I'm just saying, knowledge is power. Be prepared. You don't have to do it if you're not comfortable with it."

She's right. Thatcher did hold out on me. Why shouldn't I learn what I can and make my own decisions? I nod. "I guess it can't hurt."

Leo claps his hands together, his smile big and broad. "Hell, yes. Who feels like a coffee?"

We step into Kudu, a café where people are always hanging out, sitting around and drinking coffee. Some are students, others are townies, but it's kind of a scene. When we arrive, Leo laughs and says, "Laptop city."

"Who first?" asks Reena with a gleam in her eye.

Norris points at a redheaded girl in the corner who quickly types like her thoughts can't keep up with her fingers. We follow as Reena strolls over to the table and stands behind the typing girl.

Reena touches my forearm and a buzz jolts me, tingling its way through me, like ice cracking in the center of a frozen lake sending out jagged fissures toward shore. Cold and sharp. She stares me right in the eye, almost challenging me not to pull back. "To connect, you just have to heighten your energy," she explains. "That won't be a problem for you."

For a tense moment, I could swear I hear a spark of envy in her voice. I almost point out that it's rude to take energy without asking—wondering if they invited me along because of what I have instead of what I am. Like the girl at school who's suddenly popular because she got a sports car over the summer. I shake it off. I have energy to spare and they need it. So what? "How does this work?" I ask.

"You remember the feeling of whatever you're going to interact with," Reena explains, "so right now, I'm thinking about the light weight of laptop keys under my fingers, the way my nails click a little bit on their surfaces . . ."

She closes her eyes, puts her arms on either side of the girl, and rests her fingers on the keys. The girl is typing out what looks to be a painful history paper, but suddenly the document has a mind of its own—or Reena's own, I guess. Right in the middle of the page, new words emerge:

I'M WATCHING YOU, RED.

The girl's mouth falls open as she looks nervously around the coffee shop, like someone could have broken into her document virtually and done this.

Leo and Norris crack up at her bewildered gaze. It *is* pretty funny. I would be so freaked out. She erases Reena's typing, then takes a deep breath and starts working again.

"Not a big enough reaction," says Delia, throwing her golden curls over her shoulder. "Let's try something more drastic."

"Like what?" I ask.

They all huddle around me, like we're calling secret plays on a football field. "Put your hands in the center," says Reena. I'm wondering if we're going to do some sort of ghost fight cheer, but when I place my palm on top of the others', I feel a deep vibration, almost like we're holding on to a moving car. Tiny sparks are shooting through me, reminding me of a bug zapper that lights up every time a mosquito hits it.

I look up at Reena, and she must see the question in my eyes.

She smiles reassuringly. "We're pooling energy," she says. "That way we can do bigger things. Try anything you want, Callie. *Anything.*"

I would expect to feel revitalized. Instead I'm beginning to sag. I must not be doing this right.

After thirty seconds or so, Leo shouts, "Break!" and our hands part. I welcome the break in contact, glad all the little zaps are no longer pinging through me. Everyone turns in a different direction, but I need a moment to regain my equilibrium, so I stand there watching while they put on a show.

Leo focuses on the iPod behind the counter, changing the music from chill indie rock to upbeat hip-hop.

As everyone in the café looks up from their laptops and

conversations, Norris starts touching the strings of white lights that are hung around the café, making each of them flash in time with the music.

I laugh as the faces of the Living fill with questions. Some are smiling, some look bewildered, but everyone is exchanging glances, trying to figure out what's going on.

Delia leans over one table and blows the foam off a girl's cappuccino. As it floats into the air, her friend giggles nervously. Then Delia moves from table to table.

"Decapitate all frothy drinks!" shouts Leo.

It's like we're the guests of honor at a party, making everyone stop and stare and spin in wonder, whirling in the unknown and sharing this moment together. Suddenly my energy is boosted. I'm exhilarated, I'm energized, I'm feeling . . . *elated*.

I join in and bend down to the straw of an iced coffee at the table near me where a mom sits with her toddler. I put my lips around it and blow, making gurgling bubbles erupt in the cup. The little boy squeals with delight.

"Nice, Callie!" says Delia.

We all laugh, and I turn to see what Reena's up to. She's standing at the window looking up at the sky, not paying attention to what's going on in the café. I see the dark black mark on the back of her neck, just under her ponytail. It suddenly seems ominous, threatening.

I walk over to her to ask her about it, but before I can speak, she grabs my shoulder. A slight burning sensation where she's touching me has me gasping, and I start to pull away but she holds me fast.

She's incredibly strong for such a petite girl, and the wildness in her eyes makes me wish I weren't here.

"What are you doing?" I ask her, my voice raspy and taut.

Triumph lights her eyes as she commands, "Look."

I follow her gaze outside, where it was bright and sunny just a minute ago. Now, dark gray clouds are swirling and lightning flashes streak the sky. Abruptly, a heavy rain pounds the pavement, the sound like drumbeats in a marching band.

The Living gasp at the quick change in the weather. Chairs scrape across the floor as some get up to come to the window. They look confused, disoriented. Summer storms aren't unheard of, but this one has an almost unearthly force to it. Beyond the window, people run for cover—into stores, below awnings. For a moment, this little street in Charleston resembles the set of a disaster movie. Rivers of water flow down the sides of the street, cars stop in the middle of the road, everyone stares up at the massive web of lightning above.

Reena releases her hold on me and smiles victoriously as Norris, Delia, and Leo join us at the window.

"No way," says Norris.

"Badass." Leo enunciates both syllables.

Delia taps her knuckles against Reena's as though she conquered something huge.

"Did you do that?" I ask, pointing outside to the rain, which is lessening now to a slow drizzle. It doesn't seem possible. Touching the weather? As fast as it came on, the storm dries up. Cautiously, people emerge from the buildings. The sun pushes through the gray clouds, turning them back into harmless summer puffs.

"We did," says Reena. "I told you we're more powerful together."

"You're our lucky charm, Callie!" Leo knocks me on the arm a little too hard.

I turn back to the café. The Living are all talking excitedly about what just happened.

The barista is staring at the iPod as he switches it back to the Decemberists.

The redheaded girl is telling the guy at the table next to her about how someone hacked into her Word doc just before the storm.

A guy in the corner is pointing to his Sunday newspaper, declaring loudly that his horoscope in the *Charleston City Paper* said this day would be full of "strange occurrences."

Sunday? I shake off the sadness that more days have gone by, and fight to stay in the moment.

Now that the sun is shining brightly again, it's difficult to believe a storm was raging only a few seconds ago. It looks like nothing happened outside. A little bead of worry nestles into my chest. People were obviously scared, but it doesn't appear anyone was hurt. Their day was interrupted. No big deal. I was having fun, too. Besides, people are slowly resuming their activities, cars are moving along. I think of the words that I always see people in movies stamp onto moments in time—We Were Here.

Reena, Leo, Norris, Delia, and I—we're all dead, but we just showed this one corner of the world that we're not gone.

Then I see Leo sneaking up on the barista, who is leaning on the counter, staring out the window. Leo's exaggerated stealth is comical. It's not needed. The guy can't see him.

When Leo is close enough, when he's nudging up against the guy, he places his arm over the barista's and slowly lowers it until it disappears.

"What's he doing?" I ask Reena.

She's watching, too. Intently. "Shadowing."

"What's that?"

"Haven't you ever stood behind someone and tried to line your shadow up so it looks like there's only one person?"

"I guess so."

She shrugs. "It's the same principle."

The barista walks away, leaving Leo with his arm resting on the counter. Leo swears harshly.

"Why's he upset?" I ask.

"You want to guess their next movement, move with them. Pretend you're part of them. Shadow them—but since we're ghosts, we can shadow them closer in death than we could in life."

"And Leo's really bad at it," Delia says, chortling.

I don't get it. It seems boring and pointless to me, but I guess it's not like they can play video games. They have to find entertainment where they can.

Leo is still cursing when he joins us.

"Nice try," Norris says.

Leo gives him the finger. "I almost had it."

Norris releases his horsey laugh. "Yeah, well, *almost* doesn't count."

If looks could kill, well, Norris would be dead again.

His eyes burning with fury, Leo reaches for me and wraps his hand around my arm. It's like a tidal wave of power rolls through me, gathers up, and shoots a bolt of lightning from me to Leo. He laughs like a lunatic. I want to pull free, but he's holding on like grim death.

Everything spins around. Darkness hovers at the edge of my vision.

"Callie?" Reena's voice comes from a great distance.

I stagger, drop to my knees. Leo must have let go, because there are no more lightning bolts, no more anything. I feel like I'm sinking into an empty void. I don't want to go there. I don't know what's waiting for me, but it can't be good.

"You're okay," Reena says. "We just need to get you back to the Prism."

I try to nod, but it's as though I've turned into a rag doll, as though I no longer have any structure.

And then I plunge into the inky blackness of total oblivion.

Fourteen

"CALLIE."

The voice is soft, tender, but filled with urgency.

"Callie."

Probably my dad, trying to wake me up to tell me that I've overslept. But it's so warm here, so comforting. I don't want to leave. It's like I'm floating near the ocean floor, no sound at all except for the gentle call of my name.

"Callie."

I'm keenly aware of soft, harmonic waves flowing through me from my head to my toes. I snuggle down deeper, encompassed by comfort, compassion, love. I want to stay here forever, wrapped in this cocoon of heavenly bliss. It's unlike anything I've ever experienced before. I remember once when I was blowing bubbles, watching two of them coming together, bouncing gently off each other until one bounce joined them and they began to merge. That's how I feel: as though I'm becoming part of something else.

Slowly, with a great deal of effort, I open my eyes. I'm in my room. Relief swamps me. Just as I thought. Everything—the Prism, Reena, Leo, my death—was a dream. Thatcher was a dream, too. Sadness sweeps through me with that thought. I miss him. Strange, funny thought.

I widen my eyes, taking in more of my room. I'm not in my bed but in the window seat. I can see everything, and it's wrong. It isn't my room of this morning. It's the room that was a hodgepodge of my past.

"Callie, you're back."

I jerk my head around. Thatcher. He's sitting in my window seat, holding me in his lap, his arms tightly around me. I'm nestled against his chest. It's firm and solid, like everything else I touch within this room. I have an urge to bury my face in the crook of his shoulder.

"You're okay?" he asks, his voice rough and raspy as though he's been repeating my name for a hundred years.

I nod and whisper, "What are you doing here?"

"When I knocked, you didn't answer." He looks sheepish. "So I came in. You were lying on your bed, fading. Almost no energy at all was emanating from you. Scared the hell out of me. I've been sharing mine with you, trying to get you to respond." So much concern and worry is in his eyes that I want to weep. "What happened? It doesn't make sense that your energy would drain away while you're in your prism."

Oh, yeah. My prism. Only I wasn't here, and he is not going

to like that. I shrug and try to look innocent. As his eyes narrow, I realize there is no Academy Award in my future.

"What did you do, Callie?" he asks suspiciously.

I shake my head.

"Does this have anything to do with Reena? Was she in here taking your energy?"

"No," I respond weakly, my energy still tapped out, although I can feel it returning.

"This has something to do with her, though, doesn't it?"

"It was just some innocent fun." I cast my eyes downward, not wanting to see his disappointment.

He puts his hand under my chin, forcing up my gaze until his can lock with mine. I feel a strong buzz where his fingers touch my skin, and the gentle pleasure undulating through me increases. His jaw twitches angrily.

"Where did she take you? What did you do?" It's a harsh whisper under his breath as he drops his hand.

What's the harm in confessing? He's going to keep at it until he knows the answer anyway. I decide to leave out the part that I went to Earth on my own. He's mad enough as it is. "We were at a coffee shop. Just moved some things around."

"And it cost you."

"I'll be okay," I protest feebly.

Suddenly he's standing, his arms beneath me, lifting me as though I'm as light as cotton candy. Maybe I am. Instinctively, I clasp my hands behind his neck as he shifts my weight easily and carries me across the room.

"What are you doing?" I ask.

"Things are really bad if you can't figure out that I'm carrying you."

"Oh my God. Did you just make a joke? The always-so-serious Thatcher is teasing me?"

"Don't know what I was thinking," he grumbles. His mouth is set in a tight, worried line. A pang of guilt ricochets through me because I ignored his warnings about Reena.

He sets me down gently on my bed.

"Thatcher, Reena's my friend," I say, not certain why I don't want him to know about the others who were there. Instinctively, I know he'd be more than livid if he learned Leo was with us. "We were having fun. She brought me back when I got tired."

He steps away from me and plows his hands through his hair. "She took a lot of energy from you," he says, more to himself than to me. "Too much. Way too much."

"I'm fine. Really, Thatcher, I think I just fainted or something."

"Ghosts don't faint," he says. "What happened was not okay."

He starts pacing the floor now, clearly agitated.

"Why isn't it okay for me to have friends?"

"She's *not* your friend. Stay here," he barks, and storms for the door.

"Where are you going?"

"To make sure nothing like this happens again." Then he strides out, slamming the door shut.

"Thatcher!" I shout, certain that he's going to find Reena and have a talk with her. Although it probably won't be a talk. It'll be more of a shouting match. Oh, God, I should have told him it was Leo, not Reena. He's mad at her when she's really innocent in all this. It was Leo trying to take more energy.

I roll out of bed, my energy not fully restored, but revamped enough that I can go after him. But when I step out of my prism, all I see is the cloudy mist again, the emptiness, the gray. He's nowhere in sight. Although I have no idea where I'm going, I'm determined to find Reena and warn her that Thatcher is angrier than he was before—if it's even possible to surpass his earlier level of anger.

As I wander along in what seems to be an almost aimless route, I begin to see some grass, a bit of sky, even a pathway. I'm a little afraid, but it's the good kind of fear. The kind that rushes through me when I'm pushing my limits. The kind I used to crave.

I wonder how I'll find Reena, or anyone, in this lonely place. But then the mist swirls provocatively around me and suddenly I'm turning a corner and standing in front of a gray door, which has an intimidating wrought-iron gate over it. I hesitate. For all I know, hell and brimstone could be on the other side.

"Callie May," I say to myself. "You are no chicken."

Just as I'm about to knock, the door swings open and I jump back, crouching down instinctively. I see a swoosh of dark hair as Reena emerges. The energy in the Prism *must* work to lead me to where I think about going—it delivered me to Reena's prism. I start to stand and say hi, but before I make a sound, I hear Thatcher's voice.

"Leave her alone," he demands. Such power, determination, and fortitude ring through his voice that I slide back into the crouch, hoping the mist will hide me.

"She's a big girl," says Reena. "She can decide who her friends are. Are you bothered because she's not completely under your spell?"

"What? No," Thatcher scoffs. They're both standing in the doorway, just a few feet away from me. They're staring at each other intently. "Reena, she's a special case. You don't know what you're doing—the damage you could cause."

"Does this have something to do with her energy?" asks Reena. "She has so much. It seems almost like she's—"

"Her energy is completely standard," interrupts Thatcher. But he's told me that my energy level is high, so why is he lying to Reena?

"We both know that isn't true," says Reena.

"I don't know exactly what you and Leo are doing," says Thatcher. "But I know you're up to something—the Guides are watching you."

"Ooh, *the Guides are watching us.*" Reena's tone is mocking. "We'd better run scared now. Oh, wait, we're already dead. I guess that means we don't get scared."

"Reena, this is serious. *Stop* messing with the Living."

"I thought you were here to tell me to steer clear of Callie," says Reena. "So which is it, Thatcher? Don't think you'll get two favors out of me."

"I'm not asking for a favor. I'm issuing you a warning—stay away from Callie and stop what you're doing on Earth."

"We're just having a little fun," she says. "Haunting doesn't have to be so serious and sad all the time."

I couldn't agree more. Maybe if Thatcher would open his mind up to the possibilities and go with us, he'd see it as well.

"Besides, Thatcher," says Reena, "you're so transparent."

"What do you mean?"

"You like her."

My heart speeds up. *What?*

"I—" Thatcher begins, then halts. "She's my responsibility, but there are challenges with Callie that make it really difficult."

Ouch. Although I have to admit that I've been a pain in the butt, bucking at the restrictions, trying to find my own way to do this. I've never been one to take the path already traveled.

"You used to be into challenging girls," says Reena.

"Not anymore."

"Then why do you care if she spends time with little old me?" asks Reena in a flirty tone.

"I'm her Guide. It's my job to protect her."

"You used to try to protect me," says Reena, her voice softer.

"I still would," says Thatcher. And I wonder what he means.

They fall silent. They're standing toe-to-toe and staring each other down. I have the sense that even if I started doing cartwheels, they wouldn't notice me right now.

Then I see Thatcher reach out and take Reena's hand. He's always so careful not to touch that I feel a momentary surge of jealousy. Which is crazy. He's just my Guide, but I've started to want him to be more.

"I wish you could still merge," he says.

"I don't want to merge. You know that. I've been pretty clear about my feelings on the subject."

"I'm so sorry, Reena. I'm really sorry things worked out this way."

"Don't be sorry, Thatcher!" she shouts, pulling her hand away from his. "God, I'm so sick of you being sad. Get mad about what happened to us! Aren't you angry that we had to *die*?"

He shakes his head. "We've been over this. I won't rehash it now. Just . . . *leave Callie alone.*"

"But I enjoy her company. She's fun," says Reena. "She reminds me of me when I was *alive*—don't you think?"

My mouth drops open. *They* did *know each other before.*

Thatcher takes a step closer to Reena so that he's right up in her face. "She's nothing like you."

"Oh really?"

"She's thoughtful and funny and smart and kind and open to believing, not to bitterness."

If I were still in my body, I'd be blushing, my face heating uncomfortably. I had no idea he thought all those things about me.

"Hmm . . . I can tell how much you don't like her," says Reena. "You hate her so much you're ready to spend the rest of your death with her."

Her face lights up then, and she tilts her head at him. "Oh, I just thought of that. Is that your plan, Thatcher? From what I under-stand, she's not having any luck with her hauntings. I'm thinking that maybe you don't want her to succeed."

"What are you talking about?"

"You're the most experienced Guide, the best. But she's floun-dering. I don't think your heart is really in this little project." She narrows her eyes, runs her tongue over her lips. "Or maybe it is. Just not in the way it's supposed to be. You more than like her."

"You have"—he shakes his head—"totally lost your mind."

"You're so cute when you get rattled," Reena says. "You know I'm right. As long as those she cares about don't move on, she can stay with you, be with you. I think that's exactly what you want. Then you're no longer alone."

"I would never be that selfish, undermine her progress like that."

"Because Solus is so wonderful. But what if it isn't, Thatcher? What if you're wrong? What if you're really condemning her to hell?"

Thatcher backs up a step as though she's punched him. "You don't know what you're talking about."

"But I know what I want and I know how to get it." Reena laughs, a light, dismissive trill. "Good-bye, Thatcher." She walks back into her prism and slams the door. Crouching into a ball, I hope that he goes in the direction away from where I'm hiding.

I listen intently for Thatcher's footfall, but all I hear is silence. Duh. Walking on mist leaves no sound.

So much for warning Reena about Thatcher and telling Thatcher the truth about Leo. Reena's just trying to help me connect with those I love. Leo's trying to take advantage. I shudder at the memory of him reaching out to me in anger, of him drawing the last of my energy, plunging me into the blackness.

I know that Thatcher has kept some things from me, but I don't believe for a minute that he's deliberately sabotaging my progress. It's just that his method isn't working for me. At least with Reena's way, people know I'm there.

"He's gone."

I don't start; I don't spin around. I just work to put up my defenses. "Leo, you *are* stalking me."

I shove myself to my feet and glare at him. His hands are in the back pockets of his jeans, and he's rocking back and forth while wearing his familiar I'm-up-to-no-good grin. "I was worried. Just wanted to make sure you were okay."

"Yeah, you strike me as someone who worries a lot about others."

"I didn't mean to drain all your energy. Seriously. Reena thinks it happened because we'd already been so active. You just didn't have that much left."

"Doesn't matter how much I have left. You can't just take it."

"I know, I know. It won't happen again. Friends, okay?"

"I don't think so."

I turn to leave. I don't want to be anywhere near him.

"Hey, come on!" he shouts.

The door to the prism eases open, and Reena is standing behind the gate. Her eyes are glowing, but not in that oh-I-just-went-for-a-run way. More like in that oh-I-just-bit-the-head-off-a-live-mouse way.

Dark shadows are dancing strangely on the wooden walls behind her.

"Oh, I thought I heard voices out here. Come on in," she says, beckoning me and Leo into the darkness of her prism.

Fifteen

I HESITATE, A LITTLE shiver of warning prickling through me.

Reena tilts her head, and a warm smile lights up her face. She's so beautiful—and it's not because of her smooth, dark skin or her high cheekbones or even her lush black hair. The other ghosts I've seen look calm, pleasant, polite. But not this girl—she's got fire.

"Callie, it's all right. Thatcher won't find out," she says.

I know I should leave, just walk away, but it's almost like she's daring me to prove I'm not a chicken. She won't hurt me. I know that. Leo's the problem.

As though reading my mind, she says, "Your energy is safe in here."

With her reassurance echoing around me, I cross the threshold. Once inside, I find the space is less intimidating than it seemed from the doorway. The walls around us are a deep brown wood, which made it seem dark, and I realize that her prism is like a log cabin, with plaid curtains drawn over the windows and a big black stove in the corner where a fire throws shadows onto the wall. The crispness of late fall blossoms in here, and I wonder if we choose seasons to go along with our prisms. Mine is summer.

Reena opens the curtains and light filters in. A soft-looking red-and-white quilt hangs over a rocking chair in the corner.

"My grandparents' cabin," she says, walking over to sit down on an overstuffed sofa. "We used to spend every holiday here when I was alive."

She says that—"when I was alive"—without a trace of sadness, and I wonder if I'll ever feel that indifferent about my own death.

She pats the seat beside her. "Make yourself at home."

I ease onto the flowered cushion.

"It's nice," I say, because it is. It's warm and cozy, and I can see why Reena made it her prism.

"I like it." Then she smiles at me. "You look rested."

"Yeah. Thanks for, um, dropping me off."

"No problem. Sometimes being on Earth can be exhausting. It *was* fun, though." She studies my face. "Don't you think?"

"It was . . . interesting. But I'm not sure—"

"Thatcher got upset, right?"

"Yeah."

"What did you tell him?" Leo asks anxiously, dropping down beside me, very close, a little too close. I have an urge to edge away, to remind him to watch my personal space. He's crowding me, making me feel uncomfortable, and I can't help but wonder if, even though I can't feel it, he's tapping into my energy again.

"Not a lot. Just that we moved some things around."

He and Reena exchange a glance full of meaning—I'm not sure how to read it.

"That's good," Reena says. "He can make a big deal out of nothing."

And I can't help but wonder—

"Like what you did with the weather? It was pretty impressive."

"I've never done that before." Reena's face lights up. "It felt amazing."

"The sky was a painting. Like performance art or whatever."

"I know, right? It's all about having fun with haunting. No matter what *other ghosts* might preach."

I smile, even though I feel like I'm betraying Thatcher. I have one question I want answered, and then I'll leave. "On your neck. There's—"

"The black spot of death," Reena murmurs in a low voice that's almost seething. For a second I wonder if I've upset her, but then she breaks into a relaxed laugh and pulls her hair back, turning her head so I can see it.

It's dark and ashy, almost like she was burned with a cigar in that spot.

"It used to be the green moon," she says. "I'm sure Thatcher has told you about the mark that guides ghosts to Solus."

"Sort of. I mean, yeah, I've seen it, and he told me how it changes as you get closer to merging, right?"

"Right," she says. "Unless it goes black like mine."

"I thought you couldn't see them in the Prism. Only on Earth."

"Again, unless it's black like mine—then it shows all the time."

"But what does it mean?"

"You tell her, Leo. You earned yours first."

I twist around to look at him. His black circle is bigger than Reena's, but just as dark and ashy.

"This spot," says Leo, smiling sinisterly, and suddenly I wonder if I should be asking about the spot, if it's too intrusive of me. "This spot is a symbol of power, rebellion, a badge of honor. It means that I never have to merge with Solus. That *we* never have to merge."

Reena laughs. "Leo, don't be so dramatic!" She scoots closer to me so that I'm hemmed in. I want to make a run for it, which is ridiculous. I like Reena. "It means that we know about our lives. It indicates that we've been back."

"Back to what?" I ask.

"Back to our death spot."

"I thought you couldn't go back," I say. "Thatcher said it wasn't possible because . . . because you can't—" I don't remember him saying why we couldn't go, just that we couldn't.

"You have to understand that Thatcher has a lot of hang-ups. There's no reason for you not to go if you want to," says Reena.

I consider the implications and possibilities for a moment. I'm curious about where I died, about why Thatcher doesn't want me to go there.

"What will I see there?" I ask.

"Nothing scary," Reena assures me. "The Guides won't take

new ghosts there because it can jar your memory, reconnect you with your life, and stir up grief."

"They want the new ghosts to be mindless robots so they can finish their haunting and merge with Solus," says Leo.

Soulless. He says it in that way again.

"Right," says Reena. "But you're smart, Callie. And you already have your memories. So where's the harm in seeing where you died?"

She's smiling with encouragement, and her eyes are shining.

"You don't want to say good-bye to Earth and leave everyone you love forever, do you?" she asks pointedly.

"No," I say. "I don't want to do that."

"Right—you're choosing to be with Nick, and Carson, and your father, forever."

Reaching up, I tentatively touch my neck, wondering if the green moon tattoo is there now, if I'm willing for it to go dark.

"Forever?" I ask.

"Hell, yes!" says Leo. "And that's a good thing. Solus is where you truly die. Not here. We can still have fun, see our families, mess around on Earth, and almost live our lives."

Reena nods. "It's empowering. It's freeing to visit your death spot."

I hesitate.

"It might bring you some peace to be there," Reena continues.

"We can go right now," says Leo, standing up.

I stay seated. "I'm not sure."

Reena smiles with understanding. "Callie, would you rather go visit someone else's death spot instead?"

"What do you mean?" I ask.

"We spend a lot of time at the place where Norris died," she says. "It's kind of our hangout on Earth."

"Really?" I ask, thinking that sounds a little creepy. "Where did he die?"

"His was kind of a unique ending," Leo says mysteriously. "We'd hate to ruin the surprise."

Leo definitely has a macabre sense of humor, and I don't quite trust him. But Thatcher has no doubt discovered that I didn't follow orders and wait for his return. He may be searching for me. I'm not ready to face his disappointment.

"Yeah, let's do this," I say.

"You won't regret it," says Reena.

But some part of me already does.

Leo howls the entire time that we're in the portal, hurtling through space. It's almost like the rebel yell that the guys at school used to let out during tailgating parties—loud and long and full of fight. But when they did it, it sounded like the volume was turned up on life; Leo's yelp is more like an eerie echo of death, and I shiver as we pass through the portal, stepping out on the metal rail of a train track and stumbling down to the wooden planks.

A bony arm catches me. "Whoa there, Callie."

"Hi, Norris," I say.

He grins. "The gang's all here."

I spot Delia's blond curls before she turns around to say hello. Then Leo and Reena emerge from the portal and it closes up with a spark.

"Where are we?" I ask.

"Lyndon's Crossing," says Delia.

"Why does that sound so familiar?" Looking around at the railroad tracks, the trees growing on either side of them, I don't think I've been here.

"Some stupid kid died here a few years back," says Leo, staring right at Norris. "Train-dodging idiot."

"Shut up, man." Norris knocks Leo on the arm.

And then it hits me . . . *Norris Porter*. It happened when I was pretty young, but his death was a big deal—the train cut him in half. I remember that awful detail because I told my father that I thought maybe Norris Porter could be fixed by a magician, one who saws his assistant in two and then puts her back together. But my father shook his head and says, "No, Callie, that doesn't work in reality."

After the accident these tracks were closed for a few years. But they opened them again last summer. I guess everyone thought it had been long enough.

When Norris starts joking around about *Blood on the Tracks* by Bob Dylan being the soundtrack to his death, I ask him if it's weird to be here.

"Nah," he says. "I can't die *again*."

The rest of them laugh. Putting aside my hesitation at being here, I join in. They seem so carefree, so light, and I yearn to be a part of that, to pretend for a little while at least that I'm not dead—and forget that I should be haunting and that I've caused others pain.

Soon the *chug-chug-chug* of a train in the distance echoes around us.

"Who's gonna go?" asks Leo.

"I think Callie should," says Delia. "She's stronger than all of us."

Her eyes glimmer playfully, and I search her face. Is she mocking me? Her smile is big, though, encouraging.

I grin back. "I don't think I'm stronger than *Leo*," I say, "but I could definitely take the rest of y'all."

Norris scoffs.

"So try the train dodge," says Leo, a challenge in his eyes.

"Show her how it's done first, big shot," says Norris.

"You're the expert," Leo volleys back.

Norris laughs in that horsey way again. He doesn't seem to mind joking about his own death.

"You guys are such chickens," says Delia, stepping into the center of the tracks. "Watch this, Callie."

Her face is beaming as she stares down the locomotive that's rushing at her. Her golden hair catches the headlights, lighting up like curlicues on fire. The conductor doesn't blow a whistle, though. There's just the driving noise of the train, full speed ahead, as Delia stretches her arms out into a Y and looks up to the sky.

I always thought about trying something like this, but it seemed more foolhardy than daring. Maybe Norris's death left an impression.

My heart beats faster as the train gets closer. "She's going to get out of the way, right?" I ask Reena. "It's a dodge?"

"No need for that," says Reena.

I will myself to stand still as the engine draws near. And even though I know we're all dead, that this train can't hurt Delia, I quiver with panic.

When the front car slams into her, Delia lets out a piercing yowl. It lasts as long as the train does—I count thirty-two cars. As the final one moves past, Delia jumps off the tracks, shining like she's lit up from within.

"Woooo!" she yells.

Norris runs up to her, picks her up off the ground, and twirls her around. "Awesome." Pride rings through his voice. I scrutinize his face for signs of grief or fear—this is where he *died*, after all—but I guess it's been long enough. He's more elated than anything.

I wonder if this is what it would be like for me if I went back to that spot on Route 52. Would I find peace there, finally accept what happened to me? Would it allow me to reach Nick?

Leo folds his hands around Delia's shoulders and drops his head back as though he can syphon her exhilaration. I'm not sure why it bothers me, why I have the sense that he's trying to capture something for himself. At the same time, I'm a little envious of the way they all touch so freely.

"You should try it, Callie," says Delia. "It's a huge rush."

She appears completely fine—beyond fine, actually. Delia beams like she just had the most exciting experience of her life. Or death.

"Have you guys all done it?" I ask.

"Yeah," says Norris. "Even I've done it. The not-dying part is really cool."

I laugh along with the rest of them, but I wonder if there's a part of Norris that finds this reenactment of his death kind of creepy or sad.

We sit by the side of the tracks and talk. All the while I'm watching Norris, impressed with how comfortable he is here. Eventually, I have to ask.

"Do the rest of you guys go back to your death spots, too?"

"Ours isn't fun," says Reena, glancing at Leo.

"Ours?" I ask.

"Mine is depressing," says Delia, shifting our attention to her, and I'm left with the impression that she's trying to protect Reena and Leo, save them from a question that was intrusive. "Hospital," she says. Then she whispers, *"Cancer."*

"Oh," I say. "I'm sorry."

"It's been a while—it's okay," she says. "Plus, when I died I got all this back!" She shakes out her golden curls and they fall around her shoulders.

I don't know if I'd have been as accepting, but I understand why she craves the thrills that she probably never had in life.

"And you know what else?" she says. "I was never strong enough to do *any of this* when I was alive. But in death, I'm living it up."

Just then, the familiar *chug-chug-chug* comes within earshot. "Okay," I say. I face the tracks. "I'll go."

I'm only a little afraid—I'm used to stepping up to the edge of the cliff, but never without a safety harness. This is different. But it might be ten times as fun.

"She's ready!" shouts Leo, clapping.

Delia smiles at me. "It's a little scary the first time. Which means it's also the biggest rush."

Reena links her arm through mine and cocks her head, looking at me sideways. "You're sure?" she asks.

I watch the approaching headlights, still off in the distance. "Yeah," I say, with utter conviction.

She smiles approvingly. I experience a little prerush knowing that I'm being accepted into this daredevil group.

"Let's try something bigger," says Leo, approaching us.

"What?" I ask.

"This," he says. Then he puts his massive arms around my waist and hoists me into the air. I stiffen, not quite trusting him, but then Reena laughs as Leo carries me. He's still holding on to me from behind as he puts me down and centers us on the tracks. "I'll do it with you," he says, and immediately I'm relieved. I know I can stare down a train; I just don't know if I'll be able to stand there without dodging while it runs right through me.

Leo is a foot taller than I am, and I'm glad for his presence as I look up at the sky. I feel dizzy as I take in the line of stars that is Orion's Belt, the blurry cluster of the Seven Sisters, the crooked handle of the Big Dipper.

"It's better if you face it head-on," says Leo. I pull my gaze down to the bright headlights that are getting closer and closer. I glance over at Reena, Delia, and Norris, who are bouncing around, excited. Norris gives me a thumbs-up.

I start to feel a pull where Leo's hands are around my waist, like he's pinching me internally and drawing out some of my strength. He howls eerily up at the sky.

"We're gonna stop this freaking train!" he shouts.

"What?" I try to face him, but his hold on me is so strong that I can't budge. My nerves start pinging.

"Your energy is powerful enough, Callie," he whispers in my ear. "We can do it—do anything—together." Then, in a booming voice, he yells, "There's no limit to our powers now that we have our Lucky Charm!"

Almost frozen with dread, I'm staring at the approaching engine. Out of the corner of my eye, I see Reena edging closer to us.

"My heart is racing," I rasp.

"Your heart? Callie, you're dead. You don't have a pulse."

"Oh," I say. *Right.* Muscle memory, but wow, is it a strong memory.

The train races closer, not slowing or relenting in any way. *The driver can't see us.*

"But it feels like that, like my heartbeat is speeding up," I say to Leo, with a nervous trill.

He laughs. "Relax into it, Callie. Trust me, you only die once."

I realize how silly I sound—I know I'm imagining the heartbeat, a leftover memory. But I can feel it. The heartbeat, the panic . . . I can taste that on-the-edge coppery adrenaline that I love so much. I always get this rush, just when I'm about to do something that could—

"I can't," I whisper.

"No choice," says Leo darkly, and then there's an intense pull from the sides of my body, like the worst kind of running cramps—he's taking my energy. An eruption of fear flashes through me as a blue light streams from the spot where we're standing, streaking for the train.

"No!" I scream as loud as I can. Someone crashes into us,

shutting down the blue light and catapulting us off the tracks. *Reena.*

"Portal!" she hisses at me.

"Where?" The three of us are rolling down the edge of the tracks as the train whizzes by, mercifully untouched.

"Somewhere safe."

I close my eyes: cream walls, peach rug, daffodil bedspread, lace curtains. *Carson.* I lift my hand, full of energy, and in a flash, Reena and I are tumbling through the portal I've created, out of the way of the train and Leo's intensity, and onto my best friend's bedroom floor.

Sixteen

"NICK, *JESUS*," SAYS CARSON. She's extra pissed if she's taking the Lord's name in vain. She rolls her eyes. "Did you drive like that?"

"You said to come," he says. "I'm here. And now you're giving me a hard time?"

I stand up and help Reena to her feet. My heart is still racing from Leo's attempt to harness my energy and create a catastrophe.

"What just happened?" I ask Reena.

She smooths out her long dark hair. "Leo's excited by all the energy you have," she says lightly. "He went a little overboard."

"A little overboard? Was he really trying to *stop a train*?"

She laughs. "I know, it sounds nuts, but your energy creates new possibilities for all of us. He got carried away."

I bite my lip, thinking that's the understatement of the year. But Reena is so calm, so collected. Am I overreacting?

"Do you think he would have succeeded?"

"Doubtful."

That's hardly comforting.

"Well, thanks for saving me," I say.

"I didn't save you. Nothing would have happened to you. I just saw that you were getting scared. He shouldn't push you to do things you're not ready for."

"I did get scared," I say, feeling sheepish and a little cowardly. I never backed away from an adrenaline rush before, but something about Leo sets all my nerves on edge.

She smiles. "It happens. So where are we?"

"My friend Carson's room."

Reena's eyes light up as she takes in our surroundings, and I'm glad she's so interested in my life and getting to know the people in it.

"And that is . . ." Reena points at Nick, who looks haggard and, well, wasted.

"My boyfriend, Nick," I say quietly. "He's . . ."

" . . . having a hard time with things," says Reena, filling in my pause.

"Yeah," I say.

"He's really cute. Too bad he wasn't with you in the car."

I stare at her.

She waves a hand. "Kidding. But he is hot."

"He's looked better."

"Grief is disheveling. So what's he doing in your best friend's bedroom?" she asks, narrowing her eyes.

"Oh, no," I say hastily, realizing what she's thinking. "It's not like that. I mean, I don't know why he's here, but Carson and Nick would never—"

"It's a séance," says Reena, interrupting. "They're trying to call you back."

I focus on the details then. The glow from the more than twenty candles in Carson's room is otherworldly. She's sitting cross-legged on the floor at the end of her bed, on top of the peach shag area rug we picked out together at Urban Outfitters. Spread in front of her is a full-on mystic setup: crystal ball, Ouija board, and an old-looking book called *Summoning the Spirits*.

Nick starts to sit across from her, but Carson stops him.

"Clean yourself up first," she says, pointing to the hallway bathroom.

Nick grumbles but goes. I hear the water running, and I hope a splash in the face will sober him up.

"This girl is *serious*," says Reena.

"Yeah, she is."

I'm a little protective of Carson; I'm not sure if Reena's making fun of her. I walk over near my best friend.

"Cars, what are you doing?" I say out loud.

I settle onto the floor across from her and study my best friend. Carson is *right there*. Her face is sad but determined, and I realize something: I left her. And my goal with this haunting thing? It's to leave her again, to move on to Solus and never ever see my friend go to college, get a job, get married, maybe have kids.

"I'm so sorry, Cars. I always thought we'd be rocking on the porch together with white hair one day. I'd come back if I could."

And though it was only a whisper, her eyes pop open.

"Did you hear me?" I ask, louder this time. "Carson?"

She doesn't respond, but she looks around the room as though she's truly seeing it for the first time. Then she opens the book in front of her and flips to a page that's been dog-eared. She's concentrating on the words when Nick comes back in.

"Sit down," Carson orders. He looks at her New Age circle and bursts out laughing. He rocks forward and back in that drunk way, and for a second I'm incredibly disappointed. This isn't like him. I wish I had the ability to grab his shoulders and shake him until his teeth rattle. I've never been this angry with him.

I glance back at Reena. "He's not normally like this."

"No judgment," she says. "Losing someone is tough."

Nick stares at the circle for a moment, and I wonder if he's going to sit where I am, but he doesn't. Maybe he senses me here? He settles in on Carson's left side and closes his eyes.

"Oooommm," he hums.

"What are you doing?" Carson snaps.

"Aren't we chanting or something?" he asks.

"This isn't yoga class. We are summoning Callie's spirit."

"Right, right," says Nick, a patronizing smile on his lips. His eyes are half closed—he looks so out of it.

"We're going to bring her back," says Carson, her voice determined. "I need you to take this seriously and stop goofing around."

"Cars, I showed up, didn't I?" says Nick, slurring his words. "I must be freaking crazy for doing any of this, for even letting you believe that it's possible. . . ."

He stops and drops his head forward for a moment, and I think he might confess that he's felt my presence—I know he has. But he just looks up at Carson and says, "I came because you asked me to."

"I wouldn't have asked if I'd known you were drunk. You're lucky you didn't kill someone on your way over here."

Nick puts his hands over his face like it pains him to hear her voice. "You don't know what I'm dealing with!" I can hear the anger underneath his words.

"I know what I've heard," says Carson, her lips tight in a thin line. "But I'm giving you the benefit of the doubt because you were the other closest person to Callie, and she believed in you."

He winces.

What has Carson heard?

I glance up at Reena and see her raised eyebrows. Then she gives me a sympathetic shrug. "They do go on. They start to have experiences that we don't know about."

"I hate that part," I say, turning back to my friends.

"Yeah, it really sucks," Reena mutters.

"Fine," says Nick, and I can tell he's making an effort to be calm. "So go ahead already. Prove me wrong."

"I will," says Carson. And then she closes her eyes.

"Guardians of the spirit realm, hear my plea . . . ," she starts. She says it with a straight face, taking this very seriously as she always has. "Bring Callie McPhee to me. Other souls who hear this call are not welcome. Only Callie McPhee may enter this sacred space."

"Cars," I say, talking over her as she keeps chanting those words. "You don't need this whole setup. I'm already with you, right here!"

I look back at Reena, who's leaning against the wall with her arms folded. She's smiling indulgently.

"I know she can't hear me," I say, preempting any chastising. "But it's hard not to just talk to her."

"She can't hear you, but the more you try to connect with her, the more she'll feel you," says Reena, which is so comforting. "Talk away. It can't hurt."

"You should be a Guide," I tell her.

She laughs. "You really don't know me that well if you believe that."

"I know enough." I smile with gratitude. Because Reena is a real friend—she's helping me connect. And I know I can do it this time.

Carson's still chanting with her eyes closed, and it seems like Nick is falling asleep. His head is slumped forward at a weird angle.

I focus all my attention on Carson, pouring all my energy toward her. "This isn't going to work," I say to her softly. "It's not because I don't want to come back—I'd give anything to be alive again, to be heading out on our next adventure and to let you film my latest stunt. I'd even do dumb séances like this with you. . . ."

I look over at Nick and feel a surge of affection. Okay, he's being sort of an ass, but he's *here*. He's doing that for Carson.

"Cars, you have to help Nick deal with this. You're strong—you always have been. Stronger than me and stronger than Nick and maybe even stronger than my dad."

I pause on the last word, and when I fall silent she stops chanting, too. She looks straight ahead, almost right at me.

"Cal, are you here?" she whispers.

"Yes!" I shout.

"If you're here, give me a sign, Callie, *please*."

She's not hearing me. I need something more. Maybe I can try the candles—I've already made that work once at the fire pit. I lean over to the one with the rainbow wax at the left of her circle and concentrate. *Birthdays, trick candles, the night with Nick.* Whoosh! It's out.

"Awesome!" Reena shouts. "That's the way to do it."

With pride, I beam back at her.

Carson stares in wonder at the thin stream of smoke trailing from the wick, but I can tell she's still unsure. So I lean to the right toward a thicker scented candle she has burning, and I manage to blow out that one, too.

"You *are* here!" Carson clasps her hands near her heart. "Oh my gosh, I knew it." She glances back down at the book. "Hold on—stay here, Callie!"

Nick lifts his head up. "Huh?"

"Were you asleep?" Carson huffs. "Nick, Callie's spirit is here! She blew out *both* candles!"

Nick frowns and checks the windows—closed. "*If* that happened, it was probably the air from the AC," he says.

"It was *not*," she insists. "Now pay attention, you lush."

Quickly, she flips to another page. "Shoot. We need something of Callie's."

"Huh?"

"We need something of hers to place in the circle." Carson scans her room.

"Would this work?" Nick holds up my amber heart pendant, and Carson's eyes light up.

"Perfect." She places it between them and starts reading another incantation. "By the light of the moon and the branch of the tree, I call the soul of Callie McPhee back to me. . . ."

"Carson, stop with the stupid chants," I say. "They're not why I'm here. I came on my own. This is all just fake-magic nonsense."

But she doesn't stop—she still can't hear me. "By the light of the moon and the branch of the tree, I call the soul of Callie McPhee back to me. . . ."

She pauses. "Say it with me, Nick," she commands.

He gives her a look like *Are you effing kidding me?*

"Please," she pleads. "For Callie."

He sighs deeply and bows his head, making a curl flop over his brow. Then he joins in as they slowly say these ridiculous words together.

"By the light of the moon and the branch of the tree, I call the soul of Callie McPhee back to me. . . ."

I look back at Reena.

She shrugs. "Hey, they're trying. It's more than anyone did for me after I died."

"I know Carson seems crazy right now," I say, speaking loudly over their chants. "She's just a really determined girl and—"

My voice locks up. I can no longer speak. As Carson and Nick continue chanting, I start to feel a buzzing inside. It starts in my center—right beneath my heart, like something's shaking my core. The vibrations increase in intensity, rattling the deepest part of my being. I experience the sensation of dropping into space, like I can't hold on to anything around me. You know that feeling when you're about to fall asleep but then you wake up suddenly, like you just had a sharp fall? It's like that, but it's not stopping. I'm falling and falling and . . .

What's going on? I can only think the words; I can't voice them.

My vision goes black. I hear a high-pitched noise, and I feel severe pain throughout my body. I'm shattered, pulled apart, all my bones are broken. I can't breathe, and air is rushing around me— people are moving quickly, running and shouting. *Can I really hear them, or am I just imagining voices?* I think I hear my father.

I panic and my heart races—not in the exciting way, like when I'm taking a calculated risk, but in a full-blown freak-out. There is light and wind and sound whirling around me like I'm trapped within the center of a tornado. Fear. Raw, jagged fear pierces through me like a sharp blade, slicing open my sense of balance, my rational thought, my understanding of everything around me. I experience more absolute terror than in the moment I died. That instant just rushed past me, but this one is terrifyingly prolonged.

Just as I think I might lose my mind, I feel a soft pull, like in the tidal pools at the beach, where it seems gentle but it's actually carrying you far away. I give in to the pull, willing it to rescue me, and when I let it take hold, the pain disappears.

My eyes flash open and I'm back in my prism, in my bed, with Reena hovering over me.

I sit up, bracing myself with my hands, and take a deep breath.

"What the hell happened?" I ask her.

"I'm not sure," she says slowly. "Lie back. You've been out for a while."

Why is she treating me like I'm fragile?

"I'm fine," I say, staying upright. Truthfully, I feel full of energy, like I could fly right now if I tried.

"What do you remember?" she asks.

I search through my recent memories. "We were with Carson . . . she was chanting. Nick was there . . . and then . . ."

Reena's eyes are glowing with a golden tinge, with a heated excitement.

"Go on," she says, her voice eager. "What happened?'

"I don't know," I say. "I felt weird—like my body was shaking. And then there was a lot of pain."

Reena looks at me, her eyes widening.

"What is it?" I ask. "You don't think that what Carson was doing . . . the chanting . . . you don't think that it actually started *working* . . . do you?"

She stares back at me and her expression flickers for a moment between knowledge and disbelief. But then she says, "Séances don't work on ghosts."

"Okay." The idea that Carson's woo-woo words could have called me back wasn't one I was expecting to buy into, but . . . "It was scary," I admit. "I felt an intense pull inside me."

"How do you feel now?" she asks.

"Now?" I take stock of my energy, my being. "Normal. It's like nothing happened."

Reena nods. "You're okay. You're not as breakable as Thatcher thinks you are."

"What do you mean?"

"Just that he's overly protective, and he doesn't need to be. You're strong."

I grin, proud that Reena views me that way.

"Where *is* Thatcher?" I ask, surprised that he wasn't waiting here for me. He must have completely freaked out when he returned to my prism and discovered I wasn't there. Or maybe he just figured that I needed some space.

"There's a merging ceremony tonight," says Reena. "The Guides always have to attend, so I guess he's been . . . distracted."

"A merging ceremony . . . can anyone go?"

"Well, we don't usually attend," says Reena. "I mean, they're weird and scary and generally kind of insane."

"I'm curious," I say, because I am. Part of me wants to stay in this in-between world with Reena and her friends, who remind me so much of life and who've promised that I can stay with the people I love if I choose to. But Thatcher . . . he does care about me, and this ceremony, merging with Solus, this is what he believes in. It's what my mother believed in.

"I want to go," I say.

Reena smiles. "Okay. I'll tell the others. But don't say I didn't warn you."

Seventeen

WHEN WE STEP OUT of my prism, we're in the middle of a clearing in a giant rain forest. At least, I think it's what a rain forest would be like—I've never seen one. There are lush green leaves all around us, and they have drops of dew hanging on them, dripping slowly to the soft ground. I hear birds chirping all around us and sprinkling water sounds in the distance, but there are no clouds. Still, the tinkling melody sounds like raindrops on a windowpane.

"What's the music?" I ask.

"Mbiras," says a ghost who's standing near us. She smiles at me, and her eyes are pleasant, friendly. "They're instruments from Africa that are wooden boards with metal keys. People on Earth use them to speak to the dead—and the Guides play them up here to usher ghosts toward Solus."

She pronounces it the way Thatcher does—*Solace*—and I smile at her.

Reena takes my arm and leads me away from the other ghost before I can thank her, and we stand apart from the others. "There's a good view from here," she says.

A part of me wonders if she's trying to isolate me—keep me to herself.

With Norris and Delia in tow, Leo walks up behind us, and I tense.

"Hey," I say.

"Sorry about before at the train tracks," says Leo, and he does appear contrite. "I was really just trying to have some fun."

But he keeps doing it at my expense, like in the coffee shop. Reena's told me he takes his death harder than the rest of them. What was it she said? He's "troubled." I understand. "Just discuss it with me in advance next time? Give me a choice."

"You got it."

My shoulders relax.

"I can't believe you want to see this, Callie," says Delia.

"Yeah," says Norris. "Are you sure you're ready?"

"I don't know," I say, and I wonder if I should be more nervous. But I want to know what happens, what merging is like.

Reena is by my side. "I think after you see it, you'll understand why we want to stay in the Prism."

We're on the edge of a pathway lined with smooth white stones. The ghosts stand alongside the border of the walk, and I look around to see if Thatcher is here. Will he be angry if he sees me with Reena and Leo?

As I'm searching the crowd, everyone turns at once with a collective breath, like when a bride enters the church for her wedding. All eyes are on Ella Hartley, who's coming down the path wearing a shining silver gown that hangs around her lithe form in soft, floating waves. I realize as she passes us that the dress isn't really there—it's an illusion, an impression, but it looks very real. It ripples along the ground as she steps forward, and it seems to shimmer with every movement.

"What's happening?" I whisper to Reena.

"It's her ceremony," she says.

A prick of panic skitters through me. "Ella's? I didn't know the ceremony was for her. . . ." A current of sadness sweeps through me—this is someone I knew on Earth, someone I grew up with. We weren't close, but still.

"How does it work?" I ask.

Reena turns and looks at me. "She'll vanish. Right before our eyes."

I gulp down saliva I know isn't really there. Just another phantom sensation.

"The Guides and most of the ghosts believe she's moving on to something wonderful," whispers Reena.

"And what do you believe?" I ask.

Reena holds my gaze, utter conviction in hers. "We think that she truly dies now."

My phantom heart lodges itself in my throat as Ella walks through the crowd of ghosts. *Is everyone watching this happen like it's okay?* The ghosts around me look at Ella without expression, and when I take in their faces, I see a sea of strangers, dead strangers. I shake off a chill.

When Ella gets to the front, she steps onto a podium, turns, and smiles at everyone. I look for fear in her gaze, but I don't see any. She lifts her face up to the sky; she's beaming with radiant energy.

But I'm terrified. I have a strong urge to run.

Then a bright light shines down on Ella and the podium, and the rainlike music speeds up, its gentle rhythm getting faster and faster.

Leo, Reena, Norris, and Delia look pensive, worried, afraid. But when I glance around, it doesn't seem like anyone else is showing any fear. The other ghosts' faces are placid, smiling. Their peaceful expressions are perfectly still. The image of a cicada shell comes to my mind. They're these bugs that are like a plague some summers—making a loud buzzing sound in the evening and clinging to all the trees, everywhere. At some point, they shed their skin and just leave it hanging on to whatever surface they've chosen. The skin looks like it was in life, but it's just the shell of the being that was once inside it. It's hollow, emptied of life. Is that what ghosts are? Am I a cicada shell, my life force gone completely?

Ella's form starts to flicker, and the light around her grows even brighter. It's like she's a hologram or a website that won't quite load. The mbiras are at full speed now, plinking out a thunderstorm rhythm.

My heart races in time with the music. Ella Hartley. I'm about to witness her *disappearance*.

"Is she—" I start.

"I told you, Callie," interrupts Reena, her voice serious in a way I've never heard it. "She's going to die now."

I look at Reena's face. She's smiling, and when I look at Leo, I see that he is, too.

"But this is awful," I say. "This is . . ."

"This is what the Guides do," says Leo. "They insist that every-one merge."

"It isn't fair," I say, grabbing onto Reena's arm. "What if Ella doesn't want to go . . . what if she's—"

I look up at her again on the podium, and Ella lowers her head for a moment. Her eyes catch mine, and I think I see a shadow cross her face. It's all I need.

"Stop!" I shout. "Stop the ceremony!"

I drop Reena's arm, rushing out onto the pathway, and con-cerned murmurs rise among the ghosts. All eyes turn toward my direction.

"Ella, get down from there!" I yell, hurrying toward her. "You don't want this!"

"Callie?" Ella calls.

Then Thatcher stumbles into the middle pathway, too—he was up front, close to Ella. I see Sarah and Ryan behind him.

Leo, Reena, Delia, and Norris step out behind me.

"What are you doing here?" Thatcher asks me.

He's a furious storm ready to be released. It's obvious that he has a really tight rein on his emotions. I'm not sure I want to be around when he unleashes them. On the other hand, this is wrong. We have to make him see that. For Ella's sake.

The whole forest has gone silent. Even the mbiras are still.

"We brought her," says Reena, answering for me. Her eyes are burning gold as she stares at Thatcher and the other Guides. "She has a right to see what you're doing. What a merging is like."

Thatcher moves closer, coming toward us as the ghosts at the edge of the path watch, riveted.

"Callie, I don't know what they've told you, but none of it is true," he says. "Solus is like what you think of as Heaven; it's a beautiful—"

"Solus is a myth, Thatcher!" shouts Reena, her voice bold now. She's got the attention of the whole forest. "The Guides are perpetuating a lie—there is no such thing as Solus. The Prism is the only afterlife we'll ever know. And we're not leaving just so you and the Guides can continue sending ghosts away and keeping this world—and your connection to Earth—for yourselves."

I didn't know that her desire to stay on Earth went this deep—that she thinks Thatcher and the Guides are deceiving everyone. A rumble goes up behind her, and I realize that she has more supporters in the crowd than just the friends we came with.

I'm standing between them—between Reena and Thatcher—and I don't know which way to turn to move out of the crossfire. My request to come here, to see this ceremony, suddenly feels like a mistake. I just wanted to learn more about this world, but now it's obvious I'm smack-dab in the middle of a conflict that is much bigger than I knew.

"You think we Guides *like it here*?" asks Thatcher, his voice strained. "In this transitional space where we guide new ghosts only to see them move on? Where we form no relationships and are reminded constantly that we have loved ones who never got over our deaths?" He looks around now, at the many ghosts watching us. It feels like all of the Prism is listening to this exchange, hanging on every word. There's a celestial glow in this space and on the faces of everyone gathered here. If you were to stumble upon this scene, it would look almost holy, not like the battle it's turning into.

"That's who your Guides are," says Thatcher, his voice loud and strong. "We're the ghosts who couldn't move on, the ones whose haunting hasn't worked. Oh, we know how to help others, but we're too broken to help ourselves."

Looking around at the ghosts, I realize that most of them didn't know this—they're blissfully unaware of how things work in the Prism. They appear surprised, curious even, but unconcerned. They're unencumbered by memories, content to be haunting on the path to Solus. But the people who remember—we can't be content. We feel too much pain.

In Reena's face I see the anguish, and suddenly I wonder if more ghosts than just Leo are "troubled." Maybe we all are.

Is this what returning to your death spot causes?

"You aren't helping ghosts by forcing them to merge," says Reena, her volume growing to match Thatcher's as she addresses the crowd now, too. "If any of you are afraid of this, of Solus, you can come with us." She motions toward Leo, Delia, Norris. I notice that a few other ghosts have gathered behind her—the crowd is growing. "We'll show you what you're forgetting—your *lives* on

Earth. We can share energy; we can remain on Earth with our families and friends. With Callie, we can—"

"*Whoooooooosh!*" Sarah lets out a noise like the wind rushing through trees as she puts Reena on the ground. The force of her motion swishes by me, and Thatcher catches my arm, keeping me from falling.

Reena jumps to her feet, standing strong and ready. She smiles at me, but it's not the friendly grin I'm used to. She looks pained.

"Get Callie out of here," Sarah says to Thatcher. "I'll handle the poltergeists."

Poltergeists?

Thatcher holds tight to my arm as I try to pull away. "I'm not going with you," I say. I need to understand what's happening. Why do I feel like secrets are being kept from me?

The breath is knocked out of me as Thatcher grabs me around my waist and tugs me through a portal. As we hurtle through the darkness, I'm struggling against him, shouting, but my voice is drowned out by our speed-of-light movement.

We emerge onto what looks like a decked patio, with wooden furniture and leafy plants. A hammock is strung diagonally between the narrow walls. It's a peaceful place, but I'm not in the mood for tranquillity. "How dare you!" I spit, wrenching myself away from him.

"How dare *I*?" he shouts, nearly speechless with anger.

I cross my arms over my chest and stare out at the broad-leafed plants.

"You shouldn't have been there," says Thatcher, standing toe-to-toe with me. "It was too soon for you to see a merging ceremony.

You *ruined* Ella's transition with your impulsive actions. You're not even well into your haunting—you still have to create a real peace with Nick and Carson—you haven't started with your father yet. I've trusted you, I've revealed more to you than anyone, and—"

"You've trusted me?" I say, cutting off his rant and batting away the arrow of guilt I feel about Ella. "More like you've *lied* to me."

"I haven't—" Thatcher starts, but I cut him off again. If he's going to accuse me of a betrayal, then I'm going to confront him, too.

"The portals lead you where you need to go, Thatcher? Is that how it works?" My voice is shaking now. "Those doors are the only way I have of accessing my life, the people I love, and you withheld that from me. You made me think I couldn't control my own movements."

"I was protecting you!" he says, exasperated.

"From *what*?" I ask.

He clamps his mouth into a tight line and closes his eyes, like he's putting a lid over what he might say. Finally meeting my gaze, he reaches out and folds his strong hands around my upper arms. A flash of heat pulses through me, not the comforting heat of before. It's reverberating with his frustration.

"If you haunt on your own, there are so many things that could go wrong," he says, and his voice falters a little bit. "You don't know what a failed haunting feels like, and if I'm not there, you might . . ." He stops talking, and I wonder if he can see the truth on my face.

"You've already haunted them without me," he says. He doesn't sound mad or surprised, really, just . . . sad, defeated.

I nod and look down, still angry, but now I'm dealing with a trickle of guilt, too. "You really can read people," I say. I'm so confused. I don't know who to trust, what to believe.

"You've seen Carson?" he asks.

I nod again.

"And . . . Nick?"

I look up at him then, and I think I see pain in his eyes.

"Yes," I say.

"Your father?"

"No . . . I . . . I can't face him yet. Seeing Nick's struggles is hard enough. It must be so much worse for my dad."

"Reena will try to take you to your death spot," he says. "She wants you to become like them."

"I'm already like them," I say. "And I'm like you, too, and like the other Guides. I remember my life, I already feel the same pain you feel."

"You're not like the poltergeists," he says. "They'll probably never get to merge with Solus—their moons are dark. That's what the death spot's energy does—it makes you emotionally unable to move on."

"I know," I say. "Reena told me."

"She did?" He looks surprised. "But how could you want that?"

"How could I *not* want to stay on Earth with the people I love?"

"It isn't what you think, Callie. The people you love grow older; their lives move forward. They will *die* and you will be stuck, observing and never living, never sharing. It's like watching a movie in a theater except you're the only one. You experience no connection. It's just a yawning emptiness."

I hadn't thought about it that way. He makes it sound awful, unappealing. Needing a minute to take this all in, I study my surroundings more closely. It's small, and very private—high walls are on all sides of us. Gray stone is beneath us, a small table and two wooden chairs rest near the hammock, green plants line the area.

"Where are we?" I ask.

"My prism. It was the one place that I knew Reena and the others couldn't follow us."

"Because you've never invited them in?"

He nods, appears slightly discomfited. "You're the first."

"It wasn't exactly an invitation."

"I couldn't risk you saying no."

Any other time I might have felt privileged that he was sharing his space with me. I want to know everything about him. But I know he won't share more, not now. He won't tell me if he has to water his plants somehow or whether this place is like a patio he once knew on Earth. As I scan the area, I see nothing like a photo or even a trinket left over from life. Has he let go of everything? How can I?

"Nick's not doing well," I say, with regret, losing some of my anger at the high-handed way that he brought me here.

"He'll heal," says Thatcher. "The Living have an amazing ability to go on, and I believe that Nick has already started that process."

There's a sharp pinch in my chest. I know it's selfish, but I still hate the thought of Nick moving on, maybe falling in love again. I realize a part of me fears that he already has.

"You have to let him go, you know," says Thatcher. "No matter what Reena told you . . . you do have to let him go."

A tear slides down my cheek.

"Callie," says Thatcher, quietly yet urgently. "I'm sorry I lied to you about the portals. But everything else I've told you is entirely true."

"Thatcher," I say, wanting to use this moment, where he's open and talking about truth. "What's a poltergeist?"

He walks over to one of the wooden chairs, sits down, and leans forward, his elbows on his thighs, his hands balled tightly in front of him. As much as I'd like to relax in the hammock, I sit in the chair beside him.

"I heard Sarah say it," I explain.

He nods. "Reena and Leo, Norris and Delia, the ghosts who are with them, the ones gathered behind them tonight . . . they're the ones who refuse to merge even though their haunting is completed, the ones who can't get over dying, the ones who remember and cling to their past lives. They're *poltergeists*."

He says the word like it leaves a rotten taste in his mouth.

"And Callie, I know you think they're your friends. I know you think they're fun and that their way of haunting—moving things and all that—is worthwhile. But it's not—it's all surface level."

I nod—I've heard this from him, but I still like the way it makes me feel when I haunt that way, when the living know that I'm there. I start to say that, but when I open my mouth, Thatcher keeps going.

225

"The way I've tried to teach you to haunt—through an inner peace that comes from your unconscious—that's how we make a real connection, a soul connection. That's what gets you closer to merging. And Callie, Solus is the true way."

Leaning back into the chair, I feel like a little girl for a moment, and I hate the vulnerability that overtakes me. Watching Ella almost get taken into that white light felt so terrifying, so wrong.

"Merging isn't another death?" I ask, trying to read the drawn line of Thatcher's mouth and the twitch at the edge of his cheek. I stare at him unflinchingly.

Slowly, he reaches out and sets the hammock to swaying, and I wonder if he draws comfort from the motion. Maybe he'd like to be lying in it as well, letting it carry away his worries. "No, it's not a death. Ghosts are already dead."

"But Reena said—" I start.

"Stop listening to her!" Thatcher lunges to his feet and stalks away. "Don't you understand what she is?"

I come up out of the chair to face him. "I don't understand. You say she's dangerous, not a friend. But I know that she was your friend once, Thatcher—I've felt it. And besides, she *saved* me earlier today."

"Saved you?"

"Yes." I hesitate now, not sure I should bring up the séance. But now it's too late, and so I tell him. About Carson and the chanting, the pain I experienced and the rush of sensation and sound. And the tidal pool pull that brought me back to the Prism, where Reena was waiting.

Thatcher's eyes get wider and wider as I recount each part of the story, but I can't tell if he's surprised or afraid or just angry.

"I felt so much pain," I explain. I'm trying to put Reena in a good light. "She brought me back to my prism and took care of me."

He combs his fingers through his hair in frustration. "She didn't save you," he says. "She's only looking out for herself."

"What do you mean?"

"Callie, Reena is fixated on you. It has to do with your energy. I'm not sure what she's planning, but the way she spoke at the merging ceremony made it clear that she's leading the poltergeists to work against the Guides."

"She wants to stay on Earth," I say. "Don't we all want that? How can you ask people who've *died* not to want their lives back?"

"No one asks that of ghosts. The Guides only want to follow the natural order of things—merging is part of that. We can't have the Prism fill up with ghosts who refuse to move on because they're nervous about what's next."

"Reena doesn't seem nervous," I say. "She seems determined and strong, but *nervous* is not a word I would use."

"You're right—it's deeper than that," says Thatcher. "Reena is afraid. The poltergeists aren't happy and carefree—they are *scared*. You've been around them; you must have seen that, too. Their fear of the unknown, of merging, means that they are stuck in limbo—between the Prism and Earth. And now it seems like she's making a name for herself—and the poltergeists—by spreading that fear."

"Well, I'm afraid, too," I say quietly.

"You don't have to be," he says. I feel a current of heat when his fingers lightly brush mine, as though he wants to touch me but can't ignore the rule that it's discouraged.

"Thatcher, what happens when a ghost merges?" I ask.

He stares into space for a minute before he answers, and I worry that he's going to make something up or avoid my question. But then he says, "No one knows, but Solus has always been the next stage. You die, you haunt your loved ones to ease their pain, and then you merge."

"How can you accept that without knowing what it's like?" I ask. "How can you just *believe*?"

"It's a leap of faith," says Thatcher.

And I remember something that Mama told me when we'd go to church and I'd ask her why I couldn't see God, or the angels: "There is grace in believing, Callie May."

Eighteen

HIS SHOES ARE SPIT SHINE PERFECT. They don't need another polish. But his hands are moving methodically over the leather, like he's not even aware of their mechanics, like his thoughts are far away.

Thatcher brought me home, finally. "You have to promise to follow my instructions," he told me. "We will sit with him quietly— you will not touch anything or try to move something or show your presence physically. If he leaves the house, we will not follow him."

I nodded yes, yes, yes, so wanting to see my father, to make sure he's okay. I realize that my fear of seeing him is fading and being replaced by an intense longing. Thatcher felt it, too. But before we went through the portal, he looked at me again, worry clouding his face.

"Why don't you want to take me to him?" I asked.

"It's complicated," he said, casting his eyes downward. I put my hand on his arm, ready to follow him into the portal, and I realized that he and I were beginning to touch freely—he didn't object to it or have his guard up—and I melted a little bit at the thought of our getting closer.

Then he gazed into my eyes with such intensity. I've heard that eyes are windows to the soul. If that's true, in that moment, he touched mine. "You need to feel what healing really is—what the deeper kind of haunting can do," he said. "I have to know that you trust me, fully, at least for this moment."

"I do," I said, with utter conviction.

And now I'm watching my dad polishing his shoes in the entryway. The silhouette of his strong shoulders nearly crushes me. I feel the pain of a thousand hugs not given, of my acceptance of his stoicism after Mama died. How I wish I'd been able to bring him back from his grief.

I study his reflection in the front hallway mirror, acutely aware that I can't see myself, though I'm right beside him.

It's another reminder that *I'm not here.*

I long to nestle against his side, slip beneath his arm, but I've made a promise to Thatcher, and I know he's watching me closely, not to interfere but to be there if I need him.

"I'm okay," I say.

"I know," says Thatcher. "I can sense it. And he can, too."

With a loud sigh, Dad puts down his shoes. He walks toward the den. We follow.

His sock-feet steps echo in the lonely house with a familiar rhythm. He strides with precision, with purpose, even in our living room. I used to lie in bed and hear him pacing, and the sound of his padded footfall tugs on my heart.

"Now, let's just be with him," says Thatcher.

Dad sits down on the couch, and I join him there, hovering as we do, not really sitting here like I used to when we'd watch documentaries together with a bowl of popcorn between us. When was the last time we watched one? I was busy this spring, always out, never wanting to stop and be still when Dad would pat the cushion next to him. *Why didn't I take the time?* How did I not understand that *this*, sharing snacks and a moment with my father—not a daredevil stunt—was the best of life?

I take in a deep breath as sorrow hits me, and Thatcher moves closer, just inches from my side. The comfort that resonates through him to me is what I want to give Dad.

"Close your eyes," Thatcher says, and I do. "Don't focus on specific memories—that's been getting in your way. Just remember your love for your father, let yourself feel it."

I try. It's hard not to think of specifics if you're told not to. Memories rush at me like a tidal wave, but I think about what Thatcher said, and I try to *feel* them instead of just seeing them in my mind. So as I remember the voices Dad used to use for my stuffed animals when I was a little girl, I take the glee I felt as he dipped into baritone for Mr. Polar Bear and up to soprano for Lady Llama. And when I think of my mother's funeral, I take the security that surged through me when he held on to my hand—so tightly—at her graveside. I flash back to our last drive together, through the neighborhood on a sunny summer day, and I take pride in the look he shot me as I navigated a new clutch with ease. I draw the emotions from these memories, and I let the details fade, leaving me with the unvarnished feelings.

Dad shifts beside me, and when I open my eyes, I think he might put on a baseball game, but he doesn't. He reaches into the magazine rack beside him and pulls out an old book—an album.

When he opens it, I see that the first page holds a photo of me as a baby, in my dad's arms. I had no idea this picture existed.

"What is that book?" I ask Thatcher, but he just smiles and motions for me to keep watching.

My father flips through the pages, and there are dozens more photos that I never saw. Of me and Mama, of her and Dad. He lingers on each page, and I feel a surge of affection for him as he gently touches a photo of my mother in a white cotton dress and daisy-chain headpiece.

When I see a photo of the three of us in front of the Washington Monument, I flash back to a moment on that car trip. I was in the back in a car seat while Mama and Daddy sat up front and sang along to the oldies station. Mama's voice was terrible, but she laughed the whole way through, and it was a gorgeous sound as she tried to sing "Under the Boardwalk." Dad's voice boomed over hers for the chorus lines, and she looked at him with unabashed love in her eyes. As I watched them, I tuned in to my own happiness—the comfort and joy and wonder that filled me up when I was a little girl, back before I knew that everything would end.

The emotions are so tangible that it's almost as if I'm *living* this scene from the past. And I wish I were. I wish I could go back.

But I can't. Still, I have the emotions of that day at my fingertips, in my body, and I let them pour through me and seep out into the room, hoping my father will feel something, too.

"You were a cute kid," says Thatcher.

I smile. "I didn't know Dad kept something like this," I say. "It's so . . . sentimental."

"We all have that part of us."

I look at Thatcher then, wondering what memories make him feel this way—full of nostalgia and love.

The pages of the book rustle as Dad flips forward, and I lean closer to him. The album is arranged chronologically, and it contains photos of me even after Mama's death. A toothless me on the playground swings with Carson at our elementary school, me taking a bow after my tiny chorus role in the seventh grade musical.

When Dad turns another page, I gasp. It's a shot from last year's winter formal. Nick and I are standing in front of the Fishers' fireplace, posing in that cheesy way that every couple does—his hands on my hips. But instead of being serious, we're both making giant googly eyes and sticking out our tongues. Nick made me laugh so hard in that moment—and I had Mrs. Fisher email the photo to my dad, but he never said anything about it. He didn't acknowledge it, let alone tell me that he'd printed it out.

Dad thought I was way too young to be so serious about Nick. "Your first love isn't your last love," he told me once. I wondered at the time if he was working to convince himself as much as he was me. My mother was his first love. Was he hoping for a chance at a last love?

Dad's face softens as he stares at the image of me and Nick, so happy, so full of excitement at being together.

"You can reach him now," says Thatcher, whispering next to me. "His mind is receptive."

"Should I—" I start to reach out my hand, but Thatcher takes it and holds my fingers. I have to fight to ignore the electricity and warmth that I feel from his touch.

"Use your thoughts," he says. "Think about what you want him to know, and what you want him to feel."

I close my eyes, and I realize that I hope he doesn't blame himself, for giving me the car, for being distant. I always knew how much he loved me.

How can I convey to my father that my drive to be reckless was my own choice?

I concentrate, replaying some of my more dangerous stunts in my head—the time I set up a makeshift ramp in the backyard and launched my bike (and myself) into the river, the time I made Carson drive down the beach so I could practice bailing out of a moving car (I'd seen it in the movies, and it looked so easy), and the morning of the day of my death, speeding on the docks.

After I flash through those moments, I switch to quieter ones with my father, with Carson, with Nick—the chaste versions. The times when they each provided a safe and warm harbor, when I didn't have to put myself in danger to feel alive. As I linger in those moments, I cherish them in a way I never have before—I didn't know how to value them when I was alive. But I do now.

I open my eyes. Dad is staring as if he can see me, right at my face.

"Oh, Callie." He sighs, but it isn't a sad one. It's wistful, loving. Serene.

"He's finding peace," whispers Thatcher. "Can you feel it?"

I nod as I watch my father's eyelids get heavier and heavier. They close after a few moments. I stay still, letting the ease in the room flow through me, feeling a tranquillity deeper than I knew was possible.

"Can we stay?" I ask.

"As long as you want," says Thatcher.

We sit there for an hour while he sleeps, and Thatcher doesn't push me to go anywhere, to do anything. He just stays in this space with me, with my father.

And it means the world.

Nineteen

I WANT TO GO TO NICK NEXT, do the same thing for him, but I can tell Thatcher's energy is waning.

He creates a portal that delivers us right outside my door. I'm swamped with emotions: relief, joy, a tinge of sadness, a conviction that my dad will be all right. I'm almost bursting with a need to talk about it *and* to hold it in, savor it for a while longer. I have so much that I want to say to Thatcher, but all I seem capable of uttering is a heartfelt "Thank you."

His blue eyes warm. "You're the one who did it."

"But I couldn't have done it without you." Only now do I realize that there was a sort of underlying chaos when I was with Reena, when she was pushing me to do things her way. It's difficult to explain, but I don't think her methods would have brought my father the peace that Thatcher's did.

"You should rest," he says, as though he's uncomfortable with my gratitude.

"I—" I lower my gaze, watching the swirling mist, trying to form the right words. When I look up, his brow is furrowed, his eyes etched with concern. "You said I ruined things for Ella. Is she going to be okay?"

He nods. "There'll be another ceremony. We just needed a little time for harmony to be achieved once again."

I release a quick burst of embarrassed laughter, because I caused so many problems. "Oh, good. I was afraid she'd be sent to Purgatory or something."

"No. Solus is waiting to welcome her."

"Do you think that I could see her, apologize for what happened?"

The smile he gives me is devastating in its beauty. "I can arrange that. But you can't touch her. Your energy could unravel things."

I nod with understanding eyes, realizing that I trust him completely for the first time. "I won't. I'll follow your rules to the letter, do whatever you tell me."

He grins. "I doubt you'll go that far."

I take his jab like a good sport. It's deserved. Besides, I like it when he's relaxed enough to give me a hard time. "I will, I promise. I really don't want to mess things up for her."

"Yeah, okay. Come on."

As we walk along, I desperately want to take his hand. I think about what Reena said, that he was deliberately sabotaging my progress, to keep me here so he wouldn't be lonely. I can't see him being that selfish. Unfortunately, I *can* imagine him feeling that isolated.

"Now that I seem to have caught on to how some of this works, how long do you think I have in this realm?" I ask.

"It's impossible to say."

I wanted so badly to be out of here, to be back on Earth permanently, but now I don't know if I want to go. If I want to leave Thatcher. "I hope the next ghost you guide doesn't turn out to be such a pain."

He shifts his gaze over to me. "Callie, you're acting like this is going to be our good-bye, but we're a long way from that."

"But we will have to say good-bye eventually."

"Eventually, yes."

"How do you do that? Welcome someone here, connect with them, teach them what they need to know just so they can leave you?"

"I know something better is waiting for them. How can I deny them that? Besides, I don't connect with those I guide. There's nothing personal between us."

"Not even with me?"

"You're like no one I've ever known before."

It isn't really an answer, yet in a way it is.

Before I can respond, he swings his gaze forward. "We're here."

We're standing in front of a white door that has little sparkles, coming and going, floating around almost as though they're alive. I raise my hand to knock, but before I make contact, the door opens. Ella Hartley stands before me in the silver gown she was wearing earlier. Her eyes that I thought looked flat and dull the first time I saw her are now glowing with an inner brightness.

She smiles softly. "Callie McPhee. I was hoping you'd come see me."

"Ella, I am so sorry."

"You don't have to apologize. I know the poltergeists have a certain charisma that makes it easier to believe everything they say." She turns her head slightly. "Hello, Thatcher."

"You look lovely, Ella," he says.

Her smile brightens. "I'm happy, happier than I've ever been. Please come in." She steps back.

I shake my head. "No, I don't want to take your energy. I just—"

"Please," she interrupts, sweeping her arm to the side in a welcoming gesture. "My energy is safe."

I glance over at Thatcher, waiting to take a cue from him. I really don't want to do anything that will mess things up for Ella. He gives me an encouraging nod.

We pass through the doorway, and it's like stepping into a shower of calm that washes over me, almost taking my breath. While outside is swirling fog, in here it's like being enveloped in gossamer clouds.

"The first time I saw you at the harbor," Ella begins, "I thought we had met before, but I couldn't remember. All my focus was on my family, and my memories were scattered."

"That's okay," I assure her. "I was a little . . . scattered myself."

"Had you just arrived?"

"Yeah. Still had a lot to learn." I scrunch up my face. "Still do."

"Don't worry. You'll learn quickly, and I've heard good things about Thatcher." She winks at him. "No one under his tutelage has ever *not* merged."

Again, I can't help but wonder how many good-byes he's experienced.

"I know he's the best." And I realize that I mean the words, truly mean them. I'm not just spouting compliments to keep things from getting awkward.

"Forget everything the poltergeists told you," Ella says. "Concentrate on bringing peace to those who love you. The reward is your own peace at seeing them comforted."

"Are you scared?" I suddenly blurt out, then I slap my hand over my mouth. "I'm sorry. I shouldn't have asked."

"I'm not afraid. There's nothing to be afraid of."

"But you don't *know* what's on the other side."

She places her hand over her heart and smiles so serenely that my throat tightens. "Oh, but I do."

A leap of faith, Thatcher told me. I don't know if I'll ever be fully comfortable taking one.

"Will you come to the ceremony?" Ella asks.

"You can't possibly want me there after what I did. After I ruined everything."

"You didn't ruin anything. It just got delayed. I would so love to share this experience with you."

I look at Thatcher again, and he nods.

I smile warmly at Ella. "I would be honored to be there."

This time, I'm standing at the front beside Thatcher. We're in the rain forest again, surrounded by lush vegetation. I can hear the raindrops falling gently to the ground. Some of the Guides are playing the mbiras, calling the other ghosts here.

Ella is strolling up the path that's lined with white stones.

Something in my chest clutches at the sight of her. In spite of everything she and Thatcher told me, I want to grab her and run from here. As she nears me, her eyes meet mine, and I know that I've never seen such tranquillity.

She steps onto the platform. She's only a few feet away from me. She smiles, once again glowing with the radiant energy that seems to be such a part of her now.

She lifts her face up to the sky.

I tense—

"She'll be all right," Thatcher whispers.

Transfixed, I nod.

Suddenly a brilliant light beams down on Ella. A thousand gleaming sparkles begin dancing over her. Her smile grows wider, she spreads her arms, drops her head back.

She appears to be in ecstasy. The light bursts through her, pours over us, and a flash of calm like a prelude to Heaven surges through me. So quickly, I can't hold on to it.

But it leaves me momentarily astonished.

Ella begins to ascend. She fades. The light fades.

Then they're both gone.

The music goes silent. Not a word is spoken as ghosts and Guides begin to wander away, but there is a sense of extreme peace hovering around all of us.

"Are you all right?" Thatcher asks.

I look at him through a haze of tears. Embarrassed by my emotional response, I quickly swipe at them. "Why am I able to cry? I'm not in my real body anymore, so this makes no sense."

He appears as uncomfortable by the question as I am by the tears dampening my cheeks.

"It shouldn't be possible, but I've seen it once before—a truly powerful emotion can bring an actual physical reaction to this shell of the body."

I admit I was deeply touched by what I witnessed. And that explains why I thought I felt my heart beating on the train track. That was an extremely intense experience.

"What did you think?" he asks, and I can tell that my answer is important to him.

"It was beautiful. Ella was so radiant, filled with such joy. She looked like an angel." I shake my head. "But I'm not ready."

"I know that, but at least now maybe you can understand why ghosts strive to achieve it."

I nod. "Yeah, I . . . for a split second I felt like I was touched by Heaven."

"You were."

I look over my shoulder to where Ella was and then up to where she is now. I know it's going to be a while before I make that journey. My biggest obstacle, other than my own qualms, is Nick. I have to help him find peace, and I know that's not going to be easy.

"I want to go see Nick."

Thatcher studies me intently for a minute. "You should probably rest. You've gone through a string of emotional experiences. You're vulnerable."

"No, I'm ready. Please, Thatcher."

He releases a sigh that's part irritation with my stubbornness and part acceptance that one way or another I'm going to go see Nick. He's bound to understand that it's better if he's with me. He outlines the portal. I step through—

And am greeted by a burst of fireworks. We're standing on the water's edge, our backs to the surf. A huge amusement park is in front of us. I can hear the sounds of the midway, the rush of wheels over tracks, the screams of thrill riders. Fireworks once again dazzle through the night sky.

"Nick is here?" I ask.

"No," Thatcher says quietly. "This is a . . . a gift."

I snap my head around to study him. He's staring straight ahead, as though he's not quite comfortable meeting my gaze.

"You've been dealing with so much turmoil that I thought you might need a little escape from everything."

I think I'm going to cry again. I'm an emotional wreck. I blink back the tears. "This isn't exactly sanctioned, is it?"

He peers over at me then. "Are you going to tell?"

"Other than the fact that I don't know who to tell—" I shake my head. "No, I'm just going to enjoy the fireworks."

Another explosion of sound draws my attention to the black sky where it's lit up with red, green, and white.

"I didn't realize you were such a rebel," I say, my voice tinged with teasing and laughter. I've always loved fireworks, and sharing these with Thatcher is almost magical. My memories are so strong that I can smell the metallic blasts of powder that ignite the colorful bursts in the sky.

"What else do you do that you're not supposed to do? What

other rules do you break?" Using a portal for personal enjoyment has to be a huge no-no.

"This is a first for me."

I can't help but grin. "I'm rubbing off on you. Before you know it, you'll be as wild as you were when you were alive."

"I wouldn't go that far." He shrugs. "I wanted to give you something special, that's all."

"This is very special, Thatcher."

I feel an incredibly strong pull toward him. My gaze drops to his full lips, how soft they look. I imagine mine moving over them. I wonder about his taste, if I would even be able to taste him. Without all our senses engaged, would a kiss be anything special? And yet, I can't help but think that a kiss would make this moment perfect.

But more than Nick is holding me back.

"What haven't you told me about Reena?" I ask him.

I look right into his eyes, knowing that this question is one he doesn't want to answer.

"Thatcher, please," I say. "I want to understand you, to know you. That won't happen if you don't let me in."

"Callie—"

"I know you don't form attachments. I even get why. And I understand that I'm nothing special—"

"You're more than special. In so many ways."

"I want to know how you came to be here. I want to know everything about you."

He turns his face away from mine, staring at an explosion of color.

"Walk with me," he says.

We wander along the water's edge, but I can't feel the dampness.

I wonder if Reena hurt someone he loved once. I stay quiet, giving him space to start talking.

"I was a senior in high school ten years ago," he finally says quietly. "I went to West Ashley."

"We play them in sports," I tell him, doing quick math in my head and figuring out that Thatcher would be twenty-eight now if he were still alive. Not *too* old.

"I know. I was on the football team."

"A Wildcat," I say.

"Right." His mouth turns up a little.

Then his eyes gloss over, and I listen to the lapping of the waves on the shore, hoping it'll lure him into revealing more.

"Reena and I had been dating for almost a year," continues Thatcher.

I hold my breath and will myself not to react. I know he'll stop telling the story if I break his concentration, so I stay quiet even though my mind is screaming a thousand questions.

"It was homecoming night, after the dance, and we went out to the upper Wando River for a bonfire. There were a bunch of us there, and Reena and I decided to take out a rowboat with two other friends—Leo and Hayley."

He peers over at me to see if I get his meaning—that he, Leo, and Reena were all friends back then—and I nod my understanding, encouraging him to go on.

"We'd had a lot to drink. Just beers, but a lot. In the rowboat,

Leo and I were standing up and being stupid. It had just rained for three days straight and the river was higher than usual, rougher. We shouldn't have been out on the water."

Thatcher runs his hands through his hair and then clasps them in front of his face.

"The boat tipped over in the dead center of the river," he says softly, his voice muffled. "Any other night, we could have swum to shore, no problem. But that night, we couldn't. We didn't."

My chest tightens. "You all drowned?"

He nods.

"Oh my God. Thatcher, I'm so sorry."

"Hayley, somehow, hung on to the boat, yelling for help. But by the time anyone got out to us, she was the only one still at the surface. I don't even remember sinking down under the water."

"The three of you died together?"

"Yes."

Staring out at the ocean, I imagine the river—the way it gets so dark at night, almost black. What is it like to have that water pull you down, take away the air, fill your lungs?

"Thatcher, I had no idea—that's terrible."

"It was a long time ago," he says, brushing off my sympathetic tone. "The hardest part happened later. In the Prism."

"Were you and Reena still together?" I ask awkwardly, wondering if that's even a possibility for ghosts . . . being together.

"Yes. When we first got to the Prism, it didn't feel sad, exactly. It felt more like a new adventure. The three of us came together, so we had more of a sense of memory than the ghosts who come alone, but the memories weren't sad; they were just . . . *there*."

"What happened?" I ask.

"At first Reena was calm. Peaceful even. Her prism was this tranquil park—one that came from her imagination, I guess. We used to take walks and talk about our haunting. Hers was going well; mine wasn't. I messed things up with Wendy—I couldn't reach her. I was so afraid Reena was going to merge without me. She and Leo. Then I'd be left alone."

My heart aches for him.

"Anyway, Reena was hanging out with Leo, and they were figuring out ways to channel their energy so they could interact physically with the Living. They convinced me that I needed a different approach to connecting with Wendy." He looked at me, his eyes solemn. "I did what you wanted to do. When I was with Wendy, I moved things. I said things to her. . . . I . . ." His voice falters and I think he might stop talking altogether, but then he steels his jaw and keeps going. "It made things so much worse. She thought she was going insane; she totally closed up. It was like she put up a wall. I couldn't reach her. I can't reach her."

"I'm so sorry." I don't know what else to say.

He shakes his head. "I knew I'd screwed up, big-time. I went back to the way it's supposed to be done, concentrated on the right way. Once Reena and Leo saw Wendy freak out—they thought it was fun. They wanted to mess with people they didn't even know. But I got serious about haunting, I didn't want to have anything to do with the tricks they wanted to play. It created a distance between us that only worsened."

He grows quiet, and I know he's struggling with a bad memory. I'm afraid he'll stop now. I want to understand him as I never wanted to fully comprehend anyone—not even Nick. I want to be able to help Thatcher, but to do that I need to know everything. "How did it get worse?"

"It was Leo." His jaw tightens. "He had so many questions, even for his Guide. We couldn't remember why we'd all come to the Prism together, and it mattered to him. He found a way to get back."

"Back?"

"To the river," says Thatcher. "To where we died."

"And what happened?"

"He changed almost instantly—he was bitter, rageful."

"And he took Reena there, too," I guess.

"I watched as he got angrier and angrier—he remembered so much, and it hurt him. Reena tried to help him, I saw it, and then, in a moment, I saw her change, too. He'd taken her back. And from then on, they didn't want to be a part of the Prism—they called it 'the Prison'—they wouldn't hear anything about Solus. They wanted to return to Earth—they couldn't accept that we had died so young."

"That's understandable." I can't help it—I feel sympathy for Reena and Leo.

"It is, in a way," says Thatcher. "But we're meant to move on, to merge with Solus. If my sister, Wendy, could have accepted my death, I'd probably have merged myself—I want to be a part of Solus."

"Why just probably?" I ask.

He stops walking and looks down at the frothy waves.

"Reena wouldn't go . . . and I couldn't leave her," he says softly.

"I understand," I say. Because I do. No matter how contentious he and Reena have become, Thatcher loved her once. And I know how hard it is to let go, even when a situation is impossible.

And then, because I have to know: "Do you still love her?"

"No," he says. Then he pauses. "At least . . . not in the way I did. She's not the girl I knew on Earth."

"But you feel—"

"Responsible," Thatcher says, finishing my thought. "I feel responsible for her. And Leo, too, I guess."

I can't imagine the weight of the burden he's carrying. At least my reckless driving didn't kill anyone else. I understand him so much better now. Why he's so serious, the bad decisions he's trying to atone for, the friendships he's lost.

We stand quietly, letting the story hang in the air around us. My grandfather used to say you had to do that with the best kinds of stories, the ones that teach you something or make you think or reveal some secret about life . . . or death, I guess. You sit with them, to process.

I'm ashamed to admit, even to myself, that I'm jealous of Reena, but the bitter emotion is there nonetheless. For a while, she belonged to Thatcher. I hope she appreciated him more in life than she does in death.

When I look at Thatcher, his profile is so radiant—so *ethereal*—that I want to close my eyes for a moment and burn it into my brain.

I realize now that he understands far more that I gave him credit for. He's been through it, having to let someone he loved go.

He knows the pain and the heartache, but in some ways, for him it was worse. "Thank you for sharing."

"It's only fair," he says. "I know your story. I know what you're going through, Callie. You just need to be patient."

"Patience has never been my thing. I've always been about the rush. But I'm learning, Thatcher."

We stand there on the edge of the water, just looking at each other. I want to comb my fingers through his hair. I want to bring him comfort. I want to be his solace.

He is so very alone, and when I move on—

"So did you want to go on the roller coaster?" he asks, as though he's growing uncomfortable with my scrutiny, as though he knows the paths my mind is traveling. As though he knows they can lead to no happiness.

"It wouldn't be the same," I tell him, allowing the moment we were sharing to slip away. I don't want to make things harder for him. "I wouldn't feel the wind rushing by, tugging on my hair. Wouldn't feel the car shaking beneath me since we wouldn't actually be touching it." Just like now, if I remove my shoes, I won't feel the sand between my toes.

"Right," he teases. "I knew you were a carousel kind of girl."

"No way!" I swipe at his shoulder, and his body doesn't do the repel thing. Because we're on the same plane, I can feel him as though he's solid. But the world of the Living is something we can only pass through, not truly experience. "Never been on a carousel in my life."

"You're kidding!" He appears horrified.

"Nope. Never saw the appeal. Even as a little kid. Too boring a ride."

"It's not boring. It's . . . peaceful."

"I prefer the heart-pounding thrills." I turn my attention back to the sky. *Pop! Pop! Bang!* The fireworks light up the world.

Then they go silent, and the smoke catches on a breeze and blows out toward the ocean.

"Come on," Thatcher says, taking my hand, our fingers entwining.

"Just a little more time."

"We're not leaving yet. Come on." Together we walk onto the midway. We pass by cotton candy, pretzel, and funnel cake booths. I suddenly miss being hungry. Would love to experience those tastes again on my tongue.

I hear the calliope belting out the tinny music that plays at the carousel. Suddenly we're standing before it as the horses circle round and round.

"We're going for a ride," Thatcher says, and he urges me onto the platform.

Placing his hands on my waist, capturing my gaze, he slowly lifts me onto a horse. His hold is more than a touch; it reaches beneath the surface to a deeper level. I feel a measure of regret when he releases me. Although I'm not in direct contact with the wooden horse, my body moves with the carousel, remembering what it would have done in life. Thatcher stands by me, smiling.

"Aren't you going to get on a horse?" I ask.

"No, I just want to watch you."

I hold my arms up and release a scream like I would if I were on a roller coaster, plummeting down the tracks.

Thatcher laughs, a full, deep-throated laugh that silences me. Its richness echoes around us. I hold his gaze as we circle around. Behind him are the twinkling lights of the amusement park, the sounds of excitement, the mouthwatering smells. But they're all faint. He's the only thing that's real.

I wonder if we take our memories from the Prism into Solus. I don't want to forget him, the blond of his hair, the way it curls around his ears. I want to remember the blue of his eyes, the tiny scar on his chin. I want to treasure the way his gaze never wanders from mine, the slightly crooked smile. I don't want to lose these few precious moments of contentment that we've shared.

And he's right. The carousel is so much more than I ever expected it to be. I was so caught up in experiencing the thrills of life that I missed the small things that matter most. The carousel slows to a stop, but I don't want to leave. I just want this moment with him to go on forever.

The lights go out, plunging us into the grayness of an amusement park closing down for the night.

"We'd better go," he says, breaking the spell that's been holding us, but I can tell that he's as sorry as I am that it's over.

Twenty

THATCHER'S GIFT TO ME cost him. His energy is almost depleted as he leads me through a portal to my prism. But I don't feel tired—I feel full and vital.

And guilty.

What I shared with Thatcher was deeper than anything I ever shared with Nick. Nick and I had fun. We sought thrills, we laughed, we joked, we made out. I love him. I don't doubt that, but what I feel for Thatcher is a whole different level. Maybe it's the plane we're on, maybe it's because we're no longer alive so we don't have all our other senses to rely on, to give us the physical complements that I had with Nick, so we have to go deeper for a connection. I can't believe how much I care about Thatcher.

I still have feelings for Nick, but I have to let him go.

I'm incredibly aware now that bringing peace to those I love will mean leaving Thatcher. I'm filled with contradictory desires. I want to help the people who mean everything to me while finding a way not to leave Thatcher alone. Once my goal was to find a way to stay on Earth. I couldn't bear the thought of being without Nick, Carson, my father.

But I know they're suffering. I have to ease their pain. Especially Nick's.

Nick was the love of my life. Thatcher is the . . . I don't think I'm ready to admit that he's the love of my death, but he's very important to me. While I know he doesn't want me haunting by myself, the things I need to say to Nick, the way I need to connect with him in order to let him go—

I can't do that with Thatcher watching over my shoulder. I don't recall ever seeing Ella with a Guide, so once we learn how to haunt, like riding a bicycle, the training wheels must come off. And Thatcher taught me what I need to do—with my dad, he showed me how to bring the sense of peace not only to the person I love, but to myself.

I can do this. I need to do this. And I need to do it alone.

I pace the floor, concentrating on the images of Nick that now haunt me—the empty bottle, the bitterness on his face, the way he talked to Carson. I have to see him.

I won't do anything crazy, I reason. I'll just test things out a little bit, decide for myself how I can best haunt Nick. Thatcher has given me faith in the unconscious process by letting me see my father. And being with Reena and Leo and the others—well, they've shown me things, too. I know so much about how everything works now—I understand more. I can reach Nick this time, surely, one way or another.

When I step through my portal, I have to let my eyes adjust. It's getting dark outside, but I can hear leaves under my feet as I step along an uneven path—I seem to be in the woods. When my view sharpens, I recognize that I'm near Cotter's Pond, a little body of water in Nick's neighborhood.

I blink a few times before I see his rumpled form on the ground, leaning against a tree trunk. I move closer to him, relieved that his chest is rising and falling.

I crouch down next to him and his eyes snap open. He flips on a flashlight.

"Nick," I whisper.

He doesn't react to my voice but he slowly stands up, stretches his arms over his head and yawns. The corner of his gray T-shirt pulls up and exposes the left side of his stomach. Before I can stop myself, I'm standing, too, reaching over to touch his waist, to skim my fingers over his skin. And I remember so well how his body felt, how soft his skin was in all the right places, the little bit of hair on his stomach, how warm his chest was against mine, that I do make a connection—I touch him.

In that moment, emotions rush at me, flooding my heart with a surge of adrenaline and wistfulness and passion. I want to linger here, to put the world on pause, to stay frozen in our skin-on-skin contact. I didn't know how delicate this type of moment was until it was gone and I had to fight so hard for each one.

And I realize that I'll never know what Thatcher's skin feels like. I'll never have with him what I had with Nick. Part of me is clinging to the past and part of me wants to consider the future.

Nick flinches, looking spooked.

Come to think of it, *spooked* is the perfect word for his expression. My heart drops—I felt everything; I felt my love for him.

And he felt afraid.

"Nick," I whisper.

He doesn't realize that I'm here. I hear Thatcher's voice echoing in my head, telling me that touching is the wrong way to haunt, a poltergeist's mistake.

Nick brushes the dirt off his jeans and kicks a couple of beer cans at his feet.

I want to scream at him: *This is not you.*

We had an amazing kiss in these woods, when he took me for a walk one Saturday afternoon. I was the one who made it happen. He reached out for my hand to help me over a fallen branch, and I took it and pulled him close to me. His lips tasted like peppermint. I could feel his grin as we kissed in the late-afternoon sun. And when we finally parted, he said, "Thank God. I was waiting for that all day."

I smile just remembering it, but this scene looks nothing like that one. Nick is sad and stumbling, surrounded by empty cans and the stink of a life unraveling. Because of me.

His phone buzzes and I look over his shoulder as he checks the text.

It's from Austin Getts, a guy we've never really hung out with. He's kind of a stoner. "McCann's in 30 mins," it says.

Tim McCann throws legendary parties. The big-house-on-the-hill, teen-movie-worthy kind.

When Nick bends down to pick up his empty six-pack, I'm grateful that he's enough himself not to leave trash in the woods. But I'm still worried as he begins to head back to his car. And I'm determined not to leave his side tonight, not until I bring him peace. Until I let him go.

As Nick gets into his Camry, I pass through the door and slide into the passenger seat. "Nick, call someone to come get you. You've had too much to drink."

He looks in my direction, and for a split second, I think maybe he's heard me. But then he reaches through me toward the glove compartment. Energy ripples between us, like when you're in a pool and someone swims by you and stirs up the water, but Nick doesn't notice my presence. He grabs his iPod plug-in and sets it up, choosing Neutral Milk Hotel. Then we back up out of the driveway.

"Nick, please." To my surprise, he's driving straight, so maybe he hasn't had that much to drink. Still, he shouldn't be on the road. Maybe if I can reach him, he'll pull over.

"Since when do you meet Austin Getts at a party?" I ask.

No answer.

"You look good," I say. "Your hair's getting longer."

His eyes narrowing like he's concentrating, Nick stares straight ahead at the road.

"I thought you didn't like your hair long in the summer—last year you said it made your neck too hot." An image flashes through my mind: I'm pushing aside the fringe of Nick's hair, when it was getting long, to kiss the back of his neck. We were down by the docks last summer, and his skin was tan from the sun—it tasted like salt water because of the breeze. The way he looked at me that day, it made me feel powerful and wanted and loved—because this was my Nick, and I knew that he felt it, too. The way we belonged together. The way we just *fit*.

But we don't fit anymore. I think of Thatcher. I have memories of him now. Not as many, but they're still strong and vivid. I'm trapped between two worlds.

Tears start to sting the corners of my eyes. *I have to let this one go. I have to let Nick go.*

I stare at the dashboard for a minute while "In the Aeroplane over the Sea" plays. I think about the texts that I saw in Nick's room, and I wonder again what they meant. What secrets did Nick have from me?

That doesn't matter now, I tell myself. I have to pull it together and make this haunting work.

Some part of me wants to ignore the fact that I'm the dead girl in the front seat; I want to believe that I'm sitting here with my boyfriend on the way to a party. But he's not acting like my Nick at all. I study his face, trying to see what's changed. His eyes are more sunken and his skin is sallow. He's grieving, I remind myself, but it's more than that.

It's so quiet in the car, the silence thick and heavy. Nick reaches into the center console and pulls out a small bottle of Jameson, like those little ones on planes. At the stop sign near Tim's neighborhood, he unscrews the tiny cap and drinks it down in two gulps.

"What's happening to you?" I ask him, my voice quiet.

His eyes are glassy, and if I thought there was a chance he'd realize I'm here, it's wiped away now. He's not in tune with anything around him, let alone the ghost of his dead girlfriend in the passenger seat.

When we pull into the giant circular driveway, I see that there are already dozens of cars parked haphazardly on the sprawling lawn.

I follow Nick to the front door and enter my first postmortem social gathering.

The grand, sweeping staircase is already littered with teetering underclassmen who sit along its steps, stare out into the grand foyer, and watch the jocks funnel beer over the marble floor.

"I'm open!" shouts Nick as he walks into the fray and grabs the funnel-and-tube contraption from a wobbly Rich Langley.

And then sweet, not-a-big-drinker Nick holds the tube above his mouth and funnels the can of beer that the soccer boys pour into his throat without spilling a drop.

"Yeah, Fisher!" they shout, clapping him on the back.

Who is Nick becoming?

Shaking my head, I follow him into the kitchen. This is the kind of party where Carson and I definitely would have made an appearance, if only to gossip about people later. The short skirts and the long, blown-out hair all swirl together as I move through the house. I hear Leila Donninger fake-laughing at Mike Rutiglia's bad joke, and the shrill sound hurts my ears. Faces rush past me with caked-on sparkle, making pink cheeks shine with cheer even as black-rimmed eyes betray darker emotions.

Most people seem to avoid the spot where I'm standing, maybe by instinct or some unseen energy that I'm holding here, but others stumble right through me. When they do, I feel a slight tingle, soft and barely perceptible. I know the Living feel nothing—they don't pause or even change expression—and I'm aware again of my complete invisibility, my nothingness to them.

Danny Boyster pushes by Gina O'Neill, and I watch her face fall as he sidles up to Morgan Jackson, who's wearing a pink halter top with a low, sequined neckline that shows off her huge chest. The halter top is tucked into a tiny white skirt that would prompt Carson to say, "Pull that down before someone sees Christmas!" because it comes just under the curve of her behind. She grins and brushes against Danny while Gina turns away and flashes a bright smile in the other direction—but her watery eyes tell another story. I hear her whisper, "Morgan is such a slut," to Molly Raider, but the pain of rejection in her voice is obvious.

Everyone seems nervous, on edge, somehow more desperate than I remember. I wonder if that's because I'm watching them from the outside. *Did I use to be like this?* It all looks like such a waste of energy to me now.

I realize that getting caught up in Gina's drama made me lose track of Nick, and I do a quick walk-through of the living room again before I wander upstairs to try to find him. In the second-floor hallway there's a line for the bathroom because Tim is stingy about that—he lets partygoers use only one bathroom, even though the house has, like, six.

I pass through a door into an empty room with a four-poster bed and ivory crown molding. I imagine it's called "The Peach Room" because all the walls have a pink-orange glow.

Then I hear the toilet flush and a door open, and I realize that there's a connecting bathroom here and someone's been smart enough to find it.

I peek around the corner and watch as my best friend leans toward the mirror and reapplies her favorite lipstick—Chanel's Muse—with a deft hand.

"Carson."

Her glossy brown hair is pulled back into a purposefully messy updo and lined with fish-tail braids. She's wearing a strapless seer-sucker dress and white sling-back Tory Burch sandals—her tan shoulders and browned legs seem to glow against the pale colors of her outfit. She looks so pretty.

Smiling at her reflection, she blots her lips with toilet paper. Jessica Furlow is in here, too—she and Carson go to youth group together.

"Thanks for making me get out of my house," says Carson.

"It's good for you," Jessica says, and I feel a pang of regret that I'm the reason Carson isn't living her normal life. I have to admit that there's also a pinch of jealousy—Jessica can help her move on from losing me.

"*This* is good for you, too." Jessica smiles as she hands Carson a bottle of Miller High Life, and my best friend hesitates for just a second before she throws her head back and takes a swig. She coughs a little and says, "I don't even like it much."

I smile. *So* Carson.

"You'll get used to it," says Jessica, which kind of annoys me. But I'm not here to begrudge Carson a drink after she's lost her best friend—me.

I follow them out into the peach room, and then back to the main throng of the party. Jessica stops to talk to someone, but Carson walks gracefully down the stairs, around the girls who line the steps. She smiles at their compliments on her ensemble with signature sweetness. "Aw, y'all are so nice! *Thank yooou!*" I can tell by her tone that she's a teensy bit drunk. The swig she took upstairs was apparently not her first.

When Carson wanders into the kitchen, she takes in the scene without breaking her stride. There's a tray of Jell-O shots, and Austin Getts is mixing brownie batter with some of his friends. They're laughing hysterically, and I know that if I were alive, I'd be able to smell the pot that they mixed into the batter.

"Hey, Fisher!" Austin shouts. "We're about to bake, man."

He puts down the bowl and moves to the sliding glass door next to the kitchen, opening it a crack. Then he starts chuckling and comes back inside.

"Fisher's already wasted," he says.

Carson balls her hands into fists and marches outside. I'm right behind her.

"Nicholas Fisher!" she shouts, and it's her no-nonsense voice— the one that could snap me to attention almost as quickly as one of my father's military-style commands. Nick's condition has obviously served to sober her up.

"Hey, Cars," Nick slurs. "Come have a drink with us." He has his arm around Gina O'Neill, which makes me stop for a moment, frozen in the doorway. But he's drunk. *He's just being friendly.* Nick holds out a red plastic cup, his hand wobbling back and forth.

"You must be out of your mind," she says, walking closer to him.

"Aw, don't be pissy just because that little séance of yours didn't work," he says.

Carson rolls her eyes. Then she leans back, like a wave has hit her. "You reek! How much have you had?"

Nick looks up at the sky like the answer to her question is out there in the darkness. "Let's see," he says, letting go of Gina as he counts on his fingers. "I think I had three beers at home and then something in the car. . . . And I'm pretty sure this is my third round of jungle juice so . . . seven?"

He lets out a loud, sloppy laugh and starts to reel forward. As Gina steps away, Carson moves in and holds him up, draping his arm around her shoulder.

I cringe, hating to see Nick like this.

"Good Lord, you're *trashed*!" Carson is staring at Nick angrily, and her fish-tail braids are loose with undone pieces now. "What is the matter with you?"

Nick lets out a burp in Carson's face, and she fans her hand in front of her nose.

"Gross," she says. "Do you think Callie would want to see you like this?"

I see Gina flinch. *Good.* Part of me is happy that Carson

mentioned me, that I'm still *there* with them somehow, even if it's just in their memories. But another part of me is just plain worried. I mean, we all started drinking last year, but just for fun, just to get a little buzzed. Nick is drinking alone now, I know, and getting completely plastered at this party. Everyone else seems to think that's fine, and I feel a rush of affection for Carson, who knows this is not okay, that this isn't Nick.

"Wake up!" she shouts, slapping Nick on the arm as his eyes droop closed.

He opens his eyes wide and says, "I'd give anything if you'd just *shut up.*" Then his head tips forward and his body follows—I try to reach out, to summon enough energy to catch him, but he falls right through my arms, crashing to the deck as he blacks out.

Twenty-One

"JESUS!" Carson shout-whispers. "You are a *mess*."

She struggles to get him to his feet, and I move in, trying to help her support his weight. I can't hold him up, but I do manage to make contact with his arm enough so that she can hoist him onto her shoulder again.

Nick mumbles for her to leave him alone, but Carson has a single-minded fire in her now—I've seen it before, like after Mama died and I wouldn't come out of my house for days. She marched over to our place one Saturday afternoon with a bottle of soap bubbles and filled my room with the transparent, glossy globes. Then she said, "This is more fun outside," and I followed her into the yard and sat in the sun for the first time in a week. We were six. She doesn't take "leave me alone" to heart.

They leave Gina on the porch as Carson leads Nick through the house and past the kitchen, where Austin and his friends give him a thumbs-up. He opens his eyes long enough to acknowledge it, then slumps back over Carson, who holds his weight expertly despite his wobbly legs.

When she finally gets him past the girls on the stairs and up into the peach room, she dumps him on the bed and closes the door behind them.

I sit down by Nick's side while Carson goes into the bathroom and turns on the water.

Leaning down, I whisper in his ear. "It's going to be okay." I feel so helpless—I'm not a part of his life anymore in any tangible way, but I want him to feel that I'm here. . . .

Carson comes out of the bathroom, and I step back as she presses a wet cloth to Nick's forehead.

The anger is gone from her face; there's just sadness now.

"I get it, Nick," Carson says. "Summer's ending. School starts soon. Callie won't be there with us. It totally sucks. But you can't be doing this."

Summer's almost over? Already? And they're still floundering because I'm not mastering this haunting thing. Guilt and remorse swamp me. The time I wasted with Reena—I could have been helping them.

"I don't care about school, Carson," Nick says. "I'm just tired of thinking about her, of people telling me how sorry they are. And the whispers that it was my fault."

"Don't listen to the whispers, Nick. The accident wasn't your fault," she says softly, kindly. And for a moment, it's like she's the ghost, trying to make him realize that she's here for him.

His eyelashes flutter open and he stares up at her.

"Yes, it was."

There's so much despair in his voice that it makes me ache inside. I sit down on the floor next to the bed, close to them, and I wish I could reach out to him.

"It was her choice to drive so fast, her choice to answer the phone when she was driving. She knew better," Carson says.

For all her belief in the supernatural, Carson is practical. And she's right.

"You don't know, Cars," he says. "I was going to tell her that night, and . . ."

He falls silent, and Carson reaches up to stroke the side of his face.

"No," she says softly. "Shhh. . . . It wasn't your fault."

I look up at my best friend, so caring. Her dark brown eyes are focused on Nick, and I'm so grateful to her for doing what I haven't been able to—for bringing him out of his grief.

The way I felt with my father, that peaceful feeling—I want it now. I realize that this is the perfect moment for it, while they're here together, alone.

I close my eyes and let myself remember moments with each of them, with the three of us, and I find it easier to steer clear of the details of the memory and instead dive into the emotions that these moments stir. I fill myself with them, let those intangible and unconscious sensations take over my being and slink into the room so that all three of us—I hope—can feel them together.

There's a promising silence in the room, and I open my eyes— Carson and Nick are still. I can't help but give them one extra push, so I send a thought their way: *I'm with you.*

"She's with us." Both Carson and Nick murmur together, and they look at each other for a moment. I feel the energy connecting all three of us, almost as if it's a real thread that ties us to one another.

This is the true connection, the one I need.

"Thank you, Thatcher," I whisper.

And just as I say it, a loud crackle echoes from within my body, and I feel a lightning bolt strike through me. I close my eyes at the surge, and then it's over. When I open them again, Carson's eyes are sparkling with gold. Her face blurs momentarily, almost like I made my own vision go fuzzy, and I see a flash of familiar rosebud lips. I shake my head to clear my sight, and when I look again, it's Carson, just Carson. But her expression has changed. Her mouth is curled into a small smile.

"Nick," she says. Her voice is almost a purr. It doesn't sound like Carson at all.

He's lying back now, his head on the soft down pillow with the ruffled peach sham. "Callie's here. You felt it, too, didn't you? She's here. I have to tell her."

"Tell her what?"

He releases a broken sob. "I was going to break up with her."

I stagger back as though he's hit me with those words. Break up with me?

"If I'd told her the night before, like I'd planned, she wouldn't have been coming to see me. I called to tell her—" Another sob.

Pain is ripping through me. Is this what those texts were about? What Nick should have told me before the accident? But who is H? Does it really matter anymore? Everything I thought I had with Nick was a lie.

Carson looks in my direction, like she can truly see me. Her lips curve up in triumph.

"Well, then . . ." She straddles Nick and presses her lips to his. Her hair falls off her neck and I think I see a dark spot there, but I can't be sure. For a second my brain can't process what I'm seeing.

Carson is kissing Nick.

It's another blow. Was she the reason he wanted to break up with me? Then why didn't she know? I can't make sense of any of this; the devastation of their betrayal is fogging my mind.

I jump to my feet, my mouth open wide like the breath has been sucked out of my body. *What's happening? What's happening? What's happening?* My mind is racing and they are *still kissing.*

I try to collect myself to form enough energy to *get her off him. Think, Callie, think.*

I focus all my emotions on Nick's mind, trying to make him recognize my presence. I close my eyes and picture the day he and I drove out to the Isle of Palms together. We crossed over the bridge and onto the island, where Nick took me out to the beach and we walked for miles. It wasn't a hand-holding-at-sunset thing, it was us being funny, doing handstands, pushing each other into the water, looking for sea glass. I try to call up every detail I can remember. We finished the night by laying a blanket down in the sand and watching for shooting stars, where we kissed until I thought I couldn't breathe without his lips on mine. I'm remembering, I'm focusing. . . .

And suddenly I hear Nick say my name.

"Callie."

I open my eyes as he pushes Carson away. He jumps off the bed and backs away from her. I see Carson's body jolt, as if that same electrical charge is passing through her, and then she starts coughing. Her face looks stunned, disbelieving, as her hand flies up to her mouth.

"What are you doing?" asks Nick.

I look around the room, needing to reaffirm for them that I'm here, that the presence they felt was real. I spot a small porcelain statue of a Dalmatian on the bureau and swat at it with a palm filled with anger. It teeters, then drops to the floor with a crash.

Nick and Carson both jump, startled.

"What just happened?" she says. Then she looks at his horrified face and asks again, more urgently, "Nick! What just happened?"

He looks away from the fallen dog statue with fear in his eyes.

"You kissed me," he says.

"No," she says, pressing her fingers to her lips as if she can deny it. "No . . . I . . ."

"You did," he says. "And then I saw her . . . our day at Isle of Palms . . . I saw her."

"You're drunk," Carson says, glancing at the broken pieces of porcelain. She sinks down on the bed, holding her stomach like she's in pain. "You're confused. . . . I didn't . . ."

"Callie," Nick says again, like he's calling to me. "I'm sorry I didn't tell you the truth before. I just didn't want to hurt you."

It hurts just as much now. I know it shouldn't, but it does. How long did he feel that way? How much of our relationship was just me hanging on?

I can tell by his face that he is in a full panic. He stumbles past Carson, tearing through the door and down the stairs. I should let him go. I want to wallow in my misery.

But he's not acting like the Nick I know. There's a carelessness in him. And I know how much he's had to drink. I rush after him.

His eyes are wide open and glazed over, and he seems like he doesn't even hear people shouting for him to stop.

"Hey, Fisher! I got brownies for you . . . ," Austin calls from the kitchen.

Nick doesn't slow down for a moment, and I race alongside him, small pings of energy pricking me as I crash through anyone in my way.

He pushes by a crowd near the front door and out into the driveway, knocking into a group of freshman girls who spill their bright red drinks and then burst into laughter. Nick doesn't stop.

The driveway is long and curving, but Nick finds his way down the dark pavement, his steps falling at a rapid pace. I glide beside him, unconcerned with the physical world, just wanting to stay near him, glad that my ghostly self has the grace to do that. He fumbles with his keys at the door to his car, and he looks back up at the big house like it might be chasing him. I glance at the mansion in the moonlight, too, and I hear rooms echo with drunk laughter. When I turn back to Nick, he's got his keys in the lock.

"Don't drive, Nick," I plead. "Please . . . don't drive."

But again, I'm useless. I'm not here. All I can do are party tricks like breaking a porcelain dog. I can't stop Nick from doing something incredibly stupid.

In spite of what he said, in spite of everything, I still care about him. Maybe I'm in denial, can't truly face it, but I don't want him hurt.

He gets into his car, and I hurry to join him, passing through the door as if *it's* the thing that isn't here, instead of me. As I hover in the passenger seat, he guns the engine and peels off the McCanns' lawn.

Nick drives dangerously fast, ignoring the stop sign at the end of the street and blasting his horn at a car up ahead of him. I have to get him to calm down, to pull over.

I look out the windshield at the dark highway speeding by us, and I can't help but flash back to the truck that came out of nowhere on the night I died.

"Nick, please," I say, knowing that he can't hear me but hoping that somehow he *can*, just like I think Carson heard me, deep down, during the séance. "Please slow down. Nick, I still love you. Please, please slow down."

I'm repeating it over and over, like a whispered prayer.

Nick is driving like he's possessed. We turn out onto the old rural route, and the speedometer goes up to ninety as his jaw hardens. It's almost like he *wants* to punish himself.

How can this be happening? After all of the connecting, the haunting, the real moments between us . . . he's still so unhinged.

This entire time guilt has been gnawing at him, a deeper guilt than I realized. He wanted to talk the night he came to my room, but I wanted him to hold me. And he did what I wanted.

Now he feels responsible for my death, for not being honest with me, for harboring a secret. His unwillingness to hurt me, in the end, hurt me beyond his wildest expectations.

Why was he going to break up with me? What did I do wrong? I push back the pain, the anger, the betrayal. I have to help him, to save him.

As the car pushes past ninety-five miles per hour, I see the blind recklessness in Nick's profile, the intensity on his face. His foot is still pressed on the gas pedal. I know this moment—I used to live in it myself.

I got into his thoughts once tonight. I have to try again. I close my eyes and feel the speed of the car, but I try to block it out. I fill myself with internal emotions, not the fear and desperation that surround me in the car, but the peace and pure happiness I felt with him when we were alive. I dig deep into myself, into my *soul*. And then I call out to him.

"Nick," I say.

He turns around and smiles at me. "Callie, what are you doing outside?"

And it's like we've spun on a rotating stage set . . . the scene changes and we're outside in a lush, green garden. I'm with him—I must be inside a daydream, or a memory he's having. I have to remember that this isn't real—that we're in a car, and he's in danger. I need to save his life. But I'm so thrilled that he sees me! He hears me! I rush into his arms, hugging his body close to mine.

And though I half expect my arms to pass right through, I am suddenly enveloped by him. His soft T-shirt, his strong arms, his *smell*. He's kissing the top of my head and laughing at my ardor.

"Whoa," he says softly. "Why so intense?"

His smile is easy, like the smiles we shared . . . before.

"I love you," I say. "I will always, always love you."

"Callie, I know," he says.

The air is soft and inviting, like Charleston on the very best days of spring. Not hot yet, but past winter's chill. It's when the flowers bloom and everything feels new. It's perfect daydream weather, and of course it would be what Nick's subconscious chooses. His warm brown eyes are so alert, so *aware* of me that I want to cry with joy.

I didn't realize what not being seen by your loved ones can do to a person—it's heartbreaking, feeling like you don't exist. Like you never existed. But here I am, and here Nick is, and in this moment we can be together.

But it's not real. None of it is real.

"Callie," Nick whispers. "I care about you so much—I do."

"I know," I say, but I have to say good-bye. And I can't resist—I lean in to kiss him. It's the kind of kiss that's soft and hard all at once, the kind that makes my breath ragged with desire as I lift up onto my toes for more. My head swirls with the thought of staying with him, of keeping this moment locked in my heart so I can live within it.

But there's a nagging at the back of my mind, and my lips fall still for a moment.

He pulls away from me. "There's something I need to tell you," he says. "This isn't right. It doesn't feel—"

"Oh, Nick," I say, pressing my head into his chest again as I put a finger up to his lips. I don't want him to say that this doesn't feel real. I know it isn't. But I want it to be.

And I especially don't want him to say that he's breaking up with me, but even as I think it, I realize the selfishness of it. I have to let him go.

"It's okay, Nick," I say softly. "I know what you wanted. I don't know why, but it doesn't matter now. The accident wasn't your fault. You can let me go. It's okay."

"Callie—"

"It's okay. You need to be happy, Nick. All I want is for you to be happy. Because I'm okay where I am. I'm finding my own happiness here." Or at least now I have confidence that I will. The reality I was clutching never really existed.

I hear a blaring horn that doesn't fit with this dreamscape, and Nick hears it, too. He looks around, breaking our embrace, and I feel a rush of force as I open my eyes to see two blinding headlights barreling toward Nick's car. We are going to crash.

Twenty-Two

NICK IS IN THE REAL PRESENT NOW, fully aware of the danger he's in. He grabs the wheel and veers away from the oncoming car, back into his lane. But as he turns, the speed is too much, and the car swerves dangerously—he's losing control. No matter what I do to reach his mind, I can't save him.

But someone can. Reena, Leo—they're so strong, so sure. They can move things with their energy; they aren't afraid to do that. Suddenly I realize why Reena told me that I didn't call her that day in my prism—that I didn't have that power. Because she didn't want me to know that I truly could call for someone who would help.

And then I lift up my head to shout into the darkness.

Downcast eyes, sharp chin, a sigh that holds volumes of sadness, a hint of stubble, a shock of blond hair that falls into his face, eyes with their own storm system, electric fingers. My unconscious mind takes over, and the question of who I trust the most is answered in a single, instinctual scream.

"Thatcher!"

"Is that an open field?"

A voice shouts from the backseat, and I twist around to find Thatcher pointing up ahead and to the left.

"It's Dodsons' Farm," I say, stunned. "Mostly corn."

"But no trees or fences along the highway?" He's squinting to better identify any obstacles before us.

"It's open land," I say.

And then Thatcher's gone. I call out for him as the car shifts to the left. Nick releases his hold on the steering wheel completely, fear etched all over his face.

Looking out my window, I see Thatcher holding on to the front wheel well and slowly but surely turning the tires in the direction of the field. His face is pure concentration, but he looks calm, in control. I feel a surge of affection for Thatcher: He's saving Nick.

The Camry lurches left and pops off the road, bumping and dragging stalks of corn as it plows through the Dodsons' crop.

The stalks connecting with the metal of the car pop like gunfire. Nick is jostled and thrown as though he's a marionette whose strings have come loose.

But he was still enough of himself to wear his seat belt.

I can hear everything, but I don't feel anything. The bounce and jump of the car as it barrels through rows of corn, the sound of the hard ears on the windshield and under the tires . . . it's like I'm in a movie stunt scene.

When we finally stop, Nick's head hits the steering wheel. A trail of blood trickles down his temple, and it looks like he's blacked out. But I know he's okay. I know he's alive. I know that Thatcher saved him.

I reach over and touch the blood on Nick's forehead with my finger, tracing its dark red line carefully.

I want him to know that my death isn't his fault. I should never have made him remember being with me—he *can't* be with me, so why torture us both? I need him to move on, like he was going to move on before the accident. If I hadn't died, he would have been free. How ironic that my death tied him to me.

When I sit up, I see Thatcher staring at us through the windshield of the car. He looks furious, and I know I've disappointed him. Then, for a moment, I think I see a flash of regret in his blue eyes before they cloud over, unreadable.

Sirens blare in the distance. Whoever was in the other car must have made a 911 call. Multiple doors slam, and the shouts of police officers echo through the field. I take one more moment with Nick, smoothing his hair as he starts to stir.

The driver's-side door opens abruptly and Sheriff Curtis Simmons says, "Boy, you're gonna have to answer to Mr. Dodson tomorrow!" Then he straightens up and shouts to the other officers.

"He's okay!" I hear the emotion catch in Sheriff Simmons's voice. He's been a friend to my family all my life. He and Mama were in high school together—they're both Old Charleston. Our great-great-way-back grandparents signed the Ordinance of Secession together just before the Civil War.

A few slaps on the back happen and a big cheer goes up. Too many times in our town this kind of drunk-driving accident ends another way.

I walk up to Thatcher, who's standing off to the side in the field. His brow is furrowed, his lips tight.

"What exactly were you doing tonight?" he asks, his voice angry.

I bow my head without answering.

"What made Nick drive like a crazed lunatic—drunk, I might add?"

More ground gazing. *It was me*, I think. I had them, I was connecting and helping them in the way that Thatcher wants me to—on an unconscious soul level—and then I broke it out of anger, hurt, and jealousy. He was kissing Carson and I got so upset that I made him think of me, I made him feel guilty enough to jump into his car and tear away from the party. I turned into a poltergeist and used their tricks instead of following Thatcher's path. It's my fault.

"Callie?"

I look up at Thatcher slowly.

"You were haunting on your own?" he asks.

I shift my eyes away from his, and it's clear that the answer is yes.

"What we did for my father . . ." I start. "I wanted that for Nick, too."

"Soulful haunting doesn't have results like this," says Thatcher. "You must have been doing something else, you must have been—"

"I'm sorry," I say, interrupting him. "You're right."

"Callie, if you hadn't mishandled the haunting, Nick never would have been driving like that. He never would have—" He stops and tilts his head. "Did you say I'm *right*?"

I nod, and surprise crosses his face.

I look over at Nick leaning against the hood of his car for support. His eyes are open now, and I can see the sheriff talking to him. He's really going to be okay.

The enormity of what just occurred hits me, and I sink to my knees.

Thatcher drops down beside me.

"Did Reena bring you to Nick?" he asks.

I shake my head no, taking full responsibility.

"You created the portal," he says.

I nod yes. Then through the knot of tears in my throat, I push out the words: "He was going to break up with me."

"What?"

"Nick. He . . . he told Carson tonight. The night I was going over to his house, the night of the accident, he'd planned to break up with me. I don't know why. I don't know what I did—"

"You might not have done anything. It might have had nothing to do with you."

I stare at him through a veil of tears. "How could it have nothing to do with me?"

He looks back in Nick's direction, where the EMTs are testing his reflexes. "People break up for all kinds of reasons." He turns back to me. Sympathy and understanding are reflected in his eyes. "There's a farmhouse over there."

"Yes. The Dodsons' place."

"Let's take a walk."

We move deeper into the countryside, away from the road, away from the tow truck that's hauling Nick's wrecked Camry to Lee's Garage. The EMTs are still tending to Nick, and Sheriff Simmons is talking to them, too. I make sure we stay within eyesight of the scene.

As we walk through the Dodsons' field, gliding over the crop beds and moving slowly toward the little white house, I notice that the moonlight is so bright that it's the type of phase that would cast our shadows on the ground if we were really here. Looking down, I see the soft glow playing off the tall grass, but not a trace of me, or Thatcher, is here. We aren't trampling the vegetation or making tracks in the dirt or even rustling the corn husks. We're floating through this world, in it but not of it.

When we get to the Dodsons' farmhouse, Thatcher points to the wooden porch swing, which looks both abandoned and inviting with its chipped white paint.

"I used to love those," he says.

"I always wanted one. I asked my dad for ages if he'd put one on our porch, but he never did."

Thatcher smiles wistfully. "Come on," he says, leading me up the rickety white steps. We sit down together on the swing, hovering over it but feeling like we're really sitting. I focus on my feet, willing them to connect with the floorboards of the porch, and they do. We rock a little bit. The chair creaks, and I wonder if the Dodsons ever hear this swing moving. They must think it's the wind.

Thatcher waits. Patiently. Always so patiently. I don't even know where to begin.

"He was at a party, totally drunk before he even got there. Carson took him to a bedroom. To yell at him mostly, I think. But I managed to make them both feel my presence."

I look out at the cornfields. I can still see the emergency lights flashing in the distance. Nick is sitting up on a stretcher now.

"It was so incredible, Thatcher. Like with my father. I felt this immense relief, peace welling up inside me. All because of you." I give my attention to Thatcher, who is studying me intently.

A softness touches his eyes. "You've come a long way, Callie. But you did it on your own. I was just guiding you."

I want him to understand that to me he's more than a Guide. "After witnessing Ella's merging, after my night with you . . . I no longer wanted to remain on Earth. I wanted to be where I was."

"I'm glad," he says.

He still doesn't understand what I'm saying. Maybe I'm afraid to admit it aloud. After discovering what Nick was keeping from me, I don't quite trust my own judgment. But still I say, "It meant a lot to me, Thatcher. Everything you told me, all that we shared. I know it probably wasn't supposed to be special, but it was."

"I wanted it to be," he says quietly. "Selfish on my part."

I release a small laugh. "I can live with that kind of selfishness."

"But it's all we can have. You need to merge."

I nod jerkily. I have so many memories with Nick to take with me, so few with Thatcher. It's not fair. I want more.

I lean forward, stopping our slow rock in the swing as I look out at the near-full moon shining in the distance. For a moment I feel alive again, like I'm sitting on a front porch with a guy I like, trading stories and telling secrets. It's nice, familiar.

"Carson kissed Nick," I tell him. It just comes out, before my brain even knows I am going to say it.

"What?" Thatcher turns to me, his eyes widening. "Really?"

I feel a fresh wave of hurt as I see the scene in my mind again. "Yes," I say.

"But she's your best friend. Is she the reason he was going to break up with you?"

"I don't think so. Otherwise, wouldn't she have known that he was going to break up with me?"

"How do you feel about her kissing him?" asks Thatcher. It's such a non-guy question, and I appreciate that. He's listening.

"Angry," I say. "Sad. Hurt. Confused."

Nodding, Thatcher puts his hand over mine resting on the wooden slats of the swing. I welcome the spark it creates, because it's comforting, soft, safe. I touch my toes down to the porch again and rock us back and forth, back and forth, making the creak of the swing a little louder. It almost feels like it would feel if we were still alive.

I flash back to the peach room at Tim McCann's party. "It was right after he confessed that he was going to break up with me." I shake my head. "She seemed triumphant, like she was someone I didn't know at all."

"Grief can make people crazy," says Thatcher, his brow furrowed like he's trying to figure it out along with me.

"I know," I say, still playing the scene in my head. "But there's something else. Right before they kissed, I thought I saw . . ."

I shake my head, feeling silly.

"What?" asks Thatcher.

"Carson's face was blurred, and I saw . . . I don't know, I thought I saw Reena there for a second."

Thatcher puts his feet down and stops our rocking abruptly, turning to me. "You saw Reena? In the room?"

"That's what's so weird," I say. "I thought I saw her in *Carson*, like her face flashed over Carson's for a second. Like she was doing that shadowing thing."

"What shadowing thing?"

"I don't understand it exactly. It's a game they play where they try to line themselves up with people and follow their actions."

"And this was before the kiss?"

"Yeah, just before she leaned over Nick," I say, realizing that the moment is burned into my brain in excruciating detail.

Thatcher stands up abruptly and traces a portal.

"Where are you going?" I ask.

And then I notice that he's shaking, he's weak. He reaches out his hand to me, but quickly he sinks back down to the swing. "My energy is low," he says.

I bite my lip, worried that the strain of rescuing Nick drained him beyond what he can handle. "Take some of my energy."

"No, you need to hold on to it." With a great deal of effort, he shoves himself to his feet. "You stay here, make sure Nick is okay. Can you get back to your prism?"

"Yes. Will you come find me there?"

He nods. "I have to talk to the Guides—tell them what you saw."

"What I saw?"

"Listen, Callie—Carson didn't kiss Nick. Reena did."

Twenty-Three

IT'S HARD TO MAKE OUT WHERE I am at first, in the darkness. The air is thick with humidity, and the only lights are the stars above. Before my eyes adjust, all I can sense are shapes and sounds—echoing voices that sound like they're muffled by shadow. But then I see the glimmer of the train tracks in the distance, and I know I'm back at Lyndon's Crossing.

I'm going to find her. All this time I thought Leo was the dangerous one, but Reena was manipulating me so much more.

I felt confused for a moment, stunned, when Thatcher told me what he thinks Reena did. That she actually may have *possessed* Carson. But he was so weak that he had to go before he could tell me why, or what it meant. So after I made sure Nick was in good hands and on his way to the hospital, I created a portal.

Thanks for showing me how, Reena.

First I summoned all the pieces of her—the long black hair, rosebud lips, doll cheeks. Then I thought of the way her strong stance belies her height, the sideways hook of her smile, and the way her eyes flash gold sometimes.

The portal I traced pulsed with light, and I stepped through it. *I'm sorry, Thatcher. I have to do this.*

And now I'm here, by the tracks. As my eyes adjust, I see the glow of the poltergeists in the distance about twenty feet away—they haven't spotted me. The trees around them seem to wilt in their presence, bowing down in the humidity. I watch them for a moment, these ghosts I thought were my friends, wondering what they're capable of.

Just as I'm about to call out to Reena and face the poltergeists, I hear voices coming up over the hill toward the tracks.

"Oh, great," says Leo.

"Gotta love a Southern Saturday night." Delia rolls her eyes.

"I don't know." Reena's face glows with anticipation. "This could make the evening even more fun."

A crowd of people—mostly guys—emerges over the hill. I recognize them instantly. Tim McCann is here, and so are Eli, Brian, and Hunter—the soccer guys from the bonfire. I scan everyone's faces and spot Gina O'Neill and Molly Raider, who's been in love with Brian since third grade. This must be Tim's after-party.

They all settle at the edge of the tracks, where they stand around and take pulls on a bottle of vodka that they probably hoisted from Tim's father's stash.

"What was that kid's name again?" asks Eli. "Norbert or something?"

Norris throws up his hands. "Norbert?" The rest of the poltergeists laugh. They're nearing the group now, approaching the Living. I watch their glow start to flicker all around my classmates, and it must be a light that only those of us on the other side can see. No one reacts to it, even as Reena, Leo, Norris, and Delia surround them, standing outside the perimeter of the gathering. I stay back, watching, wanting to see how they'll interact, waiting for something bad to happen. I see them now the way Thatcher has seen them—poltergeists, enemies of the Living, and of ghosts, too.

"It was Norris," says Molly quietly. "He was friends with my older brother."

"Yeah, well, he must have been a total idiot," says Eli, passing the vodka after a long drink. "Who doesn't have time to jump out of the way of a train? They only go, like, forty miles per hour."

"The idea is to let it get as close to you as possible, big shot," says Brian.

"Yeah, *without* letting it hit you." Eli laughs.

Seeing them gathered here, I feel like I'm witnessing a moment from my former life. Sitting around, talking about nothing, but feeling on the brink of something exciting, some new possibility. Except now my life has taken this horrific turn—their circle is lit up with the ghostly glow of poltergeist eavesdroppers, and they have no idea.

I took nights like this for granted, found them boring even. When Carson would linger with other friends, talking and laughing and hanging out just to be out, I'd be the first who was ready to leave, wanting to get to something more exciting, some new thrill.

I couldn't recognize the value of simply being with friends. My skin prickles with emotion, a wish that I were on the other side of this scene. But I'm not. I'm with the ghosts.

A soft rain starts to fall, but no one makes a move to leave, and when the lights from the next train beam in the distance, everyone's heads turn toward the *chug-chug-chug*.

Eli steps forward and stumbles a little. Without saying anything, he positions himself on the tracks with his arms folded across his chest.

"Dude, get down," says Hunter.

Eli just smirks and continues to stare down the train, which is still about a minute away from where they're standing.

"Should I try it?" Leo's voice booms as he looks to Reena, and she smiles at him, the glow of her face lighting up the darkness around her.

"Doesn't it only work if we have Callie to draw from?" asks Norris.

Anger surges through me. They're talking about using my energy, just like Thatcher said.

"We've taken a lot of energy from her already," says Reena. "Let's see what happens when she's not here."

Immediately, Leo moves in. He positions himself behind Eli, standing with him.

I keep my distance, but the muscles in my legs tighten, ready to spring, and I lean forward to see more clearly. *What is Leo doing?*

As the train draws closer, the engineer sees Eli's shape on the tracks. He blows the horn in warning, but Eli doesn't move.

"Come on, man," says Hunter, moving closer with Brian. "You're drunk."

Brian reaches out for Eli's arm, intending to pull him off the tracks, but Eli swats him away.

"Get off me," he says. "You called me a wuss after the bonfire, but y'all are the real pansies." He stretches out his arms like he's yawning, and he smiles at the train's headlights, which are getting closer and closer.

The bonfire. When Reena scared him with her tricks. Thatcher's right—even joking around with them can have dangerous after-effects.

Eli's making no move to get down—he's drunk and full of bravado. He has something to prove.

The train is closing in now. The engineer has started to hit the brakes, and they're sparking on the rails.

Leo is still standing at Eli's back, very close, and he raises his arms to his sides slowly. He looks menacing, almost wild, like when I first saw him in the barn at Middleton Place.

"Eli, we all know you're not a wuss; now get off the tracks!" shouts Molly, her eyes widening. The rain starts to fall harder, in big fat drops.

Eli laughs and relents. "Okay."

But when he moves to step down, Leo's massive arms encircle him, holding him captive.

Leo's eyes close—he's using all of his concentration to physically keep Eli in place. My phantom heart pounds in my throat. *Should I scream?*

And Eli starts to panic.

"I can't get down," he says, his voice breathy and clipped. Eli is flailing now, his legs lifting off the ground as he tries to escape the hold on him. Then, a crackle zags through my body and that sharpness is followed by a blind rage, because I know what's happening—they're using me, taking my energy. In the next moment, I see something straight out of another world—Leo's glowing figure moves inside Eli, taking over first one leg, then the other, then his arms, and finally his face. Inside Eli's smile, I see the glow of Leo. A shot of icy cold dread blasts through me—they're not just trying to scare Eli. This isn't a game of exhilaration. They're possessing him.

Just like Carson.

"Stop messing around, man," says Hunter, his voice rising with every word. "Get off the tracks!"

Brian is shouting now, too, and Gina has started crying. Molly screams, and Hunter rushes up to Eli and tries to drag him to safety, but Leo stands strong, and a wide smile slowly spreads over Eli's overtaken face.

The poltergeists are watching with rapt attention. Reena's grin, the one that drew me in with such warmth, makes her face look evil in the rain, which is now pouring down on us all, soaking the Living.

"Stop!" My cry pierces the night even above the metal brakes screeching and all the frantic yelling.

Eli-Leo looks in my direction then and releases a laugh, a deep, angry chortle.

This time, I don't call for Thatcher. I've done so many things wrong—I have to make this right on my own while he regains his strength. *I have to save Eli.* The thought clicks in my brain like a bullet locked and loaded in a gun, and then I'm pure action. Energy pulses inside me, coming from the very core of my soul, catapulting me forward as if I'm propelled by an engine. It rumbles in my feet, like I'm standing at the center of an earthquake, and flies through my legs and into my chest—driving me, pushing me, as I rush at Eli's form. If I don't get there in time, he will *die.* I race up to Eli-Leo at what seems like the speed of light.

I collide with him in the split second before the train can take his body, and he flies off the tracks, into the woods. I know we're moving at a velocity that would be hard for the human eye to even comprehend, but to me, time has gone into slow motion. We fall together onto the forest floor, and when I stand up, Leo steps out of Eli like he's a snake shedding its skin. He stumbles as the wind of the slowing train rushes past us. The engineer is yelling and cursing, and Eli is crouched on the ground, coughing and sobbing. His face is stricken, shocked, but he's alive. Beautifully and gloriously alive. I feel a jealous sting at the thought that he came so close to this line, the one that I've crossed into death, and has a second chance on the other side.

Time returns to normal, and I shake out the excess energy that was occupying my body.

The Living rush up to Eli, asking him what happened, trying to figure out if they just witnessed a terrifying paralysis or the best train dodge in history. I stand close to them and hear Eli quietly repeating, "I'm okay. I'm okay." Then I turn and face the poltergeists—I came for Reena.

But what I see is her retreating, moving quickly. *Is she afraid of me?* As I watch, she creates a portal, and Norris and Delia vanish into it. Then she helps Leo, who's crawling toward her, looking as beaten down as Eli does. As she's about to step through, she turns and meets my gaze with a defiant smile.

"No!" I run at her, fast, forcing my way into the portal behind her—and then I plunge into darkness.

Twenty-Four

WE TUMBLE THROUGH TOGETHER, but this isn't like any portal I've been in—it's faster, more violent, twisting and turning and echoing with blackness punctuated by flashing white light and the sound of ghostly howls. I train my eyes on Reena's long dark hair, whipping around in front of me as she remains just out of my grasp. I reach out to catch her—I'm afraid that they'll be able to lose me and I won't know where they end up—but she eludes me. Still, I keep up, bumping and colliding with the edges of this celestial wormhole, a portal that feels like it's a bucking horse trying to throw me.

And then we stop falling. We're on the ground, on the side of a highway. The sky is clear and dark now, but the asphalt is slick from the summer rainstorm, and the puddles flash with an eerie light when a car passes by, spraying water in our direction.

The four of them stand quickly, and Leo motions for them to walk along the road. I think they might be trying to get away from me again, but when I move toward Reena, she opens her arms like she wants a hug.

Is she insane? Judging by the expression on her face, she very well may be. Does she think that using me for my energy—taking over the bodies of the living—is okay? That I'll go along with them while they nearly extinguish a life? Out of everyone in existence, ghosts should understand that causing a death is the worst wrong imaginable—we *know* what it's like on the other side of life, watching our loved ones' anguish.

No matter how much we want to live again, she can't believe that it's okay to take someone else's life. Can she? Anger pulses through me, but I hold back because I want an explanation.

So I ask her: "What was that?"

"Just a little fun," she says, dropping her arms and smiling. "Eli pulled off the best stunt ever."

I call up to Leo. "Were you going to dodge?" I ask. He's walking ahead, but he turns back and shrugs. His voice is quiet, tired, when he says, "Of course."

"You shouldn't have interfered, Callie," says Reena, and now we're all walking along this road like they're trying to get somewhere. "Eli is weak. They all are."

"What are you talking about?" I ask. "You were going to *kill* him."

"Not *kill*," says Reena. "Killing wouldn't leave us with much of a body if we let a train speed through it, would it?"

"We're trying to *take*," says Leo from ahead of me. He doesn't look back.

"You can't just take someone's body," I say.

"Ah, but you're wrong." Reena's voice is controlled but intense. "I thought it was something from the movies, but recently we've been able to play with possession. It's the only way to maintain energy on Earth that we've found. And it's all thanks to you."

"Thanks to me?"

"The energy you've shared with us has been enough—we've been practicing taking a body and staying on Earth without having to return to the Prism," she says. She sounds enthusiastic, elated even.

Delia pipes up from behind me. "We think that if we can possess a body three times—one time for each level of the soul—we can truly take it over and live an entire life again. There's a precedent for these things, you know. Possession is real."

Reena meets my eyes and smiles, but I don't return the warmth. "Callie, it's what we talked about," she says. "You'll get a second chance at being alive. Truly alive."

Her voice is friendly, encouraging. I think about the time we spent talking about our common wish for a life on Earth again, our shared experiences. But I'm no poltergeist—I would never value my own life over someone else's this way. It seems like they don't even know what they're doing—like they're experimenting with people's mortality. A chill races up my spine as that word crosses my brain.

"What happens to them?" My voice cracks. "To the souls whose bodies you take?"

Reena blinks and looks ahead down the road. "We can't worry about that," she says. "We'll take strangers, people whose lives don't mean anything, people who won't be missed."

"Like Eli?" I ask.

She grins wickedly. "After what he said about Carson, I made him my first pick."

My heart drops. He was targeted because of me. "It's *murder*, Reena," I say. "Thatcher would never—"

She starts walking away from me, moving faster to catch up to Leo, her dark hair whipping around in a circle.

"You're a rule follower after all," she says. "That's too bad."

"You can't just *possess* a living body," I shout at her back. "It isn't right. It isn't fair."

"There is nothing fair about dying young!" screams Reena as she pivots around, emotion etched in her face. "The Living don't appreciate their lives! They don't value what they have!"

Her words resonate with me—I spent my entire existence chasing thrills instead of appreciating the beauty of my world, the love that surrounded me. But that's the prerogative of the Living, to be blissfully ignorant and experience life in their own way.

"It's not up to you, or any of us, to say how people should live," I say. "Do I wish I could go back? Of course. But not this way."

Reena spins around again, striding forward so that I have to jog a little to keep up. A car passes us on the road, its headlights washing through us cleanly.

Delia falls into step with Reena, putting her hand on Reena's shoulder to calm her. "Callie, we can live their lives ten times better than they can," Delia says evenly. "Because we know what it's like to lose everything."

"Is that why you took over Carson's body?" I ask Reena, tired of their insane rationalizations, ready to call her out on what she did tonight. "So you could improve her life by making it seem like she betrayed me?"

Reena raises her eyebrows and slows her pace just as we approach a bend in the road. "What do you mean?" she asks me, but I can tell by her expression that she's playing dumb.

"I saw you. I know you took Carson."

A smile spreads across her face then; she's impressed.

"Guys!" She looks around at the poltergeists, and everyone stops walking.

"It seems like our little Callie has another special skill," she says. "She can see when a living body is hosting a ghost."

"No way," says Leo, his eyes wide as he walks back to where we're standing. "That's impossible."

"I saw you, too," I say. "I could see your face inside Eli, clear as day."

"That's unusual." Reena narrows her gaze on me. "It seems there's no end to your extra talents, Callie. Too bad Thatcher's been lying to you all this time."

"You're wrong," I say, looking at Leo, Norris, and Delia, who are standing behind Reena and watching us cautiously. "He told me why he lied about the portals—he was trying to protect me, and—"

"Protect you?" she interrupts. "Oh, how sweet. More likely he didn't want you to know why you're special."

I shake my head—she's messing with me again. "*You* used me," I say. "You've stolen my energy for . . . this. Taking over bodies, making me think my best friend would betray me."

"I've never lied to you," she says. "You can't trust the Living— don't you know that by now?" Her face flashes with sadness for a moment.

"Carson would never try to take Nick from me," I say.

Reena laughs, and it's a bitter sound, tinged with pain. "Don't be naïve," she says. "They move on, they forget you. Unless you're there with them, you might as well have never existed. I was only showing you what's bound to happen, sooner or later."

Leo, Delia, and Norris stand behind Reena, nodding, and I can see the hurt flickering on their faces, too. What happens when people move on? For most ghosts it means merging with Solus. But for the poltergeists, it means waiting for everyone to leave you behind.

Reena says, "Of course, it's already happened with Nick. If not for me, you wouldn't know that. He was going to break up with you. Don't you want a chance to get even?"

"You've totally lost it," I tell her.

Reena grabs my arm roughly, creating a zigzag of painful current, pulling me forward. "I'll make you understand," she says, her voice a low rumble. "I know you're one of us." She shoves me toward the curve in the road, and I stumble into the street.

Leo, Delia, and Norris are standing nearby, tense, waiting for something to happen. They're staring at me like I'm a bomb a couple of seconds away from exploding.

The rain starts to fall again, harder this time.

"I knew it," whispers Reena. She's right beside me, but she's looking all around us.

"Knew what?" I ask.

She steps around me in a way that reminds me of a shark circling a swimmer in one of those summer horror movies.

"Thatcher did keep a secret from you," she says, almost to herself. "Nothing's happening. This is the right spot, but nothing's happening."

Before I can stop her, she brushes my hair aside, her fingers grazing my neck like little pinpricks of fire, trying to ignite into a full blaze. "You have no moon."

"Because I've had no success at helping those I love move on."

"No, you should have something. And it should be blackening now, but there's nothing."

I feel a rush of anger—mixed with fear—shoot through me. "What are you talking about?"

"Look around, Callie," she says. "Maybe you can even find a piece of your precious BMW as a souvenir."

Then it hits me, and my world reels like I'm on a Tilt-A-Whirl. We're alongside Route 52, in the arm of the curve where I crashed. It's dark, the leaves overhead fluttering in the trees, and my head starts to spin. I hear my own laughter, I see the bright yellow bag where I grabbed my phone, I hear Nick's voice, I smell a hint of magnolia over burning rubber, I see the flash of the truck's metal grille in the setting sun . . . and I feel the crash. Spinning, snapping, banging, pounding, breaking . . . I'm up against the windshield, pinned in between my seat and the glass, which are just inches apart.

My brain is reliving my death, and instead of the jolt and tidal pull that moves me through a tunnel of white noise, this time I hear sirens and see flashing lights. Men shouting, a woman holding my hand. I look into her eyes. "Where's Thatcher?" I ask weakly.

"Callie!" Thatcher's voice breaks my reverie, strong and clear. He's standing by a portal on the other side of the road. There are no ambulances, no woman holding my hand. I'm just standing by the dark road, with the poltergeists.

"Come with me!" he shouts over the rain.

He reaches out to me.

"She's ours now!" Reena shouts.

Suddenly she and Leo grab me. Sharp pings arrow through me from my head to my toes, and I feel a huge pull inside of me. My strength is waning. I'm fading like fog dissipating before the sun.

"No!" Thatcher shouts.

I try to break free, to escape.

A great whoosh of energy hurtles past me and takes Leo with it. In that instant, I experience a surge of power. It's enough for me to wrench free of Reena's hold and stagger back. I raise my fists. I've never hit anyone, but I'm sure as hell not going down without a fight.

Thatcher must have lowered his shields, because he's grappling with Leo. Sparks are flying with each punch. Electricity is crackling in the air.

I swing around looking for Delia and Norris, but they're nowhere to be seen. Out of the corner of my eye, I catch sight of Reena barreling back toward me. I turn to face her—

I'm swept up into strong arms—

A high-pitched screech pierces the air.

"I figured it out, Thatcher!" Reena shouts. "I know why she's different."

It's almost like we're flying as Thatcher dives for the portal.

"I know what she is! I know she's—"

Blessed silence as the portal closes around us.

Twenty-Five

WHEN WE EXIT Thatcher's portal, my eyes have to adjust.

The lighting is dim—mostly candles, flickering in the distance. We seem to be standing at the end of a long hallway. . . .

As our surroundings come into view, I realize where we are. *It's a church.*

Despite the chaos of what just happened, I feel an immediate sense of calm and peace. This isn't my church, not the one where we used to go with Mama—but the feeling is familiar nonetheless. On Sundays she'd put on a flowery blouse, let me wear my favorite patent-leather shoes, and help Dad get his tie on straight. I don't remember the sermons, but I remember the way Mama's perfume smelled, and holding Dad's hand as we walked up to our usual pew, halfway down on the left side. But since she died, I've mostly been to worship with Carson's family, and then only on holidays when Dad thought it might be nice for me to be a part of the rituals and traditions of religion, even though I overheard him tell a pastor who came to visit after Mama died that he wasn't sure what he believed anymore.

I see a few figures kneeling up front, heads bowed in prayer. I notice that there are glowing souls here, too—ghosts—like the older man sitting with his hand on the shoulder of the white-haired lady next to him. She's holding a handkerchief up to her face as if she's afraid she'll cry if she lets go. His light surrounds her, though, like he's keeping her safe.

"They're haunting," I whisper to Thatcher as I gesture in the couple's direction.

"Yes," he says. "It's the third and final level of haunting—a heart connection. It's creating an internal peace for the Living, one that comes from *them* instead of from the ghost."

It does look peaceful, the two of them in a soft cocoon of light.

It also feels so far away from where I am—from what I've seen.

"Why am I not a normal ghost?" I ask Thatcher. "Why hasn't it worked that way for me? What was Reena talking about? That she had figured out why I'm special."

"I'm so sorry, Callie," he says, his voice a reverential whisper. I guess even ghosts stay quiet in church. "The Guides aren't permitted to interfere when a ghost is like you—we're supposed to teach you to haunt, just in case . . ."

He pauses, and looks me in the eyes. "There's a reason I didn't want you to draw portals on your own. I didn't mean to lie to you. I just didn't want you to come here . . . to learn the truth . . . in case the worst happened."

I tilt my head. "Reena used your lie as a way to manipulate me. But I still don't understand what you mean by—"

His face hardens as he interrupts me. "You have to believe that I had no idea Reena would use you this way. I never knew that she was capable of . . . whatever it is she's planning."

"They're taking bodies," I say.

He shakes his head no. "They're playing with possession," he says. "But they're not at the stage where they can take over a body yet, not really."

I bite my lip, not sure how he'll react to what I know. "They mentioned the three levels of the soul," I say. "Delia said that if they take a body three times, they can somehow . . . stay there?"

Thatcher's face goes ashen, his sharp jaw turns slack, and he buries his head in his hands. When he looks up a moment later, his eyes look far away. "They know," he says, his voice shaky.

"It's true then?" I ask.

He turns to me, refocusing on my face. "The Guides have known for a long time that possession was possible—it's one of the secrets we're sworn to protect, because if other ghosts knew they could find a body and stay on Earth . . ."

"It would be chaos," I finish.

"Right," says Thatcher.

"How did the poltergeists learn about possession?" I ask. I look down, afraid to meet his gaze. "Is it . . . my fault?"

"What?"

"They said it was because of me," I say. "Because of my energy."

"No, no . . . ," says Thatcher, and he inches closer to me on the pew as I look up at him again. "Callie, Reena and Leo have been searching for a way to stay on Earth since the day we died. It's not your fault."

"They think that if they live again, they'll be able to be with their families," I tell him. "They promised me that if I joined them, I could stay with the people I love on Earth."

Thatcher shakes his head.

"No—" I say. "Let me finish. I know that isn't true; I know that's not how it works. But it's an appealing promise, one that will help them recruit more ghosts who refuse to merge with Solus."

"That's a problem," says Thatcher.

"We can stop them. Together." I say it strongly, with conviction, because I mean it with every fiber of my being. I'll stand with Thatcher and the Guides; I'll let them use my energy and my ability to see when a poltergeist is attempting a possession.

Thatcher wraps me up in a hug, and I freeze for a moment. He smells like a summer breeze and fresh-cut grass . . . am I imagining that? I take another deep breath anyway and rest my head on his shoulder.

"Thank you," he whispers.

Then he backs out of the hug and stands up, holding out his hand for me to do the same.

Before I take it, I say, "You have to explain it all to me."

He opens his mouth to respond, but I stop him. "I know there has to be some sort of Guide order, or something. I know you go somewhere other than your prism when you leave me. I want to see it. I want to be a part of it all."

"Callie, I—"

"Thatcher," I interrupt. "No excuses. Just answers."

He turns his head toward the front of the sanctuary, looking out into the candlelit silence.

When he turns back to me, his face is serious. "You're the only one," he says, and my heart stops for a moment.

"You're the only ghost we know of who can see when a body is taken," he continues. And my heart beats again.

"Oh," I say. "Right."

"We have to track the poltergeists," says Thatcher, answering my questions before I can ask them. "With you, we'll know when they've attached to a body, so we have a chance to expel them."

I nod my head. "Go on."

"It's going to sound crazy," he says.

"Thatcher, almost everything you say sounds crazy."

He smiles at me.

"Okay," he says. "We've talked about how the soul is divided into three parts. All three must be taken before possession can be achieved."

"Meaning?"

"The poltergeists can't just own a body on the first try," he says. "It takes longer than that. But each time they enter someone, another piece of the soul is weakened, vulnerable. In order to achieve permanent possession, the poltergeists have to enter the same body three times."

Carson. Eli. My palms start to sweat. "What happens after the third time?"

"Then they're able to attach themselves for good. And the host soul is replaced."

"Replaced?"

"The soul dies," he says. "The poltergeist permanently owns their body."

"And the former soul comes to the Prism?"

"No," says Thatcher, eyeing me carefully. "Souls that are banished from their bodies this way simply disappear. No Prism, no Solus . . . just ash."

"Ash?"

"They blow away like dust. They cease to exist."

I drop my head, trying to take this in.

"I told Reena . . . ," I say, hesitantly looking up at him again. "I told her I thought it was murder."

"What did she say?" he asks. I can see in his eyes that he doesn't want to believe she's one hundred percent evil.

"She said she wasn't thinking of it like that," I say, standing. "She said they'll take the bodies of people who won't be missed."

Suddenly a wave of exhaustion hits, flushing my entire body of energy. I feel like I'm going to fade away into nothingness. I can no longer support myself. I'm collapsing into myself, sinking to the tiled floor. My brain is addled, slowed, and my vision goes blurry. It feels like I might pass out, so I sit back down on the pew.

"What is it?" asks Thatcher as he bends down with me.

"I don't know," I say meekly. "So . . . tired . . ."

"They must be in your prism," he whispers, his eyes widening. "They were invited—"

"Only Reena."

"She might find a way to steal your energy and transfer it to them. They'll just get stronger, and you'll get weaker. Our personal prisms are connected to us. Through your prism, they can drain all your energy. They won't stop until they have you."

"What do you mean?"

His face flickers with emotion, and I see a tiny tear form in the corner of his eye. With a shaky finger, I reach up to touch it. For once I can read his eyes, full of wanting, long-held yearning, long-denied desire, and he takes my hand, leans in, and plants a single, soft kiss on my lips. My body feels explosive with just one light touch. It's like nothing I've ever experienced.

He steps back for a moment, and he says, "Callie, I—"

But he doesn't finish his sentence; I won't let him—I just press my lips to his, and it isn't like any kiss I've ever had. It's a kiss that feels like it's been written in the stars for a thousand years, like it's filled with right now and yesterday and eternity all at once. It tugs at me with a sadness I can't explain, and in its urgency I hear a warning bell, an alarm—it's as if the fire between us is going to consume the last breaths we'll both take.

I'm melting into him and I can't feel my body. My entire being is tingling with sensation. If ghosts can feel this much, it's almost as good as being alive. Maybe it's better. My thoughts fade as I let myself give in to the pure pleasure of this moment.

When we part, confusion fills my mind like smoke. I feel foggy and lost and warm and chilled to the bone all at once. Because that wasn't just a kiss—it was a revelation.

And I know that in death I've found something true. I wonder if it's the anticipation of this kiss that has weakened me this way. When we part, Thatcher is holding me up. But instead of the elation that I feel, I see despair in his face.

"What is it?" I ask.

"We have to close your prism. It's the only way to save you."

"What are you talking about?" He doesn't answer, just shoulders my weight as he walks me down the aisle toward the sanctuary exit. It's the first time I don't feel weightless—it's almost like I have my body, my real body, dragging me down. But I go willingly—I'd follow him anywhere. I hold on to him tightly, taking in the Earth once more, knowing that I've made a decision now: I'm leaving my life here behind. I'll fight the poltergeists beside Thatcher, I'll merge with Solus, I'll . . .

The bright lights outside the door startle me. I hear the *click-clack* of sharp shoes on linoleum floors, and I squint as my eyes adjust to blinding fluorescent bulbs. As we walk together down a hallway, I see white coats, green scrubs, metal carts with needles and tubes.

We're at the county hospital—that was the hospital chapel. Thatcher leads me down a hallway, with a purpose in his stride.

I can almost feel how cold it is here, smell the disinfectant.

Thatcher turns down one corridor and then another. He knows exactly where he's going. I wonder at what's happening, but when I try to form the words to ask him, nothing comes out. My energy, it's gone.

I stumble. Thatcher catches me, supports me.

"Not much farther." His words seem to be encouragement for me, but disappointment for him. I don't understand.

Finally Thatcher urges me into a room, and as we pass through the door I see the back of my dad's proud crew cut; I take in the width of his shoulders as he sits, straight backed, in a chair by the bed.

Who's here? I wonder, and when I look up at Thatcher with a question in my eyes, he doesn't meet my gaze.

"I wasn't allowed to tell you," he says solemnly. "I wanted so badly to tell you everything, to explain it all, but it was forbidden."

He turns his eyes to me then, and I see that his beautiful ocean blues are brimming with tears. "They'll keep coming for you now, and you're so vulnerable—this is the only way I can protect you."

What?

"Callie, come back to us." I turn my head sharply at the sound of my father's voice. And as he leans forward in the chair, I catch a glimpse of the girl in the bed as he brushes her hair from her forehead.

My forehead.

I'm in the bed.

Twenty-Six

THATCHER CLOSED HIS EYES when he did it—when he drove my soul back into my body. He grimaced and released a low groan like he was in pain, and then he grabbed my arms and I felt a hard push this time, not the gentle pull of the tide that led me into the Prism, but a powerful thrust as my body lit up with pain and my mouth froze in a silent scream. *Nooooo!* He forced me to leave him, and I saw his face—tortured, regretful, full of hurt. He'll be alone in death once again, despairing and hopeless and up against impossible enemies who were once his friends. I never got to tell him that with one kiss he sealed my fate and that I'd never leave him. Because he chose for me. He chose my life. One moment he was there, sharp and clear, and then he faded—his energy lost to the strain of what he did for me—disappearing into the darkness without a word.

Beep-beep-beep-beeeeeeep!

I hear buzzing, ringing, the high pitch of machines. My head feels like it's carrying a load of bricks, and I gasp through dry and cracked lips. I thrash about, realizing I'm strapped down to something. A needle tears from my arm and a shooting pain makes its way up through my shoulder. I open my mouth to cry out, but I can't seem to do it. My vision is blurry—all I see are circles of light shining into my eyes.

Slowly, my sight clears. Through a wobbly lens, I see the world in front of me: a nurse, leaning over me and calling frantically for a doctor . . . Carson, clapping her manicured hands together and jumping up and down with excitement . . . Dad, holding my left hand in his and pressing it to his lips, kissing it over and over again.

Am I hallucinating? Did I create a portal to someone's dream?

The physical agony I feel tells me that I can't possibly be in the realm of the Prism, where there was no pain, only a slight buzzing and a fullness of energy. Now I'm depleted, hollowed out and hurting. It feels like I weigh a thousand pounds, and I can't move.

The doctor walks in and asks everyone to clear the room. I hear her speaking swiftly and sternly to my father. She pulls a curtain closed around my bed and leans over me.

"Callie, can you hear me?" she asks.

I try to say yes, but my lips are raw and ruined and my throat feels dry, dust filled, so all that comes out is a burble.

"Blink twice if you understand me," says the doctor.

I do, and even my eyelashes seem to tingle with pain.

She smiles.

I try to pull myself up, to look through the gap in the curtain for someone I know isn't there. *Thatcher.* He's gone, truly gone. Tears rush to my eyes, and the pressure they create sends a sting through my nose.

"You're awake," she says. "Take it easy, lie back."

She looks over at the nurse, who's replacing the IV into my arm.

"That's for fluids," says the nurse. "Please don't tear it out again."

I blink back the tears, wondering if I'm crazy, if I've lost him forever. But she just smiles. She sees only that I've blinked twice, agreeing.

"You were in a very serious car accident, Callie," says the doctor. "You've been in a coma for six weeks. Your family and friends are here, but I want you to rest now before they see you."

I blink twice, but all I can think is that there's someone missing, there's a dimension that feels gone, wholly and irrevocably gone, from my existence. And this body—this broken, bruised body—its injuries may be nothing compared to what my mind has suffered. Is it fractured? Have I gone mad?

"Good," she says. "Lie back, relax, and let me get one of my colleagues, okay? I'll let your dad come in in a little while."

I blink twice.

The doctor walks out, and the nurse pushes the hair off my forehead gently before turning to leave. "Welcome back," she says on her way out of the room.

Epilogue

WHEN MY FATHER COMES IN to visit me, my pain medication has been regulated according to what I've been able to blink to the doctors, and I'm starting to regain my normal vision. His face makes my heart leap. He sees me, and that makes me feel whole again, validated, *here.* Even though I'm dulled by painkillers and weeks of darkness, I remember the heartbreak of not being seen.

Dad holds my hand and tells me how much he prayed for me to come back to him, how he couldn't bear losing me, how he's going to make up for the time he spent being foolishly absent from my life.

I nod at him reassuringly, trying to smile and encourage him. I haven't spoken yet—it seems my voice is missing. The physical realities of this body, the healing I need to do, overwhelm my senses, but when I let my mind wander, it goes to one place: *Thatcher.*

A nurse brings in a tray of mashed food—like something a

baby would eat—with a glass of milk covered in plastic wrap. Is this really happening?

The tangible world is so strange to me, so precious and ordinary at the same time. All the while a thousand thoughts are racing through my brain: Where was I all this time? The poltergeists must have been a crazy nightmare my coma state brought on; the Prism isn't real, none of the things I saw were. Still, when I close my eyes, I see bolts of lightning and rain and energy—nothing is solid, nothing is clear. Except for his face. *Thatcher.* I can see him smiling softly, I can see him gazing at me, I can see him anguished. I feel his loss beating somewhere inside me, threatening to overwhelm my gratitude, my happiness at being alive after what I've heard was a terrible accident.

When Nick comes in to greet me, I'm not sure how I'm supposed to feel. Do I confront him about what I heard? How do I explain that I was there? Was I there? Or did my mind create a scenario where he was breaking up with me so I wouldn't have to feel guilty about my growing attraction for Thatcher—an imaginary guy who my coma-induced mind created?

If Nick really was going to break up with me, would he look so glad to see me? His smile is so big that it's almost cartoonish.

But what if it's true? What if he meant to break up with me, but my near-death experience made him realize what a mistake it would be, made him acknowledge how deeply his feelings for me ran?

"Callie," he says, rushing over. He hovers above me—he seems unsure how to say hello. He settles for a delicate kiss on the cheek, and I hardly feel its flutter, barely notice its touch. I don't know if I expected a spark, a pull, a flash of energy, but I find myself disappointed.

Nick sits down in the chair by my bed.

"Oh, man, I can't believe you're awake," he says, looking down at his shoes and not at me. "I mean, thank God. If you hadn't been rushing to get to my house, talking to me on the phone . . ."

I shake my head no and put one finger to his lips.

"I'm sorry," he says. "The doctor said to talk to you about happy things. Um . . . did you see my gift?"

Nick points to the window, where a shiny crystal charm hangs on a transparent string. He stands and walks over to it. The string is looped around one of the window locks, and when he touches it, it moves in the sun, catching the light and casting tiny rainbows on the walls around me.

"I put it here just after the accident," he says. "For luck or maybe just so that there would be something pretty in here for you . . . in case . . ."

He looks down at his feet, blushing. "I sound like Carson, right? Trying to bring you luck with something as silly as a prism."

A tear trickles down my cheek involuntarily, and Nick quickly walks toward me to wipe it away, reminding me of the tear I brushed from Thatcher's face just before . . .

I shake my head to clear it. *Why am I crying about a world I made up?* I wonder, chastising myself for thinking of Thatcher. Nick is real, and he's in front of me. Thatcher doesn't exist. He can't. It isn't possible.

"I don't mean to upset you, Cal," says Nick. "Maybe I should just go."

I muster a smile, and he squeezes my hand before he leaves. This touch, it's real. It doesn't make my body fill with energy, it doesn't light me up inside . . . but it's concrete, uncomplicated, solid.

I will myself to feel good about this, about being here, being with Nick. My brain must be completely muddled for me to be mourning a world that I made up in my head instead of celebrating waking up from a coma and getting a second chance at my life with the people I love so much. Mama would have taken this chance . . . I know it.

"I'll let Carson come in," says Nick. "I can almost hear her scratching at the door."

He leans over to give me another quick kiss on the cheek.

"I'm so sorry, Callie," he says, his face serious. Then he turns and walks out.

In a burst of energy, Carson pushes open the hospital curtains. She's careful with me, but she still manages to give me a huge hug—it's the kind I missed so much while I was in the Prism. I blink to erase my confusion, so I can stay in this moment—this *real* moment—with Carson, instead of going into my coma dreams again. She lays herself across my lap and stares at me with wide, excited eyes.

"Callie, you won't believe what you've missed!" she sings. "Did you know you woke up just in time for junior year? School is about to start! Way to sleep through the entire summer!"

I stifle a laugh—it hurts when it starts to bubble up, but I am glad to want to laugh again, to be alive again. The fog around my brain is lifting a little because of clear-eyed Carson, who never changes for anyone or any situation. I think of how I imagined her when I was hallucinating *(yes, that's what it was, a hallucination . . .)*—keeping hope alive that she could bring me back from the dead.

She starts going over tons of gossip that she knows I'd never have cared about, and still don't, but it's fun to hear her talk. Dad and Nick were so careful with me, so gentle. It's nice to have Carson treating me normally.

As I listen to her energetic chatter, my nagging worries start to fall away. There are no poltergeists, there is no Prism, no body possession or group of Guides. I wonder why Ella Hartley entered my subconscious with such a presence, and I make a mental note to visit her grave when I get out of the hospital.

But why is there a sting of doubt underneath my thoughts? I stare at the prism that Nick brought, zoning out a little while Carson talks. *Prove it to me, Thatcher,* I think. *Prove that it was real, if it was.*

"I guess being in a coma made you appreciate life and all that," Carson is saying when I tune back in, not so much asking me as hypothesizing out loud. "By the way, I'm never letting you take a risk with yourself again! You're too valuable as a best friend. I mean, you should have seen me without you. I was *lost*! Shuffling around the house, whining to Georgia, baking like there was no tomorrow. I must have gained three pounds!"

I widen my eyes in mock shock.

"Well, you know that's a lot on me!" she says. "I'm short! Oh, but Callie, what was it like being in a coma? I mean, do you remember what you dreamed about or—maybe it isn't dreaming, maybe it's more like a trance state?"

She pauses and leans in, whispering now. "Or maybe your spirit actually leaves your body?"

I stare at her, willing her to mention something I remember— the séance, the night in the car with the radio. Maybe Thatcher can make her say it out loud.

But she stops talking and looks up into the air like she's thinking hard about something. And I suddenly realize that I am so, so sleepy.

"Cars," I say.

Her eyes brim with tears. "Callie! You said something!"

Oh, yeah, I did.

My voice is unsteady, weak, but functioning. I guess I have a few weeks' worth of sleep caught in my throat.

"What is it?" she asks. "What did you want to tell me?"

"Tired . . . ," I start.

"Oh, my manners!" she says. "Of course you're tired, and I'm just prattling on about myself. I'm sorry, Cal, forgive me!"

She squeezes me once again around the waist and turns for the hallway.

"I'll be back every day," she says, blowing me a kiss.

Then she runs out the door, and I hear her flag down a nurse.

"She's talking!" Carson yells.

• • •

When my best friend leaves, I stare at the prism and watch it dangle in the window, catching the sunlight and sprinkling bright colors onto the tan linoleum floor. I must have known it was here subconsciously, somehow—the Prism. I created a whole world in my head, with ghosts and haunting and Guides and poltergeists. How very detailed it was! I hear myself sigh out loud as I try to accept the fact that it wasn't real.

What *is* real is that I have another shot at living my life. And I remember the regret I felt, while I was in the coma, at not having appreciated each day and the people who loved me. I make a silent vow to do that—to hold on to the little moments, the ones that I used to consider boring or trite or just plain unimportant. I don't need any more thrill seeking to make me feel alive. I just have to remember how I felt when I was . . . almost dead.

The hospital physical therapist comes in to see me a few times. While she helps me regain strength in my arms and legs—which are wobbly and thin from lack of use—she asks me simple questions. About my name, my address, what year it is, who's president. I pass that part with flying colors, and I wonder if she's ever going to delve deeper, ask me what I experienced when I was in the coma. But she doesn't. I guess the hospital is concerned with my *life*, not my death.

I started to ask my dad about the subconscious, and he gave me a long explanation about how synapses in the brain fire when someone is in a coma, how they can create sights, sounds, other worlds that seem incredibly real.

Then he warned me not to talk about much, even if it's just made up, because there are reporters who have been sniffing around, people who want to ask me all kinds of questions about my "near-death experience."

So I shut up.

"Oatmeal mush again?" I say to Patricia, the nurse who comes every morning to prop me up on pillows and check my vitals. "Can I get an extra cookie at least?"

I smile big, because I ask this every day, and every day she gives in. She feels bad for me, I think. Visiting hours are just a small fraction of the afternoon, and the TV only has a few channels.

She pats my arm as she undoes the Velcro cuff and smiles at me. "You'll be out of here soon enough, and then you can eat anything you like," she says.

"Really?" I ask.

"Tomorrow," says Patricia, her eyes shining. "We just got a release date for you, and your dad's taking you home in the morning."

My grin is huge as I lie back on my pillows. For eight days now, I've been put through a battery of tests by the doctors and fed lots of Jell-O and soft foods. The nurses agreed to take out my IV once I showed them how much I could eat. Oh, man, did I miss food! Even this hospital stuff is a taste sensation in my mouth.

What I can't stand, though, is how much everyone who visits coddles me. My dad talks softly, which is so unlike him, and Nick's only been twice, both times hovering over me like a nervous bird, like he might break me. There has been a steady parade of well-wishers—people from the church we used to go to, neighbors, Curtis Simmons and a few of the guys from the sheriff's department... even our school principal, Mr. Faulkland, who brought me a giant bouquet of sunflowers. But they all kind of stood over me, looking afraid. Like at any moment I might slip back into oblivion, and if they were there when it happened, they'd be somehow to blame. I understand how they feel, though—life is fragile, worthy of reverence and gentle care. The old me didn't realize that at all.

Still, I sometimes get tired of their nervousness. Only Carson acts like herself—lying next to me on the bed, painting my toenails while she tells me about her various boyfriend possibilities for junior year. She even tried to sneak Georgia in once ("That dog is dying to see you!" she told me), but she got caught by an orderly and was banned from visiting hours the next day, so I told her not to attempt it again. I can't live without my daily dose of Carson. It's the only thing keeping me sane.

When Dad comes this afternoon, he asks me if I want anything special for dinner on my first night back at home. "We'll eat out on the porch," says Dad. "Did I tell you I put in a swing like you always wanted?"

I flash back to being with Thatcher on the porch swing at Dodsons' Farm. A throbbing despair works its way into my heart, one that I can't quite explain. It feels like there's a part of me missing. *But it was all in my head.*

I find that I'm having to remind myself of that a few times a day—I have to fight to stay out of my thoughts and in the world in front of me. Still, I can't help but repeat my request every night when the lights go out. *Thatcher, give me a sign. Show me that it was real.* So far, nothing. Which should make me feel even more certain that it was all in my mind, that the Prism doesn't exist.

The only thing that keeps me hanging on is the dull pain in my heart, the one that feels like the ache of truth, a physical manifestation of the loss I experience whenever I think of Thatcher. On my last night in the hospital, I ask again for a sign. But this time I add, *If you're not giving me a sign because you want me to move on and forget you, I won't. Don't think you can do that to me—I will keep trying to find you.*

I'm not sure even I believe what I've said—it sounds crazy. But I know him, or the him I created in my mind, and that's the type of thing that he'd respond to. I hope.

The next morning, Dad comes bright and early, newspaper in hand.

"How are you feeling?" he asks.

"Stronger. I think they're releasing me today."

"That's the word." He hands me a bag with some clothes in it. Then he sits in the chair in the corner and unfolds his newspaper. Some habits are hard to break. Reading the news is one of them. I take some comfort in the familiarity of it. Not everything has changed.

Slipping out of bed, I'm grateful that Dad brought me my pajama shorts and tank top a couple of days ago. The hospital gown had serious fashion issues. I walk slowly to the window, holding on to surfaces along the way to steady my still-weak legs, and I study the prism that Nick brought me, the way the morning sun hits it directly and casts a rainbow of colors on my wall. Did he want to break up with me? Or was that just my imagination, too? I can't escape my own confusion. Staring at the pastel shades, I desperately wish for a sign from Thatcher.

They start to shimmer and waver.

I jerk my gaze back to the prism. It's rocking back and forth slightly as though someone blew on it. My breath catches. Dad's too far away to have had any influence on it. Did my movements stir the air and set it in motion? If so, why didn't it move right away? Why was there a delay, giving me time to study the colors before they wavered?

"Thatcher?" I whisper low, so low my dad can't hear me.

"Pretty."

I spin around. My physical therapist is standing near me, with her clipboard clutched at her side. I didn't hear her come in. I give her a soft smile. "My boyfriend brought it for me."

"I've never been a fan of prisms."

I almost ask her to repeat herself, because it sounded like she said *prisons*.

"I'm going to sign you out today," she says, handing my father a discharge slip. "I'll see you again for a couple of appointments, though. You're still not fully recovered. We've got to get you back up to full energy."

My heart stutters to a stop for a second as her gaze locks with mine. Her eyes flash gold. She smiles a familiar smile, and suddenly I'm convinced that everything I saw, everything I knew in the Prism, was very, very real.

Acknowledgments

MY PROFOUND THANKS TO everyone who helped this book take shape: Morgan Baden, Claudia Gabel, Sara Lyle, Sarah MacLean, Melissa Miller, Jan Nowasky, Micol Ostow, Doug Stewart, and the entire team at Katherine Tegen Books!